GALES
OF NOVEMBER

AARON STANDER

WRITERS & EDITORS
INTERLOCHEN, MICHIGAN

Cover photo by Mark Bear.

ISBN: 978-0997570120

Printed and bound in the United States of America

FOR BEACHWALKER

Bitsy Morgan's Wilderness Journal

I plan to make journal entries every day, just like I usually do, on our wilderness camping trip. I'm sure that every day will be filled with new challenges and struggles, and that's what I hope to capture—the raw edge of all those experiences. More than just the who, what, when, and where, I want to record the smell, taste, sound, and touch with all the nuances. Maybe when the week is over, I'll have enough material for a magazine article about kids confronting the Michigan outback in winter. Maybe I'll even get it published!

I've been camping before a few times—Girl Scouts, that sort of thing. There was some cooking and hiking, but for me it was mostly about s'mores, telling horror stories, and giggling far into the night, safe in my sleeping bag in a rustic cabin with my friends and a bathroom and our parents, including my mother, hovering close by in other cabins and RVs.

This trip will be very different; we will really be in the wild. Some of the upperclassmen told me about other Leiston School trips. Last spring, just as it was starting to get warm, there was a school trip to North Manitou Island for a long weekend. The theme of the trip—it's always about themes at Leiston—was "Reawakening: Nature's Eternal Cycle." I guess they saw lots of wildflowers, some tadpoles, and some ducks having rough sex. But when they got back, they mostly talked about the mosquitoes and the late-season snowstorm, about being cold and wet. The park rangers let them pitch their tents inside a steel building. I heard there was some switching of tent-mates during the night—mostly seniors, I think. Not that it doesn't happen on campus. I mean, not the whole night or anything. Our house parents closely monitor the dorms, but with the woods and all the unlocked buildings, kids find places to do whatever.

Most of the kids go home for Thanksgiving—Leiston is closed for the week. But going home for many of us isn't that easy. Some of our parents are working international, or there are complicated family situations. And then there are a few students from abroad, mostly Europe and Asia. Getting home and back would take much of the week, and then Christmas break is coming up just a few weeks later.

So Leiston sponsors a couple of chaperoned trips on school breaks. This year there was a museum and concert trip to New York and the winter camping trip to the Upper Peninsula.

My mother is a lawyer, an expat currently living in Beijing. I'll spend three weeks with her at Christmas. I could spend Thanksgiving with my grandmother on Long Island—that's where I usually get parked. I know she doesn't approve of my mother's lifestyle, and I don't need to hear all of that again. I could have worked an invitation to go home with one of my friends, but something didn't feel right about that. Anna, a girl from my English class, invited me to come to Maine, and Stephanie really wanted me to come to Florida, but I've only known them a few months, and I don't feel comfortable going home with them. Besides, what if I want an adventure?

So I signed up for the camping trip, a new experience. My mother has dragged me to endless concerts and museums. That's how much she knows about teenagers.

Besides, most of the other campers are, like me, on the fencing team, and I've already spent a lot of time with them and learned so much from them. I joined the team because my father was a fencer, according to my mother. He and my mother went splitsville (my mother's term) when I was three or four. I really can't remember him, and my mother has zero photographs of him, even though she has photos of me when he was still around. Mother says she has no idea where he is—he seemed to fall off the end of the universe. But fencing makes me feel close to him in some small way.

The trip leader was supposed to be Julie Jensen. Ms. Jensen teaches biology, environmental studies, and runs the P.E. program. She has been an Outward Bound instructor, a ski patroller, and a whitewater rafting guide. She was one of the first women admitted to West Point, and I can see that in her bearing. She is all about competence and goal setting. She's a real taskmaster. I know that puts some of the kids off, but I like her. You just believe in her knowledge and skill. You know you could follow her into the wilderness, and she would get you back safely.

Sadly, a couple of weeks ago, she hurt her back lifting weights and ended up having emergency surgery.

Etienne Falconet, the French instructor and fencing master—Ms. Jensen's second-in-command—is now our leader and guide. Some of the juniors and seniors said it was our lucky day. They went to Paris with Etienne on the Easter break trip last spring. They said he was a great tour director for the first few days—the Louvre, Musée d'Orsay, Notre Dame. Then he told them they would learn French faster if he wasn't around constantly assisting them. Etienne called it the "total immersion" approach to language learning.

So the kids were left to their own devices. My roommate at Leiston, Alexandra, was on that trip. Life was good, she said. Lots of drinking, eating, and shopping. Etienne reappeared the day before they were scheduled to leave and made sure everyone was packed. The morning of the departure he got everyone to Charles de Gaulle in time for the flight. When they got back to Leiston, they all followed the party line, *the best learning experience ever*. The school officials and the parents never knew what really happened.

Our first meeting with Etienne and Ms. Jensen—funny that we always call Etienne by his first name, but no one calls Ms. Jensen Julie—took place in September, weeks before we were scheduled to leave. I found out then that out of twelve students, Scott and I are the only freshmen going on the trip. That makes me a little nervous. Even though I know Scott from fencing and we're about the same age, he seems so much more mature than me. I feel like the little kid on this trip.

First we all had to sign an agreement on the dos and don'ts of a wilderness experience: leave the area as you found it, meaning no garbage or other debris; Walkmans and other personal listening devices are allowed, but nothing more than that, nothing that might intrude on natural sounds.

Then Ms. Jensen gave us a handout of required clothing and equipment. She made it clear we would need everything on the list if we wanted to go on the trip. The list was specific and arranged alphabetically: boots, hats, jackets, long underwear, mittens, sleeping bags, wet weather gear. It even included numbers for L.L. Bean, Eddie Bauer, and Patagonia products. Ms. Jensen sent the same list to our parents or guardians. The school provided tents, sleeping mats, and cooking gear.

Ms. Jensen did all the talking and answered all the questions at the meeting while Etienne hung around in the background. Occasionally she would refer to him, something like, "Mr. Falconet and I . . . ," but it seemed like she was just making an effort to include him. He would smile and nod, but most of the time he looked like he was somewhere else.

Two weeks before we were scheduled to leave, just before Ms. Jensen's accident, we had to show up at the gym with our backpacks and lay out everything from the list in alpha order. There were a few kids who didn't have some of the required stuff. Richard Gordon and a couple of the other boys didn't have all the extra layers of fleece or down specified on the list. Ms. Jensen reminded them that they couldn't go without it.

At our first meeting without Ms. Jensen, Etienne regaled us with stories of the youth hostels and small inns he had stayed at on his many treks around Europe. But I have to admit that going on the trip without Ms. Jensen makes me a little nervous.

Last night, Etienne quickly checked our packs again and said that everyone was ready. Then we met Mike Kniivila—who has been the head of Leiston's maintenance crew forever and who would drive us to the campsite—at the bus and loaded the backpacks into the back. Mike said he would drop us off at the trailhead and then drive on to visit family up near Eagle Harbor for Thanksgiving before turning around and coming back for us on the following Saturday.

We went back to the dorms, but no one at Leiston got a good night's sleep that night. Everyone was really excited, the students going home for Thanksgiving and those going on trips.

SATURDAY, NOVEMBER 17

DAY 1

We were all on the bus by seven this morning. I bet less than half of us made it to the cafeteria for breakfast. It didn't matter, though, because everyone had all kinds of extra food stashed in their carry-ons.

It was pretty noisy for the first half hour or so, then people either seemed to be snoozing or listening to their Walkmans. Somehow we organized ourselves in the bus by class year. The seniors and juniors were in the back just ahead of all the rows of backpacks. There were two serious couples in that group, kids who had been dating for a while. The freshmen and sophomores, kids like me, were in the front of the bus. Etienne was in the back; the older girls liked to hang out with him.

I was dozing when we got to the bridge. Then I was wide awake. The crosswinds really rocked the bus, sometimes violently. The world outside was cold and gray. I was happy to snuggle into my new down jacket.

Mike really had to slow down. Like the other big trucks, our bus crept across the Mackinac Bridge. It's only about five miles long, but at ten or fifteen miles per hour it seemed to take forever. Out of the windshield all I could see was the back of the truck that Mike was following. Off to the side, far below the bridge, I could see big waves pushed along by the wind. Mike said they were gale force winds, which must mean strong. He grew up in the Upper Peninsula and said he'd never seen the bridge rocking like that. He told me the story of a woman who was driving over the bridge in wind like this when her little car went out of control and flipped over the side and fell down, down into the water. It was more than I wanted to know, and I found myself gripping the edge of my seat like a vise until we got to the other side.

A mile or two after we passed the tollbooth on the other side, we stopped at McDonald's. Richard Gordon, AKA Flash because he was always snapping pictures with his expensive camera, disappeared into the woods behind McDonald's as most of us headed inside. He was our resident stoner. One or two of the other kids went off with him.

We didn't look like anyone else in the restaurant. It was midmorning, and most of the other customers were scruffy bearded men wearing camo or heavy wool jackets and big boots. Mike said it was deer season. I've never really seen hunters before. I can't imagine killing anything. I looked at these guys while I was standing in line, trying to catch bits of their conversation. They seemed quite ordinary, but I couldn't imagine anyone killing a deer.

McDonald's—heaven for some of the kids, not so much for me. I do my best to be a vegetarian—I can't stand the thought of animals suffering on factory farms. At McDonald's at least I can get hash browns and an Egg McMuffin, sans bacon. At Leiston School, the cooks, who are nice enough people, look at me like I'm a Martian when I ask if they can make something with tofu instead of meat. They're meat and potatoes people. That's what my mother says about the Midwest, people big on pork and beef, short on . . . well I can't remember quite what. She's a native New Yorker, calls everything west of the Hudson "Indian Territory."

I barely had enough time to eat before Etienne and Mike were herding us back onto the bus. Richard was the last one to board, smelling of tobacco or something more.

Then we headed north, and the view became trees, endless trees. Occasionally I saw a house or a small church or a cluster of trailer homes set back from the road. There were occasional farms, too. All of the buildings and vehicles looked old and dilapidated. Many of the houses had two or three rusting cars or trucks in the yard, like when one died, they just went out and got another. I'd never seen poverty like that before.

Hours later we stopped at a second McDonald's in Marquette, the first real city we'd seen this side of the bridge. I guess we must have been in the suburbs, because all I saw were strip malls with the kinds of chain stores you see everywhere in America.

Once we got off the state highway, the roads narrowed. And then they turned from pavement to gravel. Finally we were on a one-lane road hemmed in by trees, almost like being in a tunnel. Mike said the road was built on an abandoned railroad bed.

For the last part of the drive I sat up front alone, and I was the only audience for Mike's continuous travelogue. Mike does everything at Leiston School from fixing things to plowing snow to driving the bus to taking kids to the airport or to doctors' appointments in town. And he's good about making special stops for books, or music, or food.

Since I arrived at Leiston in September, I've been dealing with some problems. My mother thinks I'm depressed and need therapy. My grandmother, on the other hand, thinks my mother is the one with the problems, but I just follow my mother's dictates. It's much easier than fighting with her.

Mike drives me to town twice a week to see my counselor. I didn't say much in the beginning. Mike filled the silence with stories—mostly about growing up in the Upper Peninsula, hunting and fishing—so I've been curious to see the place he's described, even though at first I thought his stories were sort of dumb. He's what you might call a raconteur (PSAT word list), a modern Mark Twain. I don't know how much truth there is in his funny stories, but they've been the best part of the trips to town.

The therapist, on the other hand, hasn't been helpful at all. She says she can't help me unless I'm willing to talk to her, and so she spends the sessions mostly sitting and looking at me, waiting for me to say something.

The shadows are getting long, and Mike says we're close to our final destination, the trailhead that leads to our campsite.

So much happened as we were approaching our journey's end. I didn't have a chance to get any of it down at the time. There was no opportunity. Things were so intense, and I hope I can capture those feelings. I've never experienced anything like this before. It was so violent. The bus hit a deer.

Mike braked the bus suddenly, and when I looked out the windshield, I saw several deer sprinting across the road. The last deer was white—pure white—with a big rack of antlers.

Mike wasn't going very fast, but he still couldn't avoid hitting the buck. A shudder ran through the bus. It was like I could feel the animal's bones breaking. I could feel the pain. I screamed. I think that's what got everyone else's attention. I've never really screamed before, not like that.

Mike opened the door, and I followed him out. First he checked the front of the bus for damage, then he went to look at the deer. Most of the other kids and Etienne tumbled out after us. Mike warned us to stay back, that the deer might not be dead yet. He inspected the animal carefully. Even back a few feet, I was transfixed by the beauty of this magnificent animal. Mike rested his hand on the ribs of the deer and waited.

"Did you see it happen?" Richard asked me kind of gleefully. "That would have been so cool. What a great photo op."

"I was sleeping," I lied. I really didn't want to talk with him.

Finally, Mike looked up and said the deer was dead. As he and Etienne and Scott grabbed hold of the antlers and pulled the deer to the side of the road, I gazed into the animal's still black eye.

Mike pointed down the road. "The trailhead is only about a hundred yards ahead. You can ride or walk." The bus lumbered up the road, but I stayed behind and approached the dead buck. I reached out to touch the warm fur on its neck. What a beautiful wild thing. I wished I had the power to bring it back to life.

A few minutes later Mike, Etienne, Scott and Richard came back. I followed as they dragged the carcass up to a clearing near the trailhead. The rear door of the bus was open, and people were sorting out their packs and gear. I think everyone was shaken by the accident, but they were also eager to get started on our trek to the campsite.

Mike retrieved his own duffel bag from the bus and carefully inspected the deer. After I got my own backpack out of the bus, I drifted over to watch. I was reluctant, for some reason, to leave the buck.

"What are you doing?" asked Scott.

"I'm going to butcher the deer. No reason to waste good meat."

"That's gross," said Sarah. She's another one of the seniors.

"You flatlanders have got to understand we don't waste stuff up here," explained Mike. "You can watch or not. This is what happens to all the meat you eat. It won't take me long, and you'll be heading off into the woods with some fresh venison to roast."

I watched Mike take a knife from his duffel bag and slip the blade through the skin at the buck's lower abdomen and circle the area under its tail.

"Oh my God, did you see that?" said Samantha. "Disgusting."

"This ain't dissection, kids, this is butchering. The point is to get the innards out of the carcass without puncturing the intestines. You don't want to contaminate the meat with anything from the guts."

Most of the other kids watching dropped back, but I moved closer, oddly fascinated. Mike was so sure with his knife. He slit the buck's skin up to the neck and then cut through the cartilage at the center of the rib cage. Then he came back down to the pelvis. He popped the bone gently with a sharp hatchet, then spread the bones apart.

He looked up and saw me standing there. "Hold this leg back for me," he said, and I took hold of the dainty velvet-covered ankle. He moved back up to the buck's throat and made a small movement with the knife. He began to move back down toward me, spreading the buck's body open as he came. He pulled all of the internal organs away from the animal, making a few quick cuts to free them.

Only Alexandra, Richard, Scott and I remained, watching in silence as Mike dragged the buck's guts, steaming in the cool afternoon air, several yards away. "Now we got to drain the blood," Mike said. He rolled the deer onto its side and waited as the blood ran out onto the sand.

Alexandra reached down and dipped her fingers into the crimson pool.

"The blood is still warm," she said. "I wonder if the individual cells know it's over. I wonder if they know they're dead."

I stood there pondering her question.

"Alex, only you would think of something so dumb," snarled Richard, capturing the moment with his camera. She flipped him the bird with a blood covered finger as she walked away.

Mike took a rope from his duffel and with the help

Richard and Scott, he hoisted the deer up until it was hanging from a low tree branch. He quickly removed the lovely white hide from the deer and laid it across another low branch and then went back to work on the carcass with a knife, a saw, and a hatchet, removing the legs and large pieces of meat.

Richard had been capturing the whole process with his camera. He asked Mike to hold on a minute so he could reload, then he starting snapping away again.

Mike wrapped the two rear legs in newspaper and gave them to Etienne, along with simple instructions on how to roast the meat. Something in his tone suggested he wasn't sure Etienne could follow even these directions. Then he wrapped the rest of the meat and loaded it in the bus.

I asked him about the pelt, what he would do with it. "I've got some Indian friends—I guess I should say Native Americans these days. They say albino deer are magical." He looked over at me as he rinsed the blood off his tools and hands with water from a jug. "They say that when you see a white deer, it's an omen of things to come." He laughed. "The trouble is, I don't remember if it's a good omen or a bad one. But I hope giving them the pelt makes things right. It's not like I shot the deer. It's not like I wanted to kill him. It's just something that happened."

"So you believe this superstitious stuff?" I asked.

"Well, it's not superstitions, really. It's folkways, things native people learned over thousands of years living close to nature. They knew stuff that is lost to us moderns. Look at all the junk you guys need to spend a few days in the woods." He pointed to the pile of backpacks and gear scattered on the trailhead. "Native people only had the clothes on their backs and a few simple tools to survive in the wilderness. They knew how to hunt and fish, build shelters, and scavenge for food. If I don't come around to pick you up at the end of the week, you'll all be starving once you eat all your freeze-dried food. So who is advanced and who is primitive?"

He began gathering up his things and loading them into the back of the bus. I was suddenly feeling pretty nervous about his leaving. I studied the thick woods bordering the trail. I could only see a few feet into the trees and thick brush.

"Mike?"

He turned back toward me.

"So what do we do if we meet any of the other animals that live in these woods? Like bears?"

"Bears? What's got you thinking about bears?" He clapped a big hand on my shoulder. "You don't have to worry about them, or the coyotes or the wolves, either. They don't want anything to do with humans. Plus, the bears are denning by now. Well, usually by now they're denning up. It's been a late fall. Listen, kid, the only thing you got to fear in the woods walks on two legs and wears pants. The animals wish we'd just leave them alone."

He put the last of his gear in the bus. "You really scared of bears?"

"I've never slept outside before, not once," I admitted. I shivered at the thought that a thin nylon tent would be the only barrier between me and these woods.

Mike turned and found something in his pack and handed it to me—a canister in a canvas holder. "This is bear spray, pepper spray on steroids. Tuck this away and don't let the other kids know you have it. Can I trust you?"

"Of course," I said.

"This is how it works. You pull that white safety tab out, which lets you depress the trigger. The spray goes twenty, thirty feet. It's not a toy. It's serious stuff. Keep it hidden. It's for an extreme emergency. So I expect you will return it to me unused."

"Thanks," I said. He watched as I slipped the can into an inside pocket of my parka. It was completely hidden, but easily accessible if I needed it. Just having it made me feel better about things.

As I watched the lights on the rear of Mike's bus disappear down the road, I wished that he was going to be with us. He's a true outdoorsman, and this is his country. If there was trouble, he'd know what to do.

I'm not so sure about Etienne, not sure at all. As I looked around at the dense woods in the encroaching darkness, my thoughts were interrupted by Etienne yelling that we had to get on the move.

There's an outhouse at the trailhead, and I went to use it before strapping on my pack. Richard exited the small roughly built structure just as I got there. "If you take a big breath, hold it for as long as you can, and go fast, it's not that bad," he counseled ironically. But the skunky smell of marijuana smoke, especially when I got inside the outhouse, almost overpowered any other smell.

Richard was waiting for me as I came out the door. I was momentarily blinded by his flash and stumbled forward in the growing dusk. But before I could get very angry, he caught my arm and helped me hoist my pack onto my back.

"Look at that, Bitsy," he said. "You *are* bitsy. This thing is almost as big as you are."

It was big and bulky, but it wasn't all that heavy.

"Thank you," I said. I could see that he was totally stoned, his pupils were big pools of black.

He bowed with unexpected grace. "Always happy to help a beautiful woman."

Richard has been hitting on me since the beginning of the school year, probably because I'm roommates with Alexandra. I heard they were a couple part of last year, especially at the beginning. As the story goes, she had been dating his roommate, a senior. She broke it off with that guy and hooked up with Richard. Then she went off to Paris in the spring and got involved with Etienne.

Sarah told me that Richard hoped when he came back to school this fall he and Alex would get back to together again. It didn't happen. He was crushed. He started acting sort of crazy, although some of the kids told me his behavior wasn't much different than before. But it was bizarre enough that our school guidance counselor, probably with pressure from the teachers and other adults, sent him off to a psychiatrist. That doctor dropped him after a few sessions. Rumor had it that Richard stole a little recorder the doctor used for dictating notes. It really wasn't about the recorder; it was the confidential information on it and the fact that the doctor had allowed it to fall into the wrong hands. No one could figure out why Richard hadn't been kicked out of school. Kids have been expelled for less.

And now he is hitting on me, the lowly freshman. Alex thinks it is because of our friendship. Richard is working on me as a way of getting even with her.

The stuff he says to me, like, I know guys talk like that, but I've never been the target. The first time it happened was after fencing practice. Etienne had already left. It was just me, Richard, and a couple of other kids, including Alexandra.

Richard said he'd like to teach me about thrusting, and that he wasn't talking about his sword. What he actually said was really crude. I don't want to write those words down.

It was a bad move on his part. Like, Alex's temper is legendary. First, she gets all quiet, but you can see the tension building. Her eyes were burning into him. Then she got this tone in her voice I had never heard before. She spoke slowly and deliberately.

"Richard, back off. She's only a freshman."

"Like you weren't the school whore back then." He was just standing there with an evil grin.

We were still in our fencing clothes. Alex jammed her epee against his chest, bending it almost in half. "Touch her and you answer to me, asshole."

Richard started to say something, then he just shut up and retreated. He looked defeated.

Everyone knows she's the best fencer on the team. Even the boys have accepted that fact. Alex is fierce and fearless. Richard beat her once during practice, only once. She must have been off that day or just playing with him. He never even got close a second time.

After Richard left, she told me that if he ever bothered me again I should let her know. She'd take care of him. Those weren't her exact words. She uses the f-bomb a lot and usually with great dramatic effect. Her f-bombs aren't just swear words, they're acts of aggression, one notch below getting smacked in the face.

All new students at Leiston are assigned to an upper-class mentor, usually a senior. They room together for part or all of the fall semester, and if they get on they can continue to room together for the year.

I was assigned to Alex. Early on I could tell she didn't like the role. Fortunately, her attitude changed. I don't understand why, but she really seemed to take an interest in me, not that she lets me into her life much. There are things she keeps private. And she'll often disappear when we are supposed to be in our rooms. I hear her leave in the middle of the night and return before daylight. She is involved in a lot of stuff that can get you kicked out of Leiston, but I keep my mouth shut. We have an unspoken understanding. I'm lucky to be rooming with one of the coolest kids in the school. And I don't mind being under her protection.

As for her relationship with Etienne, I don't know.

It seems to be up and down. We never discuss it. I just guess at what's happening between them based on her moods. At the moment I think things are kind of rocky.

At the trailhead, as people were pulling on their gear, Etienne circulated, telling us we'd have to hustle if we were going to get our tents up before dark. He said that we were only going about three miles and that we should be there in less than an hour.

"I'll take the lead," he said. "Alex, you take the rear and keep it tight. Front to back, we should always be in visual contact."

"Oh, her rear is already tight," Richard said. Tony and Pete chuckled. That ended when Alex gave them the look. Etienne yelled something at Richard in French, and we all knew by his tone that he was really angry. He ordered Richard to walk behind him in line.

Then, at last, we were off, but it was hardly at a fast pace. First we crossed a wooden bridge. Everyone took their time, stopping to look at the water flowing below and the dense woods on either side of the stream. Then we moved onto the actual trail. It was just a pathway, wide enough for one person. So there we were marching along, thirteen people in single file. We had practiced this, hiking around the grounds at Leiston School with full packs, but we really hadn't covered much ground. And now we were actually carrying more weight, and it took us longer to cover even a short distance. In addition to clothing and food, we had two liters of water and a full fuel bottle for our stoves. Plus, kids had stuffed in all kinds of extra snacks. And I was as guilty as anyone else.

Behind me, Alex started grumbling. "As the crow flies, the distance is only three miles," she said. "In reality, it's a lot farther. Look at the way we're zigzagging back and forth. And this group is dogging it. We're going to be walking in the dark and setting up in the dark. This is turning into a total Charlie foxtrot." I'm not sure what that phrase means, but I can guess from her intonation.

We stopped to rest after about forty minutes and then again sometime later. We were in the gloaming, and for the first time I was starting to sense how cold it could get here. The woods that surrounded the narrow pathway disappeared into the dusk. Etienne passed out headlamps, one to each of us. He called them "head torches." His English is sometimes amusing.

Etienne explained that the batteries for the torches lose power in cold weather, but our warm bodies would keep the lights going a lot longer. He told us to tuck the battery packs inside our jackets, close to our skin.

By this point, we were all cold and tired and hungry. Earlier, I had been sweating, but now my teeth were chattering. Everyone wanted to know how much longer. Etienne joked about how the trail ended at a lake. We'd know we had arrived when our feet started getting wet.

Finally we were off again. The lights weren't very bright, but they were better than nothing. I could see the trail ahead by watching the lights, like one of those movies with railroad cars snaking through the mountains. I could also see our group starting to spread out. The sky overhead was raven black, no stars. The only sounds were our feet on the trail and the wind in the trees. And then it began to rain. Mist at first, then a steady drizzle. Alexandra and I struggled to get the hoods up on our parkas, then we moved quickly to catch up again with the glowworm in front of us.

I was thinking about that Bret Harte story we read in English class, the one with 'Poker Flat' in the title. Instead of being in New York, or home with families at Thanksgiving, we were heading toward an uncertain destiny in the middle of an unknown wilderness. My level of enthusiasm for this adventure was dropping faster than the temperature.

The rain changed to snow, then back to rain, then snow

again. Our headlamps reflected off the large wet flakes. By the time we reached the trail's end, there was a light covering of snow on the ground.

I could see the lake, or at least the shoreline, the dark water against the white band of snow. Etienne did his best to organize our campsite in the darkness. As part of our trip planning, we had been divided into six two-person teams. One team member carried the tent tied to their pack; the other carried a trenching shovel. I had the shovel; Alex had the tent. These were three person tents, the idea being we needed the extra space for our winter gear: jackets, boots, packs.

Etienne, using a bright flashlight, laid out the site—boys on one side, girls on the other. We had practiced pitching the tents in the gym at school. Then, it was a lark, lots of chatter and laughing. But in the darkness and cold, with the wind blowing and the snow falling, it took forever to lay out the tent and fit the fiberglass poles together and slide them into place. And because I mostly had to have my mittens off to do the work, my hands were frozen. By the time Alex and I got our mats and sleeping bags in place and our packs open and things organized, we had managed to drag in a lot of mud and snow.

Etienne, Scott, and Pete collected wood and built a fire. Cold and hungry, we gathered around the blazing pile of wood. As I looked at the faces of my peers lit by the flickering firelight, I was struck by how people didn't look quite okay. And Etienne, who had always seemed relaxed and in control, appeared harried. Maybe it was just hitting him that this wasn't like his treks with friends in Europe. He couldn't look forward to a cozy inn with a hot meal and a good bottle of wine.

"As you can see, I've got a big pot of water over the fire," he said. "I will be ladling it out for your freeze-dried meals. This water came from the lake. It needs to boil for at least ten minutes. I know some of you think you're starving. You're not. We've got ample food for the week, but we must follow our ration schedule. I know you have lots of other stuff you can eat while you wait."

"What happened to the venison?" Pete asked.

"Not tonight; it's too late. Also, we'll hold off building the latrines until tomorrow when we can see what we're doing."

"What are we suppose to do?" I blurted. Some people snickered.

"We talked about this," Etienne said angrily. "Ms. Jensen did a whole hour on sanitation. Tonight it's cat sanitation if you need to have a bowel movement. Every team has a shovel. When you leave the perimeter of our campsite, make sure you're with your teammate. Stay close to our campsite. Boys, stay on your side, girls stay on yours."

"What if a bear attacks me when my pants are down?" It was Richard's voice.

Etienne answered in French, but there was no mistaking his meaning.

The water came to a boil. We stood in line and Etienne ladled the steaming liquid into our pouches of freeze-dried entrées. "Give it some time. The water needs to be absorbed."

So we stood around the fire and waited. My pouch contained vegetable pasta, at least that's what the label said. By the time I ate it, the slimy concoction was only lukewarm, and the taste and texture were all wrong. Dorm food was suddenly the new gold standard. That said, I was so hungry I inhaled the contents of the package in two minutes. I would have happily eaten a second one, but I made do with a chocolate bar, some peanuts, and a couple of cups of hot water.

After eating, we scoured the area close to our campsite for enough wood to keep the fire going most of the night. And then Etienne told us it was time that we got into our sleeping bags and maybe did a little reading before we went to sleep.

After a brief excursion to the woods, Alex and I have settled into our tent. In my sleeping bag, with most of my clothes still on, I'm warm for the first time in hours. We have a candle lantern between our bags, and Alex is trying to read while I write this. I can hardly wait to tuck my arms inside my mummy bag.

Just now, Alex gave up on the reading and pulled a bottle from her pack and took a sip. "Want some?" she said. "It will warm you up and help you sleep."

"What is it?"

"Brandy. Not very good brandy, but brandy."

"Where did you get it?"

"Jack, the pizza delivery guy, the bringer of all earthly delights . . . well not all, but most." She laughed. "My dad never wonders about my fifty-dollar pizza charges. He just pays my credit card bill. Guilt money. He's still trying to keep me on his side."

She handed me the bottle, and I took a big sip—too big—and started coughing.

"Better take another," she counseled. "It will help with the cough."

I did. Alex seemed to drift off immediately. I can hear her breathing, that and the sounds of the world outside our flimsy tent—the wind and some distant howling. Coyotes? Wolves? I'm really ready to snuggle into my bag and sleep.

Sunday, November 18

Day 2

The sun was lighting the yellow nylon skin of the tent this morning when I opened my eyes. Nature was calling in a painful way, but I didn't want to crawl out of my warm sleeping bag. Finally, I couldn't stand the agony any longer. As I pulled on my heavy parka, Alexandra, who I thought was still sleeping, said, "Hold on a minute. We should go together."

We headed toward the woods in boots, jackets, hats, and mittens.

We never had cats when I was growing up, so the cat sanitation metaphor went over my head the first time I heard it. Now I understand it completely.

I was suffering as I waited for Alex to pass me the shovel. She quickly took care of business, and I tried to follow her nonchalant approach in my own shy, prudish way.

I can't say that I heard the camera shutter, but Alex was suddenly sprinting past me, and then I saw Richard running, trying to get beyond her reach. He was heading toward the lake, almost at its edge when she tackled him. She looked like a football player making a sack, wrapping her arms around him, knocking him to the ground, and then crashing heavily on top of him. I could see them struggling on the snow-covered earth.

Alex finally pulled the camera from his grasp. Using the long lens as a handle, she smashed the body of the camera against his face. She hit him two or three times. Then she slowly came to her feet and stood over him.

"You sleazy creep! Is that how you get off?" She booted him in the side. "You're sicker than I thought."

Richard just lay there looking up at her. When he finally sat up, I could see a large gash at the hairline over his left eye. The blood was flowing down his forehead and cheek onto his jacket.

Alex considered the camera. Then she walked to the edge of the lake and threw it—not a girl toss, but a low, powerful heave that propelled the camera end over end far out into the lake, where it disappeared into the cold gray water.

Richard was struggling to get to his feet. Keeping his distance he said, "This isn't over, Alex."

"Yes, it is, Richard," she hissed. "You got off easy. You better pray there is no next time."

If any of the kids had been sleeping, they weren't any longer. Everyone was out of their tents in parkas, hats, and boots, some in pants, others with PJ bottoms or long johns.

Etienne took control of the situation. He got Richard seated on a stump, and then had us gather around as he started to work on the wound. Since I was first on the scene, I ended up holding the first aid bag for him.

I was surprised that Etienne seemed to know what he was doing. First, he applied a pressure bandage to control the bleeding. At his direction, I opened some gauze bandages and passed them to him. Eventually the flow of blood seemed to slow. He asked me to open some butterfly bandages, a sort of Band-Aid with the middle cut away to make a butterfly shape. He removed the blood-soaked pads and pulled the edges of the tear in Richard's forehead together. Then he attached a row of butterflies, the thin part over the jagged cut. The wound was still seeping a bit, so he mopped it once quickly before he swabbed the area with Betadine.

That's when Richard, who had been completely stoical during the whole process, dropped a couple of f-bombs.

Etienne told him to hold on, he was almost done. He put a gauze pad over the wound, asking me to hold it in place as he secured it with adhesive tape. Etienne then helped Richard to his feet. He looked a bit unsteady.

Etienne to me. "Did you see what happened?

I gave him a quick chronology of the events. Etienne looked at Alex and then at Richard.

"This isn't over," Richard growled at Alex.

"It is over," said Etienne. "It is completely over."

"How about my camera?" Richard asked.

Etienne didn't respond verbally to the question. Everyone could tell from his expression that it would be best if Richard never mentioned the camera again.

"You better see if you can get some of that blood washed off your parka," Etienne finally said. "We don't want to attract wolves."

Etienne made breakfast—a big pot of gooey oatmeal he cooked over the fire, which we ate with the bowls and spoons from our mess kits. The oatmeal wasn't great, but it was better than the freeze-dried stuff I ate last night.

While we were eating, Etienne gave us a verbal list of morning assignments, including straightening the belongings in our tents and filling our water bottles from the lake.

"Add one purification tablet," he said, "and give it the maximum two hours to work. If you get diarrhea, this will be a long, uncomfortable week."

After breakfast Etienne organized us into a work party to collect enough firewood for several days. He parceled out the tools we needed: three folding saws and six hatchets. We started looking for wood close to the campsite but quickly found that we had to go deeper into the forest.

In the daylight, I saw how beautiful, if desolate, this area is. The lake, more than a puddle but not too large, has an island at its center. The water isn't frozen yet.

We discovered and explored the foundations of several old buildings in the woods near our campsite. They're mostly concrete, although a couple are built with lots of boulders. One is below ground level, a basement.

On our first trip back to camp, we all had armloads of sticks. Etienne just shook his head. "Great kindling, guys. But we're going to need some bigger stuff, too."

He accompanied us on our second trip, and we returned with bigger logs we had cut with our saws from downed trees that weren't too rotten to burn. But what had at first been fun had by then become just a job.

Now it's 4:00, and the shadows are lengthening, and the temperature is falling. We ended up with an impressive pile of branches and logs. Etienne built a spit over a low fire and is roasting the venison as I write this in my tent. I'll try to write more later.

Monday, November 19

Day 3

When I woke up this morning, I was zipped tight in my sleeping bag, but I didn't really remember getting here. My head throbbed—is still throbbing—and I desperately needed to make a trip to the woods. Alex's sleeping bag was cold and empty, so I slogged alone to the new girls' facilities through five or six inches of new snow. The day before, Etienne had designed and helped build a four-sided screen around a pit toilet to make sure there wouldn't be any more photo ops.

No one else was up yet, so I came back inside to write this. I wonder where Alexandra is. I'm a tiny bit worried, even though I know that she can take care of herself.

Some of last night is a blur, but I do remember how it started. We were standing around the fire, talking and warming up, waiting for dinner, and Alex bent close and said, "Cocktail time."

I liked the brandy, something I had never tasted until the previous night, so I followed her to our tent.

She poured some brown liquid into my plastic cup, doing the same for herself. "Here's mud in your eye."

When I looked confused, she shrugged and smiled. "It's something my father says," she explained, taking a sip. "Anyway, this should take the chill off."

I took a tentative taste.

"Spiced rum," she said. "Perfect before a meal."

It went down easier than the brandy. Alex poured some more into my cup, and she had some more, too. My memory of our conversation is now sort of hazy. As I remember it,

Alex was doing most of the talking. I was just basking in the glow of hanging out and drinking with the coolest girl in the school.

By the time Etienne called us to dinner, I was feeling a bit unsteady. As I was rummaging through my collection of freeze-dried entrees, Alex said, "Forget that, kid. You need some meat."

"But—," I tried to protest. I started through my litany of reasons for not eating meat.

"Deer meat is pure. No antibiotics, no chemicals. It's real food. The kind of stuff your body needs to survive in the wilderness."

We were last in line to get some venison, and even in the dull light of late afternoon, I could see the big chunk of steaming meat on my aluminum plate was plenty bloody.

"Put some salt on it," said Alex, handing me a cardboard shaker. I sat there on a log for a long moment wondering if I could put the flesh of the white buck in my mouth.

"Eat," ordered Alex. "Don't let it get cold."

It has been years since I last had any meat; I'm not sure I had even started school yet. Without the buzz from the spiced rum, I don't think I would have touched the meat from the white deer. The alcohol lowered my moral resolve. Besides, the deer was killed accidently, and I was in no way responsible for its death.

I cut off a small piece and tasted the hot, salty venison. There was an earthiness to it, something so sensual. I was soon in line with everyone else for a second slab of the forbidden fruit.

As we were eating, Richard appeared, illuminated by the flickering firelight, wearing a Mad Bomber hat. I realized I hadn't seen him for most of the day, since Etienne had patched him up that morning. He had disappeared while the rest of us were on the work detail. He must have been hiding in his tent.

Even though much of his face was obscured by the hat, I could still see the huge shiner on the left side of his face. It wasn't just around the eye. The blue-black area extended far into the cheek below.

And surprisingly, his usually surly manner seemed to be gone. He was circulating, talking to people. But then I noticed something sneaky about his manner. His eyes were glued to Etienne, and he talked or approached people surreptitiously, when he could see that Etienne's attention was pulled in another direction.

I was recruited by Melanie to buddy up for a pit stop. With our headlamps in place, we marched off into the woods.

On our way back to the circle of light around the fire, I could see Etienne, Alex, and Sarah down at the water's edge, rinsing the cooking gear. That's when Richard approached us. He had a tin of brownies and was offering them to me and Melanie. I hesitated, but Melanie squealed, "Brownies!" and took one. And even after the venison, I was still so hungry.

"If you want one, you better grab it," Richard said to me. "In fact, you should take two. Everyone else is ahead of you."

While I am a chocoholic, I don't usually eat brownies. I stick to the straight chocolate, 88%, organic. I took two brownies and ate them pretty quickly. I would have had a third or a fourth if there had been any left.

Richard circled back around as I was finishing the second brownie. "Wash those bad boys down with a hit of this," he said, holding out a bottle.

My head was still spinning from the rum.

"No, thank you," I said.

He pushed the bottle into my face, actually pressing it against my mouth. "Drink some, you'll like it," he commanded.

"No," I said, pushing the bottle away.

"Silly bitch," he snarled before he slithered away. Richard is a Jekyll and Hyde character: nice one minute, a monster the next.

I rinsed off my plate and flatware in the lake, and pretty soon Etienne had a big pot of water going over the fire. All our mess kit gear went into the boiling water. At least I can say that he's a stickler for making sure everything is clean and sterile.

My buzz from the rum was starting to wear off. I was feeling tired and thinking about crawling into my sleeping bag, writing about my day, and then going to sleep. It was pitch black by this time. Snow was beginning to fall. The only light was from the campfire.

And then the music started. I couldn't believe it. We'd all signed the agreement about not intruding on nature, and now we were listening to U2 cranked on a small black boom box that was sitting on the ground near the fire pit. People were beginning to dance.

And then I was dancing, too. And like the other kids, I was singing up to the pitch black sky, into the snowflakes that seemed to be speeding down at me. And then I noticed that I could see the words coming out of the other kids' mouths—not like sounds but like individual letters and words, like the bubbles you see in cartoons.

And then the music stopped. I could see Etienne holding onto the boom box. Kids were shouting at him, booing and worse. He looked panicked.

I lost my sense of time. I don't know how long I danced. It might have been ten minutes or . . . I just don't know. I have a vague memory of being guided back to my tent.

More later.

When I was writing, Alex came back to the tent looking for

her toothbrush. She was dressed in the same clothes she had been wearing yesterday.

"Are you OK?" she asked.

I thought about it. I really wanted a long hot bath, or at least a shower, and clean clothes and some place warm.

"I have a headache," I finally said. "And I'm dizzy and feeling kind of sick. Maybe it was the meat. I'm not used to that."

"It wasn't the meat," she said. "You ate a brownie, right?"

"Two," I admitted.

"Oh, my God. Stupid, stupid, stupid!"

I must have looked shocked.

"Sorry," she said, her tone softening. "How could you have known? The brownies, they had weed or hash and who knows what else in them. If it makes you feel any better, all of the others girls—except me—had at least one brownie. What can I say—chocolate. Did you drink that swill he was passing around?"

"No, I was already feeling strange. What was it?"

"It must have had LSD or something like that in it. People who ate the brownies were just dancing and hanging out, but the people who drank whatever it was started going crazy."

"Where was I?" I wasn't sure I wanted to know.

"I found you curled up, facing the fire, sound asleep with your back against a log. I dragged you back to the tent and somehow managed to stuff you into your bag. I have to say, you were more than a little bit belligerent. 'Leave me here. I want to sleep here,'" Alex said in a mocking tone, but her smile softened the blow.

"When I got back to the fire, things had gotten even crazier. Tony and Pete were totally stoned with freaking energy. They pulled some flaming sticks out of the fire and were spinning them around, like kids with sparklers.

Then they ran screaming down to the water and were splashing around in the shallows before they both fell in. They were laughing like they totally didn't feel the cold."

"Where was Etienne?" I was really starting to worry about the leadership on this trip.

"He followed them down there and dragged them to shore, one at a time. They were fighting back, swearing at him, tying to punch him. Then the rest of us—Scott, Geoffrey, Samantha, and me, the ones who had avoided the brownies or weren't totally stoned—hauled the guys away from the water, got them back to their tents, stripped, and into their sleeping bags. We're all bruised and battered. We took turns staying with them, sometimes holding them down till they finally fell asleep. That was just a few hours ago. I was up most of the night. The others, too. Scott and Geoffrey did most of the heavy lifting. They were the only ones really strong enough to hold those guys down."

"How about Richard? Did he take anything?"

"That bastard. I don't know what he did or didn't take. I don't know what happened to him. He was running around like a crazy man, but I couldn't tell if he was high or just playing a game. He didn't go into the water, not that I saw, anyway. Then he just disappeared. Scott said he saw him head into the woods. Etienne got into dry clothes and organized teams to sit on Pete and Tony, and then he went searching for Richard. He came back a short time later saying he couldn't follow Richard's trail. He said he'd organize a bigger search after it was light. I do know Richard's sleeping bag is gone. Arsehole knows he is in big trouble. I think he just headed out."

"Where would he go?" At this point, any respect I'd had for Richard was gone, but I was still terrified to think of what might happen to him out there alone in the woods.

"Who the hell knows? That bastard is putting all of us

in danger," said Alex. "Get lots of extra clothes on. We're going to be spending the day marching around in the woods looking for the SOB."

I can hear people moving around outside the tent now. I'd better get out there if I want any breakfast.

Later.

Etienne is looking haggard today, and he has lost his patience with us. His eyes are edged in red, and his reddish-brown beard is starting to show. He's wearing a gray and brown knit hat, made of rough yarn, with earflaps. Peruvian, maybe? As he served our oatmeal this morning, he warily scanned the surrounding woods beyond our campsite.

After breakfast, he called for our attention.

"Last night should never have happened," he said. "Nearly all of you have broken not only the agreement you signed for this trip but also the fundamental rules of our school. Some have broken these rules innocently, others willfully, and one . . ." His voice trailed off. I could see he was struggling with what to say next. "We have to pull together as a community to make sure nothing like this happens again.

"Tony," he said, "bring me Richard's backpack and anything else he might have in your tent."

Etienne unfolded a tarp, and when Tony returned with Richard's pack, Etienne emptied its contents onto the tarp: clothing mixed with some of the other gear we were required to bring along.

"You can't do that!" shouted Melanie. She's a bossy know-it-all who I try to stay away from. "You can't go through our personal belongings."

"*In loco parentis*, Melanie," Etienne responded gravely. "Your parents assign to the school the responsibility to act in their stead."

Etienne discovered Richard's many stashes of

contraband. First, there were several packs of cigarettes and a baggie stuffed with what I guessed was pot and a packet of e-z widers. He tossed them into the fire. Then he removed three pint bottles, like the ones in Alex's stash. He unscrewed each one and poured the contents into the sand near the fire. Then there were some magazines. He glanced at them briefly, muttered something that I couldn't hear, and added them to the flames.

When the pack was empty, Etienne carefully ran his hands over it, one outside and the other in the interior. He stopped, struggling to free something from a zipper compartment. I watched his right hand come out of the bag holding a dark metallic object—a gun.

What in the world was Richard doing bringing a handgun on a camping trip?

I could see that Etienne was familiar with firearms. He inspected it closely, opened it, and pushed it together again before putting the pistol into an interior pocket of his parka.

We were all witnesses to the fact that Richard had violated all the school's zero tolerance rules for drugs, alcohol, and weapons. As soon as we got back to school, he would be on the next plane home. Richard bragged that his father had bought him out of lots of scrapes. It wasn't going to happen this time.

Etienne began barking commands.

"All of you, go back to your tents. Bring me everything you have that you should not have. Everything."

Most of the kids disappeared, including all of the boys. They quickly returned and handed Etienne their contraband. From where I was standing, it mostly looked like cigarettes. There were some pint bottles, too. Alex surrendered a pint with a label I hadn't seen before. Etienne emptied the bottles into the sand and tossed the cigarettes and marijuana into the fire.

"Is that it?" he asked, holding each of us in his gaze for a moment or two as he surveyed the group. No one admitted to having anything else. I knew that if Alex hadn't given him everything, the others probably hadn't either.

"OK, gather around, everyone."

Before he could launch into his speech, Melanie cut him off. "This whole trip is a disaster. We should just pack up and get out of here before anyone dies."

At that moment I think the group was with her. We were cold and weary and not looking forward to five more days of the same.

"And what about Richard?" asked Tony.

"Screw him," Melanie responded. "Look at the shit he pulled last night. He's probably heading back to civilization. He's always got a credit card in his pocket."

"OK," said Etienne, "settle down. We're not going anywhere, not today anyway. It's too late to pack out of here. And we need to search for Richard."

"And how many of us will get lost looking for that asshole?" Melanie asked.

"No one will get lost. We will always have visual contact with one another. Now, get all your warm clothes on. Lunch will be energy bars. Make sure you have extras in your pockets. And you will need at least a liter of water."

"And if we don't want to?" asked Melanie.

"We are all going to do this, no exceptions. You have fifteen minutes. Be back here at 11:30."

Etienne had us line up, one arm length apart, starting at the water's edge. And then, with him at the center and leading us, we moved forward, the line staying at right angles to the lake. The first fifty yards or so were easy going, just brush. Then we got into the woods. Etienne slowed us down and had us close the distance between us. I don't know how far we went, probably only a few hundred yards in the dense forest. Then he stopped us, moved us south the length of the line, and the process started again. And so it went, back and forth, slowly, until we had worked our way around most of the area surrounding our campsite. Other than some rusting beer cans and other trash, we found nothing. But keeping us occupied was a good thing. We really started to work as a group.

That said, there was some grumbling along the line. Some of the kids were worried about what would happen when we got back to school.

Melanie was near the middle of the line and the center of the bitching. "If they try to kick me out, my mother will sue their ass. When she gets done with them, they will be begging for mercy." Melanie talked a lot about her mother, how she was the toughest divorce lawyer in Chicago.

Alex cut her off. "You're blowing hot air for nothing. There's no way the administration is going to kick a dozen kids out of school. That would be a budget buster."

Melanie next focused on Richard, blasting him for getting us all in trouble.

By mid-afternoon the light was fading and the overcast was intensifying. Hungry and cold, we marched back to camp. Etienne formed workgroups to gather wood and started rebuilding the campfire for the evening.

I walked to the edge of the lake. A strong northeast wind was driving waves toward the shore. The rebounding waves off the bank were colliding with the incoming waves, disrupting the rhythm, creating disorder and confusion. As I stood there I felt like I was resonating with the water: confused, bewildered, in turmoil.

Chilled, I came back to the tent to put on another layer of fleece and catch up in this journal.

I found out today that there was more to last night's chaos than Alex shared with me earlier. She has a way of trying to protect my innocence. Some people took advantage of the fact that Etienne was otherwise occupied with Tony and Pete and decided to hook up. And there was a suggestion Alex wasn't a complete innocent in that activity, either. I knew about her and Etienne, but I thought it was over.

Alex crawled in a couple of minutes ago to tell me that the water is boiling for our freeze-dried meals.

"You OK?" she asked.

"Cold," I said, not telling her about my now growing level of panic. I'm afraid of appearing to be a wimpy freshman, even though that's probably what I am.

Alex pulled a down vest out of a stuff sack, fluffed it up, and put it on. Then she reached into her pack and pulled out another one of her pint bottles. Breaking the seal, she unscrewed the cap, took a long swig, and passed the bottle to me.

"I thought . . ." I said, wondering what else she and the others had held back from Etienne's contraband raid. Then I happily reached for the bottle.

We sat in silence, passing the bottle back and forth. At one point I waved it off.

"Don't worry, there's more where this came from," she assured me.

I'm feeling so much warmer now, and I don't feel as anxious. Everything's going to work out somehow, right?

Tuesday, November 20

Day 4

I don't really know how to write about what's happened tonight—I can hardly believe any of it is real. I keep thinking of the word *prescience*—a word from my PSAT vocabulary list. I memorized the definition, sure, but I didn't really understand what the word meant until I was overwhelmed by a sense of foreboding when, after dinner, Pete called out and pointed toward the woods, and I turned and saw Richard, leading two large, scruffy men into our encampment. Between the men, hanging below the pole they were shouldering, was a deer.

A murmur of relief and gratitude went up from our group when we saw Richard. Sarah and Melissa ran forward to hug him, and Tony and Pete followed to clap him on the shoulders.

Etienne stepped forward.

"Is this yours?" the lead man asked, motioning with his head toward Richard. "We found him in the woods stoned on his ass. Kid probably would have frozen to death if we didn't help him find his way back."

"I'm afraid so," Etienne said. "I'm sorry to have pulled you away from your hunting." He shook hands with the first man, who said his name was Huck.

"And this is my brother, Judd," Huck said as the second man stepped forward to shake hands with Etienne.

"Etienne Falconet," Etienne said.

"Frenchie, huh?" Judd said. "Bet you're from Quebec."

Etienne just laughed. "Thank you for helping this young man find his way back."

"Well, we couldn't leave him out there," said Huck. "All those fancy clothes of his wouldn't have offered much protection. The wolves would have had some tender pickings."

Huck and Judd dropped the deer, then un-slung their guns and took off their big packs. Their hair was long and ragged, and their beards were filled with bits of leaves and twigs and other debris. The second man lit a cigarette, and I could see his grimy hands and long filthy nails. There was something very menacing about them.

I was wishing Mike were here. He'd know how to talk with these men so much better than Etienne.

Watching Etienne with them, I realized how small he was. He was at least six feet tall, but he was slim. These guys, Huck and Judd, were like giants, strong and tough looking, next to him. I thought about how fast Etienne was on the piste, dressed in his spotless fencing uniform. When he was on the attack, you couldn't even see the end of his foil, just a flash of steel. But these guys were a whole different game. If things went south, and he had to fight these guys to protect us . . . well, they looked like they'd crush him. And they had guns.

So many times at fencing practice he had lectured us on the importance of sizing up your opponent, how from the opening seconds of a bout you should be trying to uncover their strengths and weaknesses. As I watched Etienne talk with Huck and Judd, I imagined that was what he was doing, strategizing on how he would meet any threat that might arise. I believed that he would do everything in his power to protect us. That said, he was outnumbered, outsized, outweighed, and outgunned—although I did remember that he had put Richard's pistol into his inside coat pocket.

Judd and Huck offered to share their venison if they could use our campfire to roast the meat. Etienne agreed. They quickly chopped off the legs with an axe. There was none of the skillful butchering that Mike had demonstrated, just a kind of crude violence, like they were chopping wood. Before long they had constructed a primitive spit and were roasting the meat as they passed a large bottle of liquor, whiskey I think, back and forth.

Etienne stood with them, and when they passed him the bottle, he drank from it. Initially, I was surprised to see him drinking and talking and joking with the men. Then I realized his strategy. First, he put himself between the intruders and us kids. He created a proverbial line in the sand. His conversation and his movements were all part of a dance to establish boundaries. He may have been sharing a bottle, but he was drinking little or nothing. It was all just an act.

And Alex was stage-managing the rest of us. There was a reason she was captain of fencing team and class president. She kept us organized, boiling water for drinking and freeze-dried meals and herding us together. She kept circling like a sheepdog, keeping us in a small, observable group. Usually our crowd emits endless teenage chatter, but no one was saying much. Our attention was mostly focused on the drama unfolding before us. I think most of us were feeling anxious.

Richard, however, was really enjoying the show. Pete and Tony were hanging tight with him. In a voice just loud enough for the rest of us to hear, he was telling them that Judd and Huck were totally cool. Then he said something to Alex about how she might want to cut a couple of big notches in her belt with some real men. He pointed toward Huck and Judd. "Bet they'd be better than that lame dude." He nodded toward Etienne.

I was next to her. Alex's anger was palpable, but she stayed in control.

As Judd and Huck drank, their speech became slurred and was little more than an endless stream of profanities.

Their coordination was increasingly unsteady. I was just waiting for one or both of them to fall down and pass out.

Etienne treated them like a couple of long lost buddies. He gave the appearance of being equally inebriated. The talk among the three of them was getting louder and louder, and there was a growing hostility between the brothers. From what I could hear, they were arguing about whose bullet hit the deer. And then there was something about how the whole trip was stupid.

Meanwhile, the wind was picking up, making a howling sound through the trees, and the snow was coming down more and more heavily by the minute.

The dispute between the brothers got physical. Huck threw a punch at Judd's face, but it caught him on the shoulder. Judd kicked at his brother, only to have Huck grab his leg, toppling him to the ground. Then they rolled around awhile, almost into the fire at one point. Finally, they slowly pulled themselves erect. Huck grabbed a long thick stick from the pile of firewood. He swung it at his brother, and the rotted piece of wood snapped off near his hands.

Most of our little band dropped back and pulled close, staying on the opposite side of the fire. Richard, however, was on the other side, egging them on.

Huck grabbed another chunk of wood and somehow Judd came up with a club of similar size. They each took a couple of awkward swings at each other without connecting. At this point, Etienne tried to intervene. "Hey guys, time to stop."

Suddenly, Huck and Judd both focused on Etienne and staggered in his direction.

"Fuck you, Frenchie," yelled Huck as he swung in Etienne's direction. Etienne ducked the blow and sent Huck wheeling with a sharp karate kick to the stomach. Huck staggered backward and toppled to the ground.

Etienne turned and dropped just in time to avoid Judd's club. He sprang toward Judd, kicked him in the chest, and sent him sprawling. But by then Huck had gotten to his feet, and he grabbed Etienne from behind. Etienne struggled to escape.

At that instant Alex moved away from our group and grabbed a branch the size of a ball bat from the woodpile. I could hear the dull thud as she smashed it against the back of Huck's head.

And then Richard entered the fray, but he seemed to be going after Alex. She knocked him off his feet with the club, and then took a swing at Tony. Tony went down, too. And Judd, back on his feet, jumped on Tony with his heavy boots. I could hear a snap when he landed, quickly followed by Tony's screams of pain.

Alex swung her thick club again and leveled Judd, striking the side of his head.

While the fighting was going on, I remembered the bear spray, my security blanket. I pulled it from my inner pocket and removed the safety clip, holding the canister at the ready. Huck had managed to grab Alex around the waist from the back and was lifting her off the ground. She was swinging and kicking, but not making any contact. Finally, she squirmed free and leaped beyond his grasp. That's when I moved in and got him. The first blast was low. The second was right in his eyes. He was yelling, just screaming. I squirted him again, just to be sure. He fell to the ground and tried to wash the spray from his eyes with snow.

Then Etienne went to Tony's aid. "Take care of the guns," he shouted at Alex. I watched her grab the two rifles and, one at a time, toss them out into the lake.

When Judd came to, Etienne shouted at him to get up. I could see the fight had gone out of Judd. Huck was still on his knees, swearing and crying. Finally, he too struggled to his feet.

"You need to leave. Now!" shouted Etienne.

"It's dark," pleaded Judd, sounding defeated.

"You've got lights. Go now."

"And if we don't?"

Etienne reached into his parka and pulled out Richard's pistol.

"Now, gentlemen, now."

Judd struggled to pull on his pack and then helped Huck with his.

"How about our rifles?" Judd asked.

Etienne pointed toward the lake. "Out there somewhere."

They stood for a long while, Judd hurling obscenities and threats at Etienne and the rest of us. Finally, they moved away from the fire and headed down the long trail toward civilization. We all stood and watched as they disappeared into the darkness, but there wasn't a sense of relief. We now all understand how vulnerable we are.

What if Huck and Judd came back, especially under the cover of darkness? They had to have knives and hatchets in their packs. Probably guns, too. And if they managed to kill Etienne, well I don't even want to think about what might follow. Before I could wallow in these thoughts much longer, I was pulled into the immediate crisis.

Everyone had gathered around Tony, who had pulled his scrawny body into a fetal position. He was sobbing and crying for help. Using his hands, Etienne quickly determined the site of Tony's injury. He sent us running to get extra clothes, blankets, the first aid kit, and a camping mat.

With the help of many hands, Etienne got Tony on his back and blankets under him. He cut Tony's pants and long johns open from the ankle to the knee. I could see the leg was cocked to one side at a weird angle. Then I saw the piece of bone sticking through the skin. Blood pooled below Tony's leg on the blanket.

Etienne told Alex to untie and pull off Tony's boot.

Then he told her to pull Tony's foot slowly and gently toward her. The bone slipped back beneath the skin. Tony cried out in pain. Most of us were sobbing.

Etienne covered the wound with gauze bandages that he secured with a big piece of cloth from the kit. Several of us helped lift Tony's leg a couple of inches so Etienne could push a mat under his leg. Tony's body tensed as we lifted, his face contorted with pain.

Etienne rolled and folded the mat into an improvised splint, using a small fleece blanket for padding, and triangular bandages to pull it together. While Tony was still in pain, it was clear that he was much more comfortable as soon as the splint was in place. Then, using an improvised litter, Etienne, Scott, Pete, and Richard got Tony back to his tent and covered him with an unzipped sleeping bag, pieces of clothing, and anything else that might help him retain body heat.

Etienne called us all together at the fire.

"Tony needs to be in a hospital," he said. "Tomorrow morning, I'm going for help."

"What?" Melanie said, panic in her voice. "You can't just leave us here."

"I'm sorry, Melanie, I have to," Etienne said.

"Why can't we all go?" Melanie demanded. "I've had it. We've all had it."

"We have no good way of carrying Tony. I don't want to aggravate his injury, and it would take far too long to get the group to safety, especially if it continues to snow this way. You have enough food and supplies for many days. With any luck I'll be back before dark tomorrow or sometime the next day with help. Everyone's just got to stay calm and follow directions."

There was no dancing about the fire tonight. The wind continued to howl, and snow cascaded around us. Etienne suggested that we all settle down in our tents—do some reading and sleep as much as possible. He said he and the older kids would take turns keeping watch in case Tony needed anything. I wonder if he's worried about Huck and Judd returning.

So here I am, alone in our tent, inside my sleeping bag. At least my headlamp still works so that I can write this. I don't know how I'm going to sleep—I'm so worried about Tony and what's going to happen to him. How long will it take Etienne to find help and bring it back? Will he even be able to do it? My mind just keeps going over and over these problems.

In addition to my PSAT study guide, I brought two books with me: a new Stephen King novel and *The Russia House* by John le Carré. I'm too spooked to read King right now, so I guess I'll try the le Carré.

It's snowing so heavily now and the wind is blowing so violently that we've had to move our tents, in the dark, to the foundations of the old buildings in the woods. I've never been this cold, never. I'm shivering so hard, I don't even know if I'll be able to write this.

I fell asleep before I'd gotten through two pages of le Carré. I awoke to the roar of a violent tempest. I could feel the force of the wind against the tent's flimsy nylon skin. Alex's sleeping bag was empty, and that made me even more frightened.

Then Alex crept into the tent. "Get dressed," she ordered over din of the storm. "We've got to move the tent. It will blow away out here."

Struggling against the wind, we pulled the tent and its contents through the heavy blanket of new snow into the protection of one of the old foundations. We got our tent against a north wall, somewhat sheltered from the wind. Then I helped Alex, Etienne, and the other kids move the remaining tents into the spaces between the old stone walls. Most of us were involved in moving Tony—some of us carried him, moaning, while others dragged his tent through the snow.

I've got to stop writing now and try to get warm.

Wednesday, November 21

Day 5

Etienne left this morning.

When I came out of my tent—dressed in nearly everything I brought with me—Etienne had shoveled out a small corner of the foundation in the lee of the wind and partially covered it with a tarp. He had us huddle around him, our bodies pressed close so we could hear him above the wind. Everyone was there except Tony.

"Today you have to work hard as a team," he said. "Everyone needs to stay close by, preferably in your tents. Your job is to keep warm, to stay hydrated and nourished. The only reason to leave this area is to toilet. And even then, go in pairs, and stay close to the tents. Don't wander away for any reason. You could get lost in the storm. Does everyone understand? Alex and Scott will be in charge."

Etienne gathered up his pack. There was a lot of grousing. I could tell most of us were quite panicked. Sarah and Melanie seemed close to hysteria.

Soon Etienne was bidding us *adieu*. We watched him fight his way through the deep snow and disappear into the storm, and I wondered how he would make it to the trailhead, let alone to the road to summon help. We gathered at noon and before dusk at the shelter on the lee wall to heat water for our meals. There was no campfire or big kettle of water anymore, just our little gas stoves set up as close to the wall as possible. Then everyone disappeared again to the protection of their tents.

With Etienne's departure, Sarah and Richard moved into his tent. In fact they all but disappeared. They were

50

obviously otherwise occupied and thankfully not creating havoc. Scott, Geoffrey, and Alex took turns looking after Tony and keeping him company.

Now the sun is setting, and there's no sign of Etienne. I've spent a few hours alone in this tent today, trying to read but being constantly distracted by thoughts of all the bad things that might have happened to Etienne, thoughts about what we will do if Tony takes a turn for the worse and we have to try to get him out of here ourselves.

Today it stopped snowing, at least temporarily, and we were able to dig our tents out of the drifts. As I pulled myself to consciousness this morning, I was struck by the overwhelming silence. The roar of the wind was gone. I remembered Alex being curled close to me in her sleeping bag during the night, but now her bag was empty. As I pulled on my clothes and jacket, I noticed how distorted our tent was—the fiberglass poles were bent at odd angles, straining against the weight of the snow. Once I crawled out of the tent, I saw that Alex had had to tunnel her way up through a thick layer of snow that had drifted against the tent during the night.

Alex organized a digging crew, and much to my surprise, Richard was standing next to her, looking eager to help.

As we started clearing the deep snow from our campsite and the paths to the nearby latrine areas with our little trenching shovels, it seemed like a Sisyphean task (another PSAT wordlist term I now understand intimately). After several hours of work, we had created only a small oasis in the sea of white. Perhaps the most important thing about the shoveling to me was the heat I was generating. I was starting to warm up under all the layers of down and fleece.

By lunchtime, as we heated water for our meals on our little stoves, the mood of the group seemed to be lifting, at least for awhile.

The late risers—Pete, Sarah, Doug, and Melissa— who had made no effort to help with the shoveling, now wandered out to take advantage of our work. In the early part of this trip we had worked as a team, gathering wood, keeping the campsite clean, even looking for Richard after he disappeared. That was what this adventure was supposed to be about, teamwork.

Richard appeared, cigarette in hand, to get some water for a freeze-dried meal. "So Alexandra, where's our rescuer?" he asked in his slimy sarcastic tone. "He was supposed to be back with the cavalry last night."

She tossed some f-bombs in his direction. "If it weren't for you, we wouldn't be in this situation. None of it."

"Alex, that's not true. Shit happens. It has happened to us. I'm not the cause. And I am as worried as you are. Look at us, a group of kids stranded in the wilderness, food running low. We could end up like that Chilean soccer team. Who would we eat first?" He paused and looked around. "Probably should start with Bitsy. Young and tender, bet she'd be a tasty bit."

"Richard, you freaking idiot. This isn't the Andes. One way or another we're getting out of here. Etienne will get help or Mike will come looking for us."

Richard continued on, ignoring Alex's remarks. "Come to think of it, you'd be a tasty—"

He didn't get to finish his sentence. Alex came flying at him, knocking him down, grabbing handfuls of snow and pushing them in his face. Then Pete jumped on her back, knocking her to one side. Scott then intervened, pulling Alex away from the other two and creating a barrier by standing between them.

Richard took his time getting back up. As he brushed the snow away he said, "See what I mean," he said, addressing all of us. "Our fearless designated leader is beginning to lose it. We're starting to go native, separating into warring tribes."

I thought he was going to launch some sort of

insurrection then and there, but he didn't. Richard was off in another direction; his attention was focused on Alex. "You're so fiery, Alex. That's what Etienne likes about you."

"Enough," said Scott. "Let's get lunch cleaned up and move some more snow. We don't want to look like complete fools when the rescuers arrive. Remember *Lord of the Flies?*"

This afternoon it was my turn to sit with Tony. Before I went into the tent, I asked Alex how he was doing.

"He needs a hospital," she said.

As soon as I settled in near him in the cramped tent I could tell that he was scared. I could see it in his face and hear it in his voice. And I think I was infected by some of his fright.

I had never really talked with Tony before. He was always in Richard's company, and I tried to avoid them. So my attempts at making conversation were lame. When I asked some questions about his hometown and family, all I got were one-word answers. Finally, I asked if he would like me to read some Stephen King.

"Yeah, that would be good."

So I started from the beginning of the book. Even though King is sometimes too scary, I like him a lot. I like the way his sentences roll forward, pulling you into each scene. I could tell Tony was getting into the story. He seemed to began to relax a bit.

After about a half an hour Steve came in to relieve me. Before I left, Tony reached out to me. He held my hand for a long moment. "Thank you. That was good." Separated from Richard, Tony seems okay. Maybe we'll become friends.

I stood outside of his tent for a long moment and thought about his situation. Other than trying to keep him fed and warm, there was nothing we could do for him. None of us.

Then it started to snow again. I came back to the tent and crawled back into my mummy bag to write this.

Before long it was easier to just pull my arms into my sleeping bag and doze. In my dreams Etienne and the cavalry arrived bearing chocolate croissants and steaming cappuccinos. Within hours we were sitting in a hot tub at a Marquette hotel celebrating our survival.

Later:

We had to shovel out our cooking area again tonight before we could boil water for dinner. The first fifteen or twenty feet of the lake have frozen, so now we have to melt and boil snow, which takes a lot longer and uses much more fuel. After dinner it took me twenty minutes to transform pots of snow into boiling water and fill my vacuum bottle for the evening.

Now it's getting dark, and the blowing snow is making it hard to see. I came in to the tent to count how many meals I have left. There are more than enough to get me through to the weekend. I started with a huge stock of granola bars. Unfortunately, they're mostly gone. I had half of a chocolate bar that I should have saved but couldn't help eating just now. Life without chocolate, things were looking grim.

Alex just came in and offered to share the last few swigs from her remaining bottle. It was lovely, cinnamony and sweet, giving a momentary sensation of warmth. If there had been more, I would have happily consumed a whole bottle and gladly embraced the oblivion it provided.

All my life I've been surrounded by adults—my mother and grandmother, relatives, teachers, doctors—all these people made the important decisions for me. Now, with things falling apart, I'm with a bunch kids. We're on our own and totally out of contact with the rest of the world. Our best hope is for Etienne to bring help soon. If he doesn't, we still have a few days before our scheduled pickup. I wonder if Mike can even get the bus close to the trailhead. He will probably have to leave it out at the highway and make the long trek in. And what will he find when he finally gets here?

And what happens if Huck and Judd come back before we get rescued? I don't even want to think about that.

When Alex came in here, I hid my journal under my sleeping bag and pretended to be reading *The Russia House*. Yesterday, Alex asked what I was writing, and I got the feeling she didn't want me chronicling our adventure-turned-nightmare. So I told her I was writing a short story for my English class.

"Hmm," she said. "I'd love to read it sometime."

"Sure," I said. "It's pretty rough right now, but I'll let you know when it's ready."

I'm not sure why I lied. Maybe it's because she's asked me about my journal writing several times this fall. She seems a little paranoid about it, like I might be writing about her. Anyway, I guess now I'm going to have to write a short story—maybe about the white buck.

Friday, November 23

Day 7

It was still snowing when I woke up this morning, and our tent had partially collapsed. Some of the fiberglass rods had snapped under the weight of the snow. I had to dig my way out of the tent like a swimmer paddling to the surface of the water.

I don't have the heart to write any more. We'll spend the day just like we spent it yesterday—clearing out the snow from our campsite, boiling water for our yucky freeze-dried meals and for drinking, and hoping today's the day Etienne will return with help.

Later:

Late this morning, out of the storm, Mike appeared on snowshoes, in his red hunting jacket and a fur hat, a heavy canvas pack on his back. We all surrounded him, babbling with excitement.

Once we'd calmed down a bit, Mike asked, "Where's Etienne?"

"Tony got hurt," Alex said, "and Etienne went to get help. You didn't see him?"

"No, but don't worry. It's a big white world out there."

His response didn't make sense. If Etienne had made it out, certainly he would be back by now with people to rescue us.

"What happened to Tony?" Mike asked, opening his pack and passing out Hersey bars and bags of roasted peanuts.

"His leg is broken," said Alex. "Badly."

"When are we getting out of this hellhole?" asked Richard.

Mike gave Richard a long look before following Alex to Tony's tent. When they emerged again, Mike looked scared, and that sent my anxiety level off the charts.

He gathered us together. "Tony needs to get to a hospital ASAP. I'm going back as fast as my legs will carry me and get some help out here. While I'm gone, pack up and be ready to go. I'll try to have someone here before dark, but that may not happen. You may have to spend another night."

We all groaned in unison. It was the only thing we all had agreed on in days.

"Why can't some of us go with you?" asked Melanie.

"You'd never make it without snowshoes. I've just walked ten miles in from the highway." He paused and looked around. "Here you got food, shelter. You will be perfectly safe. The sooner I get going, the sooner we'll be getting you out of here."

Then Mike was gone. I just ate the chocolate he gave me, allowing each section to slowly melt in my mouth. In spite of everything that's happened, this might be the most difficult time of the trip, these hours spent wondering when we'll finally be rescued.

Saturday, November 24

Day 8

Yesterday, I had almost given up hope that Mike would get back before the next day. In the fading light of the late afternoon, I starting hearing the snarling screams of what I assumed must be wolves or coyotes finally closing in on us. But then I saw the approaching headlights. A long column of snowmobiles snaked around the last curve of the trail and parked near our bunker. The riders where wearing helmets, mirrored glasses that hid their faces, and heavy black nylon snowsuits. Mike stood out in his red hunting jacket. He had a pair of ragged ski goggles pulled on over his fur hat. I don't know if I've ever been happier to see someone in my life.

"Thank God," Alex said as she bounded through the snow to greet our rescuers.

Mike led two people in red parkas with white crosses on the back over to Tony's tent. I thought the smaller person was probably a woman, because of her size and the way she moved, and when she emerged from Tony's tent without her helmet, I saw I'd been right. She was young and fair skinned and had lots of blond hair.

She asked Alex and me to help drag a toboggan from one of the snowmobiles through the deep snow back to the tent. The woman and her partner secured Tony on a backboard and then carefully loaded him into the toboggan. They must have given him some painkillers, because he was out cold. They covered him with blankets and a silvery windbreak. After he was strapped in, Alex and I helped pull the toboggan back out near the snowmobiles. Then it was attached to one of the sleds—that's what the emergency responders were calling the machines. Two of the sleds headed down the trail, the first one with the toboggan attached, a second one following.

Then Mike told us to take down our tents. Alex and I folded up our tent as best we could; some of the poles were broken, others bent. Most of the tents were goners, I think. I wondered which of our belongings had disappeared into the snow and would show up in the spring.

Our rescuers had brought several of the big plastic toboggans, and we piled all of our packs onto them. Some of the kids rode out with the packs. Others, like me, got lucky and hitched rides on the snowmobiles. Mike waved me over to his machine. We were the last sled on the trail. He took a few moments to do a final check of the area before we headed out. It only took us a couple of minutes to catch up with the others.

I was getting pretty cold by the time we finally reached the highway. Our bus was there, along with a whole line of emergency vehicles. I don't really remember the ride to Marquette. I just remember climbing aboard the warm, familiar vehicle and suddenly feeling safe and secure. When I awakened, Alex told me that I had gone out like a light before the bus was even moving.

We're staying in an older hotel in Marquette. In our room, Alex quickly headed for the shower. When she was finished, I took a long, hot bath. I would have stayed there for hours, but she roused me, saying we needed to go to dinner.

Mike must have organized everything. We all had dinner together in a small dining room. There were platters of burgers, baskets of fries, and Coke and other sodas. My vegetarian ways are disappearing. I didn't even ask the servers if there were any non-meat alternatives. I don't know what's going on with me.

We all stuffed ourselves with the hot, greasy food like it

was the best thing we had ever eaten. For dessert, the servers offered pumpkin pie with whipped cream. Mike excused himself before we finished eating, saying he needed to run over to the hospital to check on Tony.

When he had gone, Alex stood up and raised her hands to quiet the room. She said there were things we needed to talk about while Mike was gone, before anyone from school or any of our parents showed up. Then she invoked her favorite Latin phrase, her satirical take on the Leiston School motto—*Fidelitas et Integritas*, Fidelity and Integrity. Alex's phrase, laughingly delivered, was *Mendacium Donec Moriamini*, Lie Till You Die. It wasn't the first time I had heard it. She had it tacked to the wall in our room at school. And during the first week in September, as part of my orientation as her roommate, she explained to me what it meant.

Alex's take on life as a teenager is that the adults at the school—teachers, administrators, counselors, dorm parents—don't have a clue what is really going on with us. As long as we are smiling and pleasant, we can get away with almost anything. That said, if any of us were ever completely honest with these adults, we would jeopardize our private world. She stressed that, especially now, it was important to tell the adults what they wanted to hear. And we had to keep a united front.

"We all broke one or more of the zero tolerance rules," Alex said. "If it ever gets to the headmaster what really happened, there's a chance that most or all of us will get kicked out of Leiston. So let's just review the verifiable facts. We went camping. We did everything as planned. Then we got hit by a badass storm. Tony got his leg caught between some logs in the deep snow. He could feel the leg break when he fell. Etienne went to get help. We waited for him to come back."

"Tony's going to stay with that story?" Samantha asked.

"He's already been admitted to Dartmouth," Alex said. "That goes away if he gets kicked out of Leiston."

Richard stood. "Alex is right," he said. "As long as we all stick to the same story, everything will go on as normal. But if we don't, all of our lives will be turned upside down."

"What about Judd and Huck?" Pete asked.

"Don't mention them," said Alex. "We don't want cops looking for them. They could make our whole story come undone."

"But look what they did to Tony," Scott said. "They shouldn't get away with that."

"At this point, Tony's collateral damage," Richard said.

"And Etienne," Pete pressed. "Where the hell is he, anyway? And what do we say?"

"We say exactly what happened," Alex said, a pained expression on her face. "Tony got hurt. Etienne went for help. We don't know what happened to him."

"But what if he reappears and messes up our story?" Pete asked.

Alex and Richard looked at each other. They were finally working together. Richard said, "Listen, Etienne is a good guy. I don't think he'd rat on us. And he's got as much to lose as we do for letting things get so out of hand. If he backs up our story, he might end up being seen as a sort of hero."

"But what if he's dead?" asked Sarah.

A long silence followed. Of course we'd all thought of that possibility. Finally Richard said, "We'll just have to wait and see."

I watched Alex move away from the group. She stood for several minutes at a window peering out into the darkness. From her facial expression and body language, I tried to sense what she was thinking and feeling. The only word that comes to mind is despair.

Reunion

1

~

FRIDAY

Ray Elkins, the Sheriff of Cedar County—a small, thin peninsula that juts out into northern Lake Michigan—pulled off the pavement onto a snow-covered two track, eventually coming to a stop in a small clearing near the beach. Simone, a cairn terrier who had been snoozing in a tightly wound ball on the passenger seat, was up, looking out of the window as soon as he pushed the transmission into park. Then she leaped into his lap and waited for him to open the door. When he didn't move quite fast enough, she emitted a sharp command bark, signaling her impatience.

As Ray swung the door open, Simone scrambled out of the vehicle. After doing a slow down dog, she sat and waited for him to attach a lead. He reached back into the vehicle for a flashlight, and then he followed her enthusiastic pull toward the big water.

Ray paused for a long moment and surveyed the scene from the top of the last small dune before they reached the water. The lake was flat, unusually still, the surface mirroring the gray sky above. His eyes ran across the darkling plain, the lake disappearing into the mist, the Manitous only silvery shadows in the dull light. The steep faces of the dunes were cloaked in darkness.

As he looked at the quiet water, he knew that it was the proverbial calm before the storm. Some hours before, the National Weather Service had issued a Winter Weather Advisory. The time frame for the warning was from 6:00 p.m. Friday evening—tonight—to 6:00 p.m. Sunday. In the early hours of a storm, the NWS estimates for the number of inches of snow were exactly that—estimates.

Ray knew from long experience that, depending on the track of the storm and the many other variables that influenced its intensity, they might get only a few inches, or they might get two or three feet. The heights of the drifts were affected by wind speeds, and this storm warning predicted possible gusts of greater than sixty miles per hour.

The weather on the Big Lake was mercurial, but in November it was even more so. As the Arctic blasts moved south at the beginning of winter, the icy winds stirred the still warm water in the gigantic cauldron into deadly gales.

In the nineteenth century, before roads and rails started to crisscross the region, the Great Lakes were the avenues for transportation and commerce for a rapidly growing nation. November, the last month of the shipping season, was always the most perilous. Sailors demanded triple wages for that time, knowing that before ice finally closed the lakes, scores of ships would be destroyed and countless mariners and passengers would die in the bitterly cold water—some pulled to the bottom with the sinking wreckage, others quickly taken by hypothermia as they clung to bits of flotsam.

Ray coaxed Simone in a northerly direction, eventually freeing her from the leash. She sprinted ahead twenty or thirty yards, looking back over her shoulder occasionally to check his progress, then waited for him to catch up.

Ray was searching for the remains of the *Jennie and Annie*. It had been reported in the local paper that a recent storm had washed away part of a beach, exposing timbers from the 1872 wreck. He spotted part of the ship's keelson and the lower portion of some of the ribs at the base of a steep dune. The old timbers, some with iron fasteners still in place, were in shallow water a few feet off the beach.

Ray took his time looking over the remnants of the sailing ship. He had seen period photos and drawings of ships of that era. This had probably been a three-masted schooner. He visualized what the lake had looked like the night the *Jennie and Annie* foundered. He could almost hear the sound of the howling gale. He imagined the sailors' desperation and fear as they fought to save a ship tossed about by huge pounding waves. Ray closed his eyes and thought about the last few seconds when the battle was finally lost, when the boat broke apart or capsized. The crew would be struggling to find something to hold on to—pieces of the mast, barrels, anything that would support a man. They had only minutes to get to shore and find some protection or their lives would quickly drain away.

Simone was impatient. She gave Ray a sharp bark.

"You know, this ship went down in a storm out there more than 140 years ago."

Simone whimpered.

"Ten people went into the water, probably wearing heavy wool clothing. The temperatures were at or below freezing. Three people made it to shore; the rest perished in the icy surf within sight of the beach."

Simone responded with an impatient yelp, looking up at him, her head cocked to one side.

"I don't know if any dogs were on board. The history of the sinking is sketchy." He knelt and scratched Simone's head. "But if there were any dogs on board, they would have probably made it. In fact, they would have been standing on the beach shaking the water out of their coats as the survivors staggered onto shore."

Simone had had enough. She ran past Ray, heading south. It was time to get back in a warm car and head home for supper.

Later in the evening, a few minutes before 11:00, they left the house for Simone's last walk of the day. As predicted, the wind had picked up, and the driveway was already covered with several inches of snow.

When Ray awakened in the middle of the night, he could hear the storm still raging. He thought about Hanna Jeffers, his love interest of many months. She had flown out to Palo Alto to meet with a former colleague and discuss a possible research fellowship. Ray wondered what would be the outcome of this visit. He wanted to be supportive of her continued professional growth, but he was also afraid of losing someone who had become an important part of his life. He pondered what it would be like without Hanna, then tried not to think about the possibility.

Before going back to sleep, he glanced at the radar image on his phone. A heavy band of clouds extended from Lake Superior down over all of upper Michigan. *It will be a quiet weekend,* he thought, *schools closed and most people hunkered down until the storm blows through.*

2

~

U nlike the other participants coming to the Leiston School reunion, Dr. Alexandra Bishop made her own travel arrangements—flying to Traverse City, then picking up a rental car. Since graduating from Leiston, Alex had never returned, ignoring all previous reunions. Having her own transportation would enable her to leave if she found the gathering brought back too many bad memories.

Before driving to the site of the reunion, she first wanted to visit the Leiston School campus and wander the grounds. This would be a sentimental journey, the locus of a number of pivotal events during her late adolescence.

The shadows were already growing long on the late fall Friday afternoon when Alex rolled up the long curving entrance road. She parked near the side of a classroom building, an imposing Georgian mansion that was once part of a wealthy Chicago family's north woods estate. As she started her walk she noted there were no students about—Thanksgiving break had already started.

Alex walked across the leaf strewn lawn, an oak leaf carpet of reddish brown. She headed toward a cluster of small buildings some distance from the mansion. Her first stop was the workshop building. During her time at Leiston it was used by both the students and maintenance workers.

She pushed open the door at the center of the building. "Hello?" she shouted to the shadowy interior. No response. Alex felt along the wall until she found a light switch. A bank of overhead fluorescents sputtered to life. Moving to a large workbench near the center of the room, she paused and carefully took in the interior.

Not much had changed. The benches and power equipment

appeared about the same. The hand tools, however, were scattered about instead of being neatly put away. She thought about Mike, the person who had been in charge when she was a student. He had insisted on order and cleanliness. "Everything in its place," was his mantra. Anything less and you were banned from the workshop.

Alex reflected on all the time she had spent in the shop. One memory pushed the others away: the evening she had the place to herself. It had been during her senior year . . .

Under the ruse of needing to tune her skis, Alex had convinced Mike to let her into the area just as he was leaving for the day. She had built a friendship with Mike over her four years at Leiston. Among other things, he had taught her how to sharpen and wax her skis and repair her fencing equipment, so when she appeared at the end of his workday carrying her ski bag, he seemed to think nothing of letting her stay after hours. Mike's parting instructions were something to the effect of, "Alex, everything in its place, lights off, and door locked on your way out."

After Mike left, Alex dragged her ski bag to a bench in the far corner of the shop. Leaving the skis in the bag, she removed her practice epee. Setting the battered aluminum guard on the workbench, she loosened and rotated a vice, then secured the end of the epee's blade in the protective copper-clad jaws, carefully positioning the rubber knob at the end of the blade just beyond the jaws. Then she pulled off the rubber safety tip, exposing the flat end of the blade.

With slow, careful strokes, she filed the end of the weapon to a narrow point. Then she honed the surfaces of the point using one of the whetstones Mike kept on a bench near the sink. Alex dabbed some rubber cement on the blade and into the hole of the safety tip. As she waited for the glue to set, she returned the tools she had used to their designated storage places. Then she slipped the rubber tip back onto the blade, squeezing it against the steel, securing it, at least temporarily.

As she reminisced about that day, Alex ran her hands over the scarred wooden top of the old workbench. She reached out and touched the vise, feeling the cold, steel jaws. Then she retreated, stopping at the door, turning back, and slowly looking around a final time before switching off the lights.

Alex started across the lawn in the gloaming toward the fencing building, a long low structure with an arched roof. When she reached the building, the main door was locked. She checked the other door at the back of the building. It too was secured.

Alex climbed a small rise and looked down on the structure. She could feel her body tense as she remembered that evening a quarter of a century earlier. It was after dinner, during the hours designated for study time or tutorials. She had slipped out of her dorm for a clandestine meeting with Etienne, the fencing master and French teacher.

Etienne was waiting for her, working though his warm-up routine. She remembered giving him a quick smile before disappearing into the women's locker room. A few minutes later she joined him on the piste.

The fact that Etienne didn't like chatter before a bout, even a practice bout, worked to her advantage. She didn't have to feign friendliness or any sort of affection. She could concentrate on her carefully conceived plan without Etienne's charms softening her intent.

They came to the center of the piste for the prefatory salute, then moved back and pulled their masks into place.

En garde!

She mirrored his position, blade forward, alert. Alex was only a few inches shorter than Etienne's six feet, her reach almost as great as his. For the first minute or two their blades didn't even touch as they moved tentatively back and forth along the piste. Then they parried at the center for several moments before Etienne sprang forward and ran past her, the tip of his blade striking the center of her heavy canvas jacket, the blade bending as he pushed the tip against her thick plastic breast protector.

"Caught you napping, *n'est-ce pas?*" he said in a mocking tone.

Etienne's second touch was even faster, a quick parry, then a low thrust that grazed her knee. Etienne suggested that they could find more pleasurable ways to amuse themselves, something that had become the normal outcome of his special tutorials since the beginning of the fall semester. In the warmer weather they had just headed out into the woods with a blanket. But since late fall their assignations had taken place in a storage room after Etienne had locked the doors and turned off the lights.

Etienne had been her first real lover, not some fumbling schoolboy who didn't quite know what he was about. And even after all these years she couldn't help chiding herself for her silly romantic ideas that they were a couple, that they would stay together after her graduation and maybe even get engaged.

She had been enraged when she found out she was only one of Etienne's many lovers. Sneaking into his cottage one evening hadn't resulted in the welcome she had expected. And finding him in bed with Mrs. Dorenbock, the married and somewhat matronly algebra teacher, had shattered all her illusions.

After Etienne's second touch, Alex remembered how she had turned briefly toward the back wall of the gym and pushed the razor-sharp end of the epee through the rubbery glue and then through the surface of the protective tip. She stood looking at the glazed-block wall for a moment longer, unsure how she wanted to proceed. Then she faced Etienne, sword at the ready. They danced on the piste, keeping their distance, blades not making contact, faking attacks, moving back and forth. Then Etienne bobbed his head slightly, a telltale tic just before he lunged. Alex parried his blade easily and then slashed her epee across his chest, the razor sharp protuberance just long enough to slice through the first layer of his heavy canvas jacket.

Etienne froze. Then he dropped his sword, pulled off his glove, and lifted his mask. He explored the long tear in the white canvas, looking at his fingers for traces of blood. He glared at her as he stooped to retrieve his blade. She thought he seemed both angry and hurt.

"Why?" he demanded.

"You can figure it out, asshole." She held him in her gaze.

"It's not what you think," he said, reaching for her.

Alex pushed him away. Her fury was a firewall against his entreaties.

As Alex settled back into her car, she thought about that long ago evening and the events that followed. She hesitated for a long moment at the stop sign at the end of the drive. Then slowly started up the road toward the reunion.

3

ometime after noon on Saturday, Ray drove from his home
to his office at the Cedar County Government Center. It was
clear that the road commission plows were struggling to stay
ahead of the heavy snow. He only saw a couple of other vehicles as
he crept along the normally busy highway. Simone spent the trip
curled up in the passenger seat. There was nothing worth barking at
in the swirling white world beyond the car's warm interior.

Ray settled at his desk and started to go through the stacks of
papers, carefully organized and placed in order of priority by his
secretary. The first set of papers required his immediate attention,
but nothing more than his scribbled signature, over and over and
over again: requisitions, leave and vacation requests, and a few
dozen letters.

The next set of folders were related to budgetary matters; he
had put off looking at them for weeks. He spread the papers on
his conference table and started scanning the preliminary budgets
developed by his department heads, each of whom had provided
a wish list of needed items in rank order. Ray looked over the
requests. He was the final arbiter of where the limited dollars to
replace equipment would be spent. It was a difficult task. The marine
division's old dry suits leaked. He had seen the patches. The road
patrols' laptops had celebrated more than four years and could no
longer handle software updates. He made his own list, focusing on
which items directly affected the health and safety of his staff. His
musings were continually interrupted by calls from Central Dispatch
advising him on the status of the roads and progress of the storm,
which was continuing to strengthen. Thom, one of the dispatchers,
briefed him on conditions in the more northerly counties as well as

reports from neighboring counties and the Michigan State Police. After a conference call with emergency managers in the five-county region, Ray ordered that all roadways in Cedar County would close to nonemergency personnel at 5:00 p.m. and stay closed until further notice. There should be absolutely no unnecessary travel.

Thom emailed Ray a Declaration of Weather Emergency Statement for his approval. It was boilerplate—only the dates and times had been inserted—and the full National Weather Service Winter Storm Warning was appended at the end of the message. Ray sent back his approval, knowing that within minutes the notice would be popping up on phones, social media, and the broadcast outlets.

As Ray returned to the task at hand, he was interrupted by the sound of a familiar voice. Simone jumped out of the chair where she had been sleeping and went into full greeting mode.

"What are you doing here?" asked Ray. He had dropped Sue Lawrence, the department's one detective, at the airport early Friday morning. She was going to spend Thanksgiving week with her boyfriend in Chicago. Harry was finally going to introduce her to his family.

Ray looked at Sue. She appeared exhausted and glum. Her normally impeccable grooming was in disarray.

"It's a long story," Sue said. "The real question is what are *you* doing here? Remember the pledge we took? We were going to have lives and not work all the time." She sat down on the floor and let Simone climb into her lap.

"Was she a good girl?" Sue asked. She and Ray co-parented Simone, a dog they had rescued at a crime scene. But Simone spent the majority of her time with Sue.

"Hard not to be good. She was only with me for a day."

"Did she eat her prescription diet, or did she dine on lamb chops or perhaps some wild-caught salmon?"

"I don't understand why you're back."

"It's a long story and a rather ugly one."

"How did you get here? Everything seems to be closed."

"From what's-his-face's apartment, I went to O'Hare. I got the only available seat on the last flight to Traverse City last night. Then it became the usual Delta connector dance. First we had to wait for an aircraft, and then we had to wait for a crew from Minot that was delayed by weather. The crew arrived sometime after midnight.

"By then the weather up here had deteriorated, and they cancelled the flight. So I got together with three men I met in the departure area, and we rented an SUV. The roads were bad all the way. We got stopped for hours in a truck pileup just beyond the state line. Then we crept the rest of the way, taking turns sleeping and driving. The high point of the trip was slipping into a ditch near Reed City and waiting for a tow truck."

"Were you at the wheel?"

"It was glare ice, Ray. There were several other cars in the same ditch. Anyway, I'm exhausted, and I need a shower and some clean clothes. Do you think we can get home in this mess?"

Ray's phone, set to vibrate, pulsated on the conference table. Sue watched his eyes and listened to his end of the conversation. His last words before ending the call were, "I'll try to get in there. I've got some snowshoes in the car."

Ray looked over at Sue. "A forty-two-year-old female was found dead in her room sometime earlier today at the Leiston Conference Center. The victim was attending a reunion or retreat. No one has been available to respond to the 911 call. The Aral Township EMS unit is at the medical center in Traverse. They say the roads are impassable. They are going to wait out the storm in town. The road patrol unit in that sector is out of service—he's in a ditch. The other two units are assisting with accidents. In addition, our always reliable medical examiner, Dr. Dyskin, is downstate somewhere. That said, even if he were here, we'd have great difficulty getting him to the site."

"What's the Leiston Conference Center? Part of the school?"

"Remember that big trophy house that went up on the Big Lake about a mile west of the school?"

Sue nodded. They had been there investigating stolen building materials while the house, built by a Leiston alumnus, was under construction. "Rumor has it that it became a bargaining chip in a hostile divorce. Apparently the husband deeded it to the school rather than letting his wife have it. The school has turned it into a conference center, hoping to generate some revenue. It's supposed to be quite the joint."

"Did I just hear you say you were going to try to get there?" She gave him a long knowing look. "That's sort of crazy."

"Someone has to," said Ray.

"Well, if you're going, I might as well go, too. I've got snowshoes in my truck, too. If there is anything suspicious, you're going to need me. How about Simone?"

"We can leave her at Central Dispatch or drop her off at the jail. They'd be happy to look after her."

"I vote for the jail," said Sue. "The dispatch people live on cheese curls and doughnuts. Our correction officers will follow my feeding instructions and give her 24/7 attention."

Ray gave her a look.

4

~

Ray retrieved his snowshoes and stowed them in the back of Sue's department assigned vehicle, a black Chevy Tahoe with Cedar County Sheriff Department medallions on the front doors and "Crime Scene Unit" in gold letters on the rear quarter panels.

Sue started the engine and then helped Ray remove a thick layer of snow from the roof, windshield, and hood.

"How do you like your new ride?" asked Ray as he settled into the passenger seat of the new vehicle.

"It's clean. It smells good. Everything works. There's a lot more room in the rear for gear than in the Jeep. More road clearance, too. That said, it rides like a truck. The stability control doesn't seem to be as good."

Sue backed out of the parking space. They both felt the wheels spin as the vehicle started to climb over the mound left by the snow plow. Picking up speed, Sue made a hard left turn at the end of the parking lot, skidding sideways before regaining traction.

"Maybe you need to drive a little less aggressively?" suggested Ray.

Sue didn't respond. She turned right onto the highway, heading west. The roadway had all but disappeared in the heavy snow. Sue drove slowly, her eyes locked on the road straight ahead.

"So what happened in Chicago?" Ray asked. "I thought you were going to meet the family." A long silence ensued.

"I hope we don't end up spending the night in a snowbank," said Ray.

"No problem. I've got a case of Clif Bars in the back, bottled water, lots of extra clothing, and a full tank of gas. I'd prefer my own bed over sleeping in the car, especially tonight, but we've both done worse."

"So what brings you back so soon?"

"You just can't let it go, can you?"

Ray said nothing. He just stared out of the windshield.

"Toothbrush, a green toothbrush," she finally said.

"What are we talking about?"

"I found a green toothbrush."

"I'm still not following."

"Yesterday . . . seems like a million years ago. I took the train from O'Hare. Caught a cab to what's-his-face's apartment—it was early afternoon by then. He said he'd be home in time to take me to dinner. So I was unpacking, hanging things up, you know. I took my toiletry bag into the bath. I was getting ready to brush my teeth when I noticed it. A green toothbrush in the place where I always put my toothbrush. At first I just thought it was peculiar, that's all."

"Still lost," said Ray.

"He uses an electric toothbrush. Even when he comes to visit. Brings it with him."

"Maybe he bought you a new brush?"

"It wasn't new, Ray, I checked. But initially I didn't think too much about it. Then I opened the drawer I use, and there's an open Tampax box."

"Perhaps you left some on your last visit?"

"No, Ray, these were not mine."

"Maybe his sister was visiting?"

"He doesn't have a sister."

"Or a cousin or an old friend from college needing a place to crash. I'm sure there is a perfectly innocent explanation for the toothbrush and the other things."

"Yes, the other things. Shampoo in the shower with a name like Blond Sexy Hair. The bottle was three-quarters empty."

Ray waited, and eventually Sue continued. "I just had this

feeling that something wasn't right. In September he was all excited about having me meet his parents at Thanksgiving. And when he last came up here, everything seemed OK."

"How long ago was that?"

"Five, six weeks ago. And then we were both busy. He was traveling. We talked on the phone, but recently not as much. It's like I was suddenly putting the pieces together. Either he's two-timing me, or he's gotten involved with someone else and hasn't had the guts to tell me. I've just had this feeling for weeks that something wasn't right."

"So what did you do? Call him on it or what?"

"It was a fight or flight moment. I went for the flight, or at least tried to."

"Did you leave a note?"

"No. He had given me a key to his apartment on a lovely Tiffany ring. I left the key and the ring on his kitchen counter."

"And he hasn't called you?"

"No."

"And you haven't called him?"

"No. What do you think?"

"Does the radio in this thing work?"

"I haven't tried it. Instead of trying to find some music, why don't you answer my question?"

After a long gap in the conversation, Ray said, "I think you are probably right about things being amiss. The toothbrush and all, maybe it was a staged scene. You two have been dating awhile. Meeting the parents is often a prelude to the relationship moving forward. Maybe he panicked."

"Maybe."

"He's met your parents?"

"Yes, early last summer. What do you think?"

"I don't know. I'm sure he's picked up on the fact that you see everything. You are so good at working a scene. Of course you're going to see the toothbrush and the other stuff." Ray thought about it for a moment. "Here's my best guess, trying to put myself in his shoes. He figured that once you found the incriminating evidence, one of two things was going to happen: you would stay at the apartment and confront him, or you would do exactly what you did, run. My question is why did you choose the second course of action?"

Sue didn't answer. In the heavy snow, nothing looked familiar. Ray glanced down at the GPS, noting the crossroads on the map. They were two miles from the school, and the entrance to the conference center was a mile beyond that, up a long winding drive that climbed to the top of the dune.

The drifts on the road were growing. Ray could feel the SUV bottoming out.

Sue struggled to control the truck. Finally, they came to a halt, suspended on a drift. Sue rocked the vehicle back and forth, finally getting enough traction to back up. Then she accelerated forward, trying to break through the drift. The truck lifted skyward briefly, then dropped and slid off the road into a deep ditch, grinding to a stop and listing toward the passenger's side.

Sue looked over at Ray. "You okay?" she asked.

Ray nodded.

"So much for the premium snow tires," she said as she switched off the engine.

5

~

The last few miles to the conference center were a long slog in fading light, high winds, deep snow, and heavy gear laden packs. Ray and Sue, using snowshoes and poles, took turns breaking trail, staying near the center of the now impassable highway. The final few hundred yards, up the steep drive, were the most difficult. They had to work around the edges of several deep drifts, elegant sculptures formed in the leeward side of the rolling terrain. A series of marker lights—some visible, others just parts of subtly glowing mounds of snow, signaled the margins of the drive.

As they rounded a sharp curve near the crest of the hill, the mansion came into view. Sue waited for Ray to catch up.

"Just as I remember. It's quite the joint. Looks like a really big frat house," she yelled over the roar of the wind. The glow from the many windows provided them with a sense of the structure's size and shape.

They stacked their snowshoes, packs, and poles near the entrance, then Ray pulled a tall oak door open, exposing the expansive interior, where rough-hewn oak beams supported the ceiling two stories above.

Following the sounds of voices, they started to cross the wide entrance hall that occupied much of the central part of the building.

"Sheriff, over here."

A man who appeared to be in his late forties slowly crossed the hall toward them from the left.

"I was hoping you could get here," he said as he and Ray shook hands.

"You remember Gary Zatanski. He used to be a cop; now he's head of security for Leiston School," said Ray, turning to Sue.

"Yes," she responded. "It's been a couple of years. I'm Detective Sergeant Sue Lawrence."

"Of course," Zatanski responded, shaking her hand.

"Did you make it up the drive?" Zatanski queried.

"Not even close. We're in a ditch near the old Grange Hall."

"You had quite a hike."

"Yes. What have you got?"

"Well, I've got a dead body, unfortunately," said Zatanski. "It's in one of the guest cottages out back. Sorry to have to take you outside again."

They could hear the sounds of people chatting and laughing in an area on the north side of the entrance hall as Zatanski guided them to a door at the rear of the building and back into the storm. They circled a swimming pool, where a diving board hung above tall drifts, and slogged through deep snow to a cottage fifty yards south of the main building. They followed Zatanski into a living room at the center of the building. A large stone fireplace covered part of the south wall. The back wall, mostly glass, faced west toward the lake.

"There are two master suites in this unit, A and B," Zatanski said, indicating two doors on opposite sides of the living room. "She's in A."

"Before we go in, what can you tell us about the deceased and what happened?" said Sue as she extracted an iPad from her pack.

"I got a call from one of our housekeeping staff mid-afternoon. I was down at the school at the time. The housekeeper, Gladys Thompson, was trying to finish up and get out of here. I guess there was one hell of a party at the main house last night, and people didn't start getting up till noon. Gladys said this room was the last. Only one of the two suites was occupied. Gladys said she knocked on the door, but no one answered. She used her pass key but couldn't get in because the security chain was in place. She said she came back a couple of times. Gladys was in kind of a panic. The weather, you know. I told her to get on the road. I could make up the room if need be.

"I was right in the middle of something, so I didn't get started up here right away. I mean, it didn't sound like anything serious. Then I hiked up 'cause I knew my pickup wouldn't get through all the snow. I found the door just like Gladys said, the security chain in place. Rather than busting it out, I went out through there." Zatanski pointed to a set of sliding doors at the back of the cottage. "I thought maybe the slider in the suite might be unlatched." Zatanski paused briefly. "Each one of the suites has doors like this that open onto the deck that runs along the lake side of the building. As it turned out, the slider wasn't latched. I just pushed it open. As soon as I flipped on the lights I saw the body. The woman was on the floor. I felt for a pulse, but I could see she was dead. I took a quick look around. There was some suspicious stuff on a dresser, like she might have been doing some coke. Then I just backed out the way I came in. I didn't touch the interior doorknob or nothing. Given her age and all and the circumstances, I dialed 911."

"Any footprints out on the balcony? Any sign that anyone else had been there besides the occupant of the room?" Sue asked.

"Not that I could see. But truth be told, I wasn't looking, not on the way out. And the way the wind and snow are whipping around, things get covered fast."

"Do you know the name of the deceased?" asked Sue.

"Bitsy, Bitsy Morgan. That's the name on the room assignment sheet."

"And the other people here?"

"They're a Leiston School alum group, twenty-fifth reunion."

Ray followed Sue through the door leading to the balcony. They cautiously moved forward to the sliding glass door. Once inside, they pulled on latex booties and gloves. Sue switched on all of the lights and slowly surveyed the scene. The body was lying on the floor next to the king-size bed that dominated the room. Ray held his position near the door while Sue began to photograph the scene, starting from a distance and then moving close to and around the body.

"I wish Dyskin were here," she said, referring to the medical examiner.

"He's talked you through this so many times. It will be OK," said Ray, keeping his distance. From his vantage point he could see that the woman was small and compact. She was lying face down, turned slightly to one side, her right arm over her head, and both legs slightly bent, the left more than the right. Hiking boots, showing little wear, covered her feet. She was wearing a pair of close-fitting jeans and a brown wool sweater. Near the neck and at the wrists he could see the collar and cuffs of a red-and-charcoal-checked flannel shirt.

Sue continued to snap pictures, pausing from time to time to record her observations on an iPad. Then she looked over at Ray. "I need your help rolling her over."

Working in unison, they gently rolled the woman onto her back. Ray remained in the kneeling position for a long moment. His eyes swept from her face to her feet, then back again. He slowly stood and backed away, allowing Sue to continue photographing. He always had difficulty dealing with death.

Finally she stopped and looked over at Ray. "You OK?"

"Yes. What do you think?"

"Unremarkable. No signs of trauma. I'll bag her hands as a precaution. Then let's process the rest of the scene."

"I'll request a search warrant before we do anything else."

As soon as Ray got off the phone, Sue pointed to the dresser top, the one large flat surface in the room. "Look at the way her things are arranged. Nothing appears to have been opened. It looks like she walked in, leaving her carryon and backpack near the door. Then she came over here and put her purse and computer bag on the dresser. Somewhere along the line she tossed her coat on the bed. Other than that, the bed looks untouched."

Sue walked into the bathroom, switching on the light and a noisy fan. She switched off the fan. When she reappeared, she said, "A soap pack was opened and a hand towel looks used. She probably availed herself of the toilet and washed her hands. But no toothbrush or comb.

"Here's my scenario, which we can easily check. The woman

arrives from the airport or wherever. Brings her things in, makes a pit stop, and heads out to the party. Sometime later in the evening she returns to her room and dies from some still unexplained cause. Let me check the purse for ID."

Ray watched as she extracted a wallet from the purse and looked through the contents. "Elizabeth Morgan, Burlington, Vermont." She passed a driver's license to Ray. "One and the same, wouldn't you say?"

"Yes," Ray answered, passing the license back to her. "We should get one of the guests to ID the body before we wrap it up. And we could use some help finding next of kin."

Ray pointed to the items on the dresser that Zatanski had mentioned—a smart phone, a baggie, a small Swiss Army knife, and a piece of plastic straw.

Sue moved close and inspected the items. "I don't know," she answered.

She approached the body again and, dropping to her knees, she carefully examined the nose of the deceased with a flashlight. "There's no sign of powder on the skin surrounding the nose, nothing clinging to nasal hairs. I don't think this woman was doing cocaine. That setup on the dresser looks hokey to me. You?"

Ray nodded.

"What the hell is going on here?" Sue said.

"Let's get those things in evidence bags and out of sight," Ray said. "I don't want them visible when we bring in someone to ID the body."

6

~

Gary Zatanski was sitting on a couch in the living room when they disengaged the chain on the door and exited the bedroom. "What do you think happened?" he asked.

"This is one of those incidents where we depend on the skills of an experienced medical examiner," Ray said. "There is nothing about the decedent, Ms. Morgan, that suggests foul play. Sue has checked the body from head to toe. There's no evidence of any trauma. And you saw the interior of the room. It doesn't look like there was a struggle of any kind. The autopsy will tell the tale. I wish we had a way of transporting the body tonight."

"How about the drug paraphernalia?"

"I have a testing kit in my truck," Sue said. "But that will probably have to wait till morning."

"What do we do with the body?"

"We will get her in a body bag," explained Sue. "Is there a place we can store the body, like a walk-in cooler in the kitchen?"

"No," said Zatanski, "nothing like that. This was built as a resort home. High-end kitchen appliances but none of the commercial kind of stuff. If we could get the body down to the school, especially now that everyone is gone for a week . . ."

"That's not going to happen tonight," said Sue. "If you can help us get the heat turned off, we can get some windows open and this place cooled down. Was Ms. Morgan the only one staying in this cottage?"

"Yes, most of the people are in the main house. It has eight master suites. Most of the guests doubled up. Ms. Morgan apparently decided to come at the last minute. There were no vacant rooms in the main house, and the overflow ended up in the guest cottages."

"And the heat?"

"Everything is zoned, that's not a problem."

"Gary, do the other guests know what's happened?" asked Ray.

"No."

"You haven't told anyone?"

"That's correct."

"How about the housekeeper, the one who called you?" pressed Sue.

"She was gone by the time I got here."

"And she didn't suggest there might be something amiss?"

"No, she would have let me know if she had found a body, trust me."

"And none of the other guests wandered out here to look for their former classmate?" Sue asked incredulously.

"When I was in the bedroom, someone knocked on the door. They just knocked. They didn't try to get in or anything. I didn't answer. I was still just trying to take in the scene. Then I called 911. After that I stayed close, hoping someone from your agency would be able to get here. I saw my job as protecting the scene. I didn't see any reason to say anything until . . .well, I just wasn't quite comfortable with the situation. You guys know how to handle these things."

"We can do that," said Sue. "And I need someone to ID Ms. Morgan's body."

"Anything else?"

"We need a work area and probably a place to sleep tonight."

"The other suite in this cottage is vacant. It's got two queen-size beds, and this couch," he patted the couch on which he was sitting, "opens into a bed, too."

"Well, it's better than sleeping in a truck, don't you think, Ray?"

"Sure," Ray said. "Gary, before Sue makes her announcement, can you tell us whatever you know about the reunion and the other guests?"

"Well," Zatanski said, "it's the twenty-fifth reunion of a group of students that went on a wilderness camping trip in the U.P.

during Thanksgiving week and got buried by a winter storm." He looked at the swirling snow outside the windows of the cottage. "Go figure, right? Anyway, they got stranded out there, and their faculty chaperone went for help, but he never came back. Then Mike Kniivila, the school bus driver who had dropped them off, got concerned about their welfare and came back to check on them. And he was the one who organized the rescue, which happened with a lot of help from the local authorities. I guess one of the kids was hurt somehow."

"That sounds pretty dramatic," Ray said. "I don't remember hearing anything about it. I wasn't living up here at the time, but this would have been big news. I can't believe my mother wouldn't have sent me clippings."

"I guess the school was able to keep the lid on it," Zatanski said. "That wouldn't happen today, would it? Not with iPhones and social media. I've heard bits and pieces of the story since I started working at Leiston. Most of the people who worked at the school back then are long gone."

"And the missing teacher?" asked Sue.

"I don't know. I heard the guy might have been involved with one of the students. He was foreign, European. Maybe he called the headmaster at some point to say he was alive. I'm not sure."

"So give us some numbers. How many people are in the group?"

"There are twelve former students—but that's including Ms. Morgan. And then Mike Kniivila, the bus driver, was invited, too. He's the hero of the story. Mike's retired now, but he was still on staff when I was hired. He told me about the trip once over lunch. Said the school administration did a hell of a good job keeping most of the story out of the papers and off TV. You know, that kind of thing is an enrollment killer."

"Anyone else?"

"The person who organized the event is one of the campers, Richard Gordon. He is something else. I guess he's richer than God—hedge funds, whatever that is. He flew in his personal chef and kitchen crew on his private plane, so there's five of them we've got lodged in the staff quarters. He also has a couple of personal assistants—they seem to be at his beck and call. They're housed in the owner's wing, which is where his room is, so they can be available to him. His pilot, copilot, and steward are in a guest cottage, much like this one, on the north side."

"Gary," Sue said, "when you were in Ms. Morgan's room, you said that someone knocked on the door, so we know that someone was looking for her. Did that person call her name, anything like that?"

"Yes, it was a woman's voice. She said, 'Bitsy? Are you in there? Are you OK?'"

Sue peered at Zatanski for a long moment. Ray was familiar with the look. Sue was trying to suppress her irritation.

"Let's get her bagged. Then it's time we let everyone know what's happened," said Sue.

7

Ray and Sue followed Gary Zatanski out into the storm. They trudged through the deep snow and fierce wind to a door on the lake side of the mansion. Ray was third in line as they approached the loud chatter and music emanating from the great room. Three large couches were arranged in a U facing a massive stone fireplace that bisected the tall glass walls that faced the lake. Dozens of bare Edison-style bulbs in ceramic fixtures mounted along the heavy oak timber frame gave the room a warm golden glow. There were people sitting on the couches and propped up on pillows on the thick carpeting between. A tall thin woman with a tray was delivering drinks and collecting empty glasses.

Gary Zatanski approached a man seated with his back to them on one of the couches. "Mr. Gordon?" Zatanski said, and the man turned abruptly and gave him an irritated look. "May I talk with you for a moment? It's important."

Coming to his feet the man looked past Zatanski at Sue and Ray. "You know this is a private party, right?" he said. He towered over Zatanski. His straw colored hair covered part of a large forehead. His skin had a whitish pallor, with soft blue eyes set deep in a long face.

"Ah, sure," Zatanski said. "But this is Sheriff Elkins and Sergeant Lawrence, and they need to talk to you all about something important."

Gordon gave Zatanski a long look, then he led the three interlopers away from the invited guests to an adjoining hallway.

Ray took the lead. "Mr. Zatanski contacted us earlier this afternoon. He had discovered a body in one of the guest cottages. We have briefly examined the body and, based on picture ID from her wallet, tentatively identified the deceased as Elizabeth Morgan. Mr. Zatanski has told us that she was a member of your group. We need someone who knew this woman to provide positive identification."

Gordon looked off into the distance and didn't respond for several moments. Finally he asked, "How did she die?"

"It appears that she died of natural causes," answered Sue. "But we won't know anything for sure until after the autopsy."

Ray watched Gordon closely. He thought the man looked genuinely shaken by the news.

He noted Gordon's pupils appeared to be dilated.

"What do I do now? How can I explain this? Maybe you could tell the . . . I mean you must know how to do this."

"Yes," answered Ray. He looked over at Sue and nodded.

Gordon led the trio back into great room where a tall, attractive woman came to his side. "Get the music cranked down," he ordered. She scurried away.

A hush fell over the crowd as soon as the music went silent.

"Listen everyone," said Gordon, "something most unfortunate has happened. Gary Zatanski, the security director for Leiston School is here with some law enforcement people. He'll explain."

Zatanski moved toward the crowd a step or two. "The people with me, Ray Elkins, the Sheriff of Cedar County, and Detective Sergeant Sue Lawrence, they'll brief you on what's happened."

Sue moved forward. Ray scanned the crowd as she started talking.

"Mr. Zatanski made a 911 call to our Central Dispatch this afternoon. He reported finding the body of a woman in one of the cottages here at the conference center."

A low, painful moan emanated from the group. "Who?" someone demanded in a far corner.

"Normally, a road patrol officer and the township EMT crew would respond to this type of call," continued Sue, sticking to her script. "Because of the weather, they were not available. So we responded to the call."

Ray glanced at the crowd. The woman who had been ordered by Gordon to silence the music was rapidly working with her thumbs on her phone.

"When we arrived on the scene, we checked the deceased. Based on information Mr. Zatanski provided to us and a Vermont drivers license found in a wallet, we have tentatively identified the deceased as Elizabeth Morgan, also known as Bitsy Morgan."

The group seemed stunned. Ray heard someone murmur, "Oh, poor Bitsy."

"What was the cause of death?" asked the woman making notes on her phone.

"It appears that she died of natural causes."

The questioner followed up with, "So we're OK here?"

"There are no signs of foul play. Let me repeat, it appears that Bitsy Morgan died from natural causes."

Ray surveyed the group. He briefly fixated on a familiar profile. *Sarah James, what's she doing here?* he thought. The woman seemed to be studiously avoiding eye contact with him.

"At this point we would like someone familiar with the deceased to identify the body. Would one of you be able to help us with that?"

"Alex, you knew her better than the rest of us," said Gordon. "Besides, you're a doctor. You know how to deal with this kind of thing."

A tall woman with a graceful, athletic bearing stood. She glared at Gordon briefly, then moved in Sue's direction.

Ray stood in the background as Sue and Dr. Alexandra Bishop entered suite A in the guest cottage. He watched as the woman approached the body and knelt on the carpet. Sue unzipped the body bag, revealing the face and a bit of the upper torso. Alex carefully scanned the countenance of the deceased. She stood and moved back, taking one long last look. "Yes, that's Bitsy—Elizabeth Morgan." She slowly turned and left the room. They followed her out.

Alex collapsed on a couch in the living room and wiped a few tears away with her hand. Sue brought her a box of Kleenex. She wiped away a few more tears, then blew her nose.

"Can I get you some water?" asked Ray. "There might be some coffee or tea in the kitchenette."

"No, I'm fine," Alex responded, regaining her composure. "I just need some time to collect myself."

"For the record, can I have your contact information?" asked Sue. As Alex responded to her questions, Sue entered the data on her iPad.

"I came looking for her this afternoon when she didn't show up for brunch. It wasn't really brunch time. It was well into the afternoon. I wasn't feeling too well. I'm not used to heavy drinking, gave that up after college. I'm embarrassed to say that it took me a while to notice that Bitsy was even missing. But when I came looking for her, there was no answer. I thought, well I don't know quite what I thought. Poor Bitsy, dying alone."

"So you knew where her room was?" Sue asked.

"Yes, she sent me a text when she was close, so I was out there to meet her. One of the staff guys, a young man, walked us over to the cottage and carried her luggage. We just stopped there for a few moments and came back over here. We all had a late dinner."

"She said she needed a few minutes, you know. And I said I'd meet her back at the reception," Alexandra said, toying with a single braid of thick blond hair. Ray noticed her hazel green eyes.

"So you spent the evening with her?" asked Ray.

"We were part of the group. There was lots of food and champagne. People were floating around. Eventually I lost track of her. I got into a long conversation with another of my classmates. And after some time I wandered off to my own room."

"And you had no further contact with her."

"Correct."

"What can you tell us about her?" asked Ray.

"My senior year, we were roommates. Bitsy was only a freshman, sort of lost and lonely early in the semester. That's why the dorm parents paired us up. At first I was ticked at having a freshman roommate. But we got on surprisingly well. Bitsy was like an adoring little sister. It was probably a big ego boost for me. I'm sure I wouldn't have understood it that way at the time.

"Anyway, I was a fencer, and she became a fencer. She sort of followed me around. Some of the kids joked about me being a role model." Alex bit her lip, then continued. "You know how it is with teenagers. I spent most of my time when I was at Leiston breaking rules and doing my best not to get caught. My nickname was 'The Great Deceiver.' It's printed in the yearbook under my picture. I was good at conning the adults. In truth, I was probably the antithesis of a role model back then. My relationship with Bitsy . . . I think that started a change in my behavior. Early on I was probably a corrupter of sorts. Like I know Bitsy got her first taste of alcohol with me. But I did start to feel responsible for her, almost against my will. Maybe that was my first glimpse of adulthood. She was really naïve as a freshman, as green as they come. I reluctantly morphed into a role model of sorts. It's tough to give up your Peter Pan persona and stagger into the adult world."

"So you two stayed in touch?" ask Ray.

"We did. Letters after I went off to college the next year. Then phone calls. E-mails for the last decade or so. I have to admit that Bitsy was the one who kept it going. She reached out to me every few months or so."

Do you know if Ms. Morgan had any medical problems?"

"A couple of years ago in an email she mentioned that she had had some sort of cardiac episode. Apparently, as an infant, she had a congenital heart defect surgically repaired. She had never mentioned this to me before. Anyway, something happened and she ended up in an ER. I told her to go to Cleveland Clinic and get a complete workup."

"Did she?"

"No. After that one episode her primary care physician said it probably wasn't anything to worry about."

Alex straightened herself and looked over at Ray. "I should get back to the others. People will want to know what's happening. Such an awful thing."

"Just a few more questions. Then we will let you go," said Sue. "I would like to get a timeline for yesterday. When did Ms. Morgan arrive at the conference center?"

"She got here around 8:00, maybe a little later. She came commercial and had to catch a cab out here."

"Commercial?" probed Sue.

"Richard Gordon, the person who organized this weekend, has a private jet. He arranged several pickup points so people wouldn't have to fly commercial—three on the East coast and one in Chicago. Most of the attendees accepted his offer for free transportation. He also arranged for a shuttle service from the airport."

"And Ms. Morgan wasn't part of this plan?"

"She wasn't planning on coming. She arranged her own transportation just a few days ago."

"You suggested that there was a fair amount of drinking," Sue said.

"You know how it goes. The cocktail party started soon after we arrived. Dinner was being held until Bitsy got here. And then things went far into the night."

"Can you remember whether or not Ms. Morgan was drinking heavily?" ask Sue.

"I don't think so. That would've been out of character. But to be perfectly honest, if she was I didn't notice."

"Was anyone using recreational drugs?" Sue asked.

Alex was slow to respond. "Not that I saw. If anything was going on, it was being done out of sight."

"This might help us in establishing time of death," said Sue. "When and where did you last see Ms. Morgan?"

"I'm not sure. Around 11:00 maybe?"

"What time did you reassemble this morning?"

"It wasn't this morning. Not for me, anyway. I wasn't moving very fast. It was well past noon by the time I made an appearance. Richard was right there with a little hair of the dog. We were a sorry looking lot. I thought Bitsy was probably just really tired from the trip. Also, she seemed a little overwhelmed by all of us. She's a gentle person, maybe even fragile—certainly not as extroverted as some of us."

"We will have to notify next of kin," said Sue. "Do you have any idea who we should call?"

Alex didn't answer immediately. "I'm embarrassed to say that I'm not sure who you should call. She did say that her grandmother died; that was a few years ago. Her mother was an international lawyer and maybe still is, I don't know. Bitsy mentioned visiting her in Paris, but I think they just planned to meet there. I mean, I would say we're friends—we were friends—but we only spoke every few months or so."

"Anything else you can tell us about her?" asked Ray.

"I don't know. I mean, she wanted to make the world a better place. She worked at a nonprofit that focused on helping children in poverty."

"Do you know if she was married or if she had any children?"

"She was married, but that was years ago, someone she met in the Peace Corps. I never met the man. They didn't have any children. I think the marriage only lasted a few years. I asked her last night if she was dating. She said she was so busy with work that she really didn't have time."

"This is been very helpful, Dr. Bishop," Sue said.

"Please, call me Alex."

8

~

Gary Zatanski returned to the cottage as Alexandra Bishop was leaving. He stopped briefly just inside the door and knocked the excess snow from his boots.

"Did she hold up all right? It's never a pleasant task."

"She did fine," said Sue.

"Pretty woman. She's a doctor? A physician?"

"Yes," answered Sue.

"That's the amazing thing about Leiston," said Gary. "Probably other schools are like it, too. They seem to be just a bunch of regular high school kids, not too different from anyone else. But when they come back to campus a few years later, like the tenth reunion, they are doctors and lawyers and other educated, mostly successful people. I guess parents know what they're doing when they spend the dollars to send the kids here."

Gary paused a long moment, then asked, "Did you ask her about the drug paraphernalia? Did she think the woman had been doing coke?"

"Dr. Bishop thought it would be out of character," Sue said.

"That's the answer I would've expected. If they had been using cocaine, no one would admit to it even if you caught them in the act. At the school I'm always catching kids doing bad shit, and they look me right in the face and lie without even flinching. And now that we have surveillance cameras all over campus, I can confront them with video evidence, and they'll still proclaim their innocence. They think they can get away with anything. I was rattling on about this with my wife; she's a school counselor —in town, not at Leiston. She set me straight. Said this was normal adolescent behavior.

When I argued that me and my friends didn't do that when we were teenagers, she mocked me, saying memory was the first thing to go."

Zatanski slowly came to his feet. "But, I don't think she's got it quite right. It's probably a race between your hair, your knees, your memory, and your eyesight. Did I mention hearing?"

"Any idea when we'll be able to get the body out of here?" Zatanski asked.

"Your guess is as good as mine," said Ray. "Last I checked the severe weather warning was in force until sometime Monday. Then the process of digging out begins."

Zatanski passed Ray a paper sleeve with two key cards. "I programmed these to open the main door and both suites. Anything else I can do?"

"We're set. Thank you for all the help."

"OK, then, I'll head over to the house and see if there's anything that needs my attention. I'll try to rustle up some food, too. You guys must be starving."

Ray waited until Zatanski left before asking, "What do you think of Dr. Alexandra Bishop?"

"Smart, professional, very self-aware. She looked me over. She looked you over. She carefully scanned the room and brought the same level of observation as she studied Morgan's body."

"And the things she told us?" said Ray.

"She told us what we needed to know, nothing more. Perhaps that's the way people in her profession are trained to deal with law enforcement."

"And the question about drugs?"

"I don't know. The possibility is there. Coke is the recreational drug of choice for affluent people in their age group. Given our recent plague of cheap heroin, snorting a few lines of cocaine seems rather innocuous."

"Yes," agreed Ray. "But the bag, the white powder, what's that all about?"

Sue thought about his question. "I don't know. It makes my head hurt. I am so tired, I'm hungry, and I need to shower. Clean clothes would be nice, too. That stuff, maybe it was someone's idea of a joke, planted there during the course of the evening. Who knows, it might've been tied to something that happened on that camping trip or at school years ago. Then Elizabeth Morgan ups and dies, and we busy ourselves speculating on why the stuff is here."

"Since we have the search warrants squared away, let's move Morgan's bags to the other suite. I'd like to go through them to see if I can determine a next of kin before calling the Vermont DMV."

Ray and Sue were about to return to the main house to find some dinner when there was a knock on the door of the cottage.

Ray opened it and carefully scanned the woman standing before him. She was dressed in a white fur-trimmed ski parka and tight stretch pants. He thought she looked like a bar bunny at a chichi ski resort.

"Hello, Sheriff Elkins. I'm Jennings Bidder," she said. "I'm Mr. Gordon's special assistant for media engagement and his personal lawyer. May I speak with you and Sergeant Lawrence for a moment?"

"Certainly," Ray said and stepped aside so she could enter the cottage.

"Is it OK if I take your pictures?" she asked, lifting her phone toward Ray's face. "I like to have the faces as I add people to my contact list. And I'd just like to double-check the correct spelling of your names."

"No problem," said Ray as Bidder took his picture and spelled his name. He was quite impressed when Sue obliged straight-faced.

"Special assistant for media engagement. That's an impressive title," said Ray. "What exactly do you do?"

"In the old days my kind of work was referred to as public relations. But the news and communication landscape has made a tectonic shift in the last decade. As I'm sure you know, print and network news are quickly fading away. Engagement now happens via the Internet and social media. My job is to positively engage Mr. Gordon and his firm with his many friends and the stakeholders of his numerous ventures. Certainly, Sheriff Elkins, you have moved your department in this direction to keep your citizens informed."

"Yes," answered Ray, not bothering to elaborate. He looked over at Sue, who was visibly biting her tongue.

"I'm wondering," Bidder said, "how Ms. Morgan's death will be reported to the media."

Sue looked over at Ray before responding. She might as well have sighed aloud. "It probably won't be reported to the media. It appears as though the woman died of natural causes. If a person dies as a result of a criminal event or something like a traffic accident, those deaths are part of our routine media briefings. Not something like this. Death notices and obituaries are usually handled by funeral homes."

Ms. Jennings' thumbs tapped the face of her phone furiously as she took notes. Ray couldn't help but notice how attractive she was.

"I'm curious why you seem so concerned about this," said Ray.

"Sheriff, I'm not overly concerned. It's just part of the environmental scan I do to be sensitive to possible media events. Mr. Gordon is a public figure. People in his position always have detractors looking for any new little tidbit they can use against him. My job is to be out front, making sure that there is nothing in his environment that might be used to tarnish his image."

"I see," Sue said with fake solemnity. "Would it be possible to get a list of everyone attending this event? I'd like their contact information, too. After we have the autopsy results, you can inquire about exactly what happened to Bitsy Morgan."

"Yes, that would be terrific. In spite of your reassurances as to the cause of death, there is some anxiety. I've got that data on my laptop. I'll send you a copy in a few minutes.

"Mr. Gordon would like you to join us for dinner this evening. As you know this is a private party, but given that we are all captives of this weather, he wants to share our food and drink with everyone in the facility." She gave them a quick once-over. "And don't worry about the dress. We're all quite casual."

Sue followed Ray's eyes as Bidder departed. "Nice pants, huh?"

"Is that a New Yorker's view of how to dress in the north woods?" he asked.

"Could be. Then again, it might be New York bar pickup apparel." Sue stood and looked at Ray. "I'm not really concerned about my attire. But I'm a bit worried about my smell. And please don't quote Samuel Johnson to me."

Jennings Bidder found Richard Gordon standing at the bar in the great room with several other people. He hoisted a martini glass in her direction. She refused the offered drink, then moved her head in a way that signaled that she wanted to talk to him.

Richard joined her near the wall of glass at the front of the great room. Illuminated by exterior floodlights, snow swirled in an Arctic *Danse Macabre* just beyond the safety of the building.

"Anything?" he asked.

"Not that I could sense. They seem straightforward enough."

"Damn bad luck. Why did she have to show up and croak? I don't know why I thought she should be invited. She never looked like she comprehended what was going on around her. Kind of a ditz, really."

"You gave me a list of names. I found them and ways to entice them to come to this event. I got them all here. Not an easy feat going into a holiday week," she reminded him. "You can relax. The county mounty and his sidekick see it for what it is, a death from natural causes. Once the autopsy confirms that, there will be no further interest. Relax, Richard, there isn't going to be a Hyannis Port moment here."

"But it looks like the weather will keep them here all night—the body, too. That's hardly the ambience I wanted to create."

Jennings moved closer to her boss. "You never told me what this is all about. Perhaps if I knew . . ."

"Your job is to ensure that nothing embarrassing surfaces as I move forward into new endeavors. If nothing comes up this weekend, there's nothing more you need to know. Stay close to the sheriff. Make sure he and his deputy are appropriately wined and dined. As much as possible, stay between them and the rest of the group. You don't need to know anything more."

"If I had a better idea of what I was protecting you from, I could sharpen my antenna."

"You're not listening," he said, jabbing his index finger against her sternum. "Stay with the sheriff. Get them fed and off to bed. And later tonight I have to renew an old acquaintance. Keep your distance."

9

Jennings Bidder was at their side as soon as they entered the great room. The lighting was more subdued than on their earlier visit, most of the illumination now coming from clusters of candles arranged on dining tables and at the buffet line.

"Sheriff, Sergeant, you've arrived at the perfect moment. You're next in line. Allow me to introduce Michel Daudet, Mr. Gordon's personal chef. I have you seated over there," she said, pointing to a table off to one side, separated from the rest of the party. "And I'll be joining you for dinner. What would you like to drink? Matt, our bartender, is very knowledgeable. He personally selected the spirits we will be serving this weekend. We also have a superb selection of wines to go with the different entrées. Sergeant Lawrence, perhaps you would like a glass of Champagne. We're serving a 2006 Dom Pérignon. We also have a local sparkling wine, Cremant, that Matt is very impressed with."

"I'd like a Diet Coke, Ms. Bidder, if that's possible."

"Jennings, please call me Jennings. And the Diet Coke, that's easy. Would you like it with a twist of lemon, or perhaps lime?"

"Lemon would be wonderful. And lots of ice, please."

"And Sheriff, you look like a single malt aficionado, probably on the peaty side. Matt has brought along some particularly rare single malts that are impossible to find outside of New York. He also has a bottle or two of a legendary bourbon, Pappy Van Winkle."

"Mineral water would be fine, thank you." Ray could hardly hold back a smile as he listened, noting Bidder's patronizing tone. He loved being treated like a provincial.

Ray and Sue settled at their assigned table. The bartender brought their drinks himself. "Perrier for you, sir. And a Diet Coke with a twist for the lady. If you require refills or anything thing else, just give me a nod or come to the bar."

"Did you notice his hair color?" asked Sue, after the bartender had departed.

"Sue, it's dark in here. What did I miss?"

"Blondish with a hint of red, maybe. I think that color is called strawberry blond. I wonder if it's his natural color. And so thick and wavy. Very handsome."

"You seem to be on the road to recovery," he responded as he slowly scanned the other people in the room, his view limited by the subdued candlelight. At the center of the room near the windows facing the lake was a large dining table. Eleven chairs were occupied. The twelfth chair, at the foot of the table, was empty. The conversation seemed subdued. The loud rock music he had heard earlier had been replaced by bluesy jazz playing in the background. Richard Gordon was at the head of the table. Ray could see Alexandra seated on his right. She seemed to be mostly listening rather than being actively engaged in conversation. He could see Sarah James sitting at Alexandra's side.

A second, smaller table was off to the side. Ray didn't recognize any of the table's occupants. He and Sue, occasionally with Jennings' company, were at the third table, also at a distance from the main table.

When the food arrived, Sue wolfed down an artfully plated trio of appetizers. She was carefully scooping up the last few crumbs as Ray was still pondering the presentation. His approach to eating the pâté was far more meditative. He carefully sampled it, noting flavors and textures. Then he worked his way through the serving, pausing at times to cleanse his palate with sips of water.

"I bet Matt could bring you just the right wine," said Sue, observing his progress.

"Yes," he admitted.

"The fish eggs on that little potato pancake are good, too. And those little toasty cheese things, I could eat a pile of them."

Ray nodded his agreement.

"Of all the places to get stranded in a blizzard, you really know how to pick them. Do you sense we're being isolated from the other guests?" asked Sue, giving Ray a wry smile.

"Our minder, the incredibly socially adept Jennings Bidder, will be here momentarily. Maybe you should ask her."

"Everything to your liking?" Jennings asked as she settled in across the table from them just as the entrées were served. Glasses of wine appeared soon after the entrées touched the tablecloth. The waiter had disappeared before Ray could protest.

"Sorry about that," Jennings explained. "The wait staff is instructed to bring specific wines and vintages with each entrée. Chef Michel doesn't trust Americans' taste in wine. He says he doesn't want his food ruined by the wrong wine. How was your appetizer, Sheriff?"

"Superb," Ray answered.

"I'm not trying to lead you astray," said Jennings with a seductive smile, "but you should really try the wine. Just a sip. I think you'll find it enhances the flavor of the food."

"It's OK to sample it a bit," encouraged Sue. "We're not driving tonight."

Ray thought about it for a long moment, then picked up the glass, holding it by the stem. He examined the color and clarity from the flickering light of a candle. He brought the glass close and slowly inhaled the aroma. Finally, he tasted the wine, letting it wash around his tongue and palate before he swallowed.

"Well?" pressed Jennings.

"Lovely," said Ray. "An excellent choice. Thank you."

"When do you think we can get out of here, Sheriff? We had hoped to start sending people out after brunch tomorrow. We start with the Chicago people, that's such a short hop. Then the plane was going to pick up our East Coast guests, and finally Mr. Gordon and his personal staff. The rest of the staff people fly out sometime on Monday."

"That's probably not going to happen," said Ray. "First, as you can see, it's still snowing. At this point most of the roads in the region are impassable—and will remain so until it stops snowing—and the airport is closed. The latest bulletin I saw indicated that the storm will continue into Monday morning. After that the road crews will be able to catch up. It usually takes a day to get the primary roads cleared and another to get all the secondary roads open."

"We have people who need to be at work on Monday in New York, Washington, and Chicago."

"It's not going to happen," said Ray. "Hope your chef has some extra food."

"That's my next worry," said Jennings. "Excuse me," she said, leaving her entrée half eaten.

Ray watched her cross the room to Richard Gordon. She bent toward his ear, her hand on his shoulder. Then he rose and they moved into the shadows.

"Guess she missed the weather in her environmental scan," said Sue.

Ray looked in the direction of the head table again. He saw Sarah's familiar face in the golden glow of the candlelight. She was as beautiful as he remembered.

10

R ay was on his feet, moving across the room toward the head table. The chair where Richard Gordon had been sitting was still vacant. He could see Gordon off in the shadows near the front wall in conversation with Jennings Bidder.

He placed his hand on the left shoulder of Sarah James. She jumped at his touch. Then she turned in his direction, rising to her feet, reaching for him, encircling him with her arms. Ray wrapped his arms around her. He felt her body relax against his. The fragrance of her perfume triggered a wave of emotions.

"Of all the gin joints in all the towns in all the world," she whispered in his ear.

"Why are you here?" Ray asked.

"Let's get out of here so we can talk," she said, leading the way. She paused briefly at the bar, taking two glasses of champagne off a tray, and then led him into a nearby room, closing the door after they had entered. She handed him a glass of champagne, and he took it without hesitation.

"Sarah, what are you doing here? Why are you avoiding me? You won't even make eye contact."

"I'm sorry, Ray. I was just embarrassed."

"Embarrassed about what?"

"Embarrassed that I was such a shit in ending our relationship. You see, I hadn't been totally honest with you along the way. I was involved with a man in Chicago long before I moved there. And I'd probably been less than honest about lots of other things as well. One lie always leads to another."

She paused and held him in her gaze. "Those were special times we had. My feelings for you were real. It wasn't all a lie.

I was very confused." Her words were slightly slurred. She sipped her champagne.

Ray remembered Sarah's intensity, her ability to create an almost instant intimacy. He wanted to enclose her in his arms, yet he pulled back a step.

"How do you fit with this group? Are you still doing work for the school?"

"Richard Gordon enticed me to show up. I'm a Leiston School alum. I was a member of the infamous wilderness camping trip." She took another sip of the champagne, then drained her glass. Looking at his glass, she asked, "Are you going to drink that? It's going flat."

Ray passed her the untouched glass. "As I recall, you told me that your son wasn't doing well in a public school somewhere downstate. You said you took a job up here because you thought he'd have greater success at Leiston. You never mentioned that you were an alum."

"Probably it never came up," she said. "It was hardly important to what was going on at the time."

Ray let it go. "So tell me about Chicago," he said. "How's the job, what's going on in your life?"

"The job is good. I'm now the business manager of the law firm. And my son is doing great. I was able to help him get through Columbia, where he flourished. His father didn't contribute a dime. I was hoping he would come back to the Midwest. It hasn't happened."

"And what about your new relationship?"

"He was a lawyer in the firm. After he broke it off, some of my colleagues told me that was his usual MO. Dear Tom, he falls passionately in love, for months is seen floating on air proclaiming that he has finally met the one, and then suddenly he disappears. And that's exactly what happened. I was sure we were going to marry, and suddenly it was over. Around the office it was pretty clumsy for a month or two. Then he changed firms. It worked out OK, I'm seeing someone new. I would've brought him with me if Richard hadn't insisted on a 'no spouses or partners' weekend."

Sarah moved close again, putting a hand on Ray's shoulder, her body brushed against his.

"So you were on this wilderness camping trip. You all must have bonded pretty strongly to get together again after twenty-five years."

"It probably looks weird to outsiders. Not too long after we graduated, Richard went on to make a whole lot of money. He did it the old-fashioned way. He inherited a fortune from his grandfather. And he did well with that. He's a smart guy. From our first senior class reunion five years out, he started underwriting the events. We didn't come back here before. We usually went someplace on the East Coast, from Maine to Florida. But this is a different kind of reunion, just for those of us who had been on the winter camping trip, including the few underclassmen who were with us. We did have a special bond, at least at the time." Sarah looked away. "Maybe the luster has worn off. And now Bitsy is dead. I wish I hadn't come."

"Why's that?"

"Some things are best left in the past. I mean, it was good to see these people again, but an evening would have been enough. And now we're trapped here. And Bitsy is dead. It's all too much . . ."

She slid into Ray's arms and held him firmly. He remembered how much he loved the feeling of having her close. He allowed his body to melt into hers.

"At the end of the camping trip," Sarah said, pulling away a bit, "before we were rescued, I thought I was going to die. Lots of us thought that. Everything was spinning out of control. We were all going to end up freezing to death. They were going to find our bodies clustered together in those crappy little tents."

"You never mentioned any of this to me."

"I hardly ever talk about it. I don't even want to remember it. Then Richard has this great idea that we should celebrate our survival. He sends us retro backpacks, like the ones we carried back in the day, with our names embroidered on them. Then he has this faux yearbook put together with lots of photos from the trip. They were early pictures, when we were still having fun. Lots of smiles.

"And then he lays on the pressure. Personal phone calls and the extra enticements: transportation in his private jet, a luxury setting, the promise of great food and wine. We all sort of caved. The senior class reunions were always great fun. I convinced myself this one would be, too. But it's not."

"What's going on?"

"I don't know. Something seemed wrong from the time we arrived." She paused for a moment. "To start with, we all had way too much to drink last night. I was still in recovery mode this afternoon when your colleague announced the dreadful news of Bitsy's death. I didn't know how to feel. So I have more guilt than grief."

"How well did you know Bitsy?"

"I hardly talked to her at all. I was a senior; she was a freshman. Even in a small school there's a great divide. She was small and slight—she still is, was—and she seemed naive to me, but what did I know? I was too arrogant to comprehend that I was pretty clueless myself about the ways of the world."

Sarah took his hand and held it in hers. "So this has all been about me. What's happening with you? Married?"

"Hardly."

"Seeing someone?"

"Yes."

"You're a lovely man, but you're so laconic. You don't give anything away. Just the facts." She paused for a moment. "Anyone I know?"

"No."

"Not your sergeant?"

"No, a kayaker."

"I've thought about you so much, Ray," she said, moving in close again. "Leaving you was probably the greatest missed opportunity of my life." She reached up and pulled his face toward hers. Their lips touched, their bodies pressed closer together.

"Spend the night with me, Ray. I need you." She kissed him again, her tongue caressing his lips, her body melting into his.

After a long embrace, Ray put his hands on her shoulders and created a little distance between them.

"Dear Sarah, you are very beautiful, and you are also very drunk."

She planted her right hand on his sternum. "Elkins, you are such a pain in the ass. I'd almost forgotten that." She moved toward the door, turning back to him to him for a moment before she exited. "We'll always have Paris," she said in a bitter, mocking tone.

Ray stood for a long moment. He wanted to follow her. He waited until the impulse faded.

11

Sue looked over at Ray's half-eaten meal. He was suddenly up and gone, without excusing himself or explaining. She watched him cross the room and stop at the side of the head table next to a familiar face. She had noticed Sarah James earlier and was sure that Ray had seen her, too. Sue had been meaning to mention Sarah's presence; she was just waiting for the right moment. In the press of other events, that moment had never arrived.

As Sue watched Ray and Sarah exit the room, a fresh glass of Diet Coke was set before her on the table. She looked up, expecting to see the young woman who had brought their entrées. Instead, it was the bartender, Matt.

"I noticed that you have been suddenly deserted."

"Yes." She smiled in Matt's direction. "Join me if you like."

"I can do that for a few minutes. The bar business has all but collapsed for a bit."

"So, you work for Mr. Gordon?" she asked. She glanced at his strawberry blond hair again and wondered if she would have the nerve to ask if the color was natural or chemically enhanced.

"No. I bartend at a neighborhood kind of place in New York. Jennings Bidder, Mr. Gordon's personal assistant, is sort of a regular customer there. She's gotten me some extra work doing private parties for Mr. Gordon. The money is really good. Every little bit helps. New York is so expensive."

"So why do you stay there?"

"I started law school at NYU, then took some time off to try my hand at acting. That didn't work out. Maybe I'll go back to law school next year. I'm not sure."

"Jennings is an extraordinarily attractive woman," Sue observed, watching his reaction closely. "Are you two a number?"

"We're friends," he said, not giving anything away.

"But she gets you some good gigs?"

"Yeah, small parties, intimate affairs."

Sue liked his smile. It engendered warmth and friendliness. She focused on his eyes, a soft gray highlighted by his reddish eyebrows.

"Where I grew up," he said, "if you had people over, you just put out a few bottles and some mixer. And that's presupposing you were affluent enough to serve liquor. Otherwise, it was just beer and wine. These people are entirely different. They expect high-end liquor, premium wines, and champagne. And they just assume that if you're having a party, you'll have a bartender."

"Do you often travel as part of Mr. Gordon's entourage?"

"No, this is a first. It's turned out to be quite an adventure. I got to ride in Gordon's newest personal jet. It's going to be hard to go back to commercial. Mr. Gordon's crew made one flight just carrying beverages and food for the event, and that's in addition to a lot of stuff they had shipped FedEx. And the prep for this goes back months. Right after Jennings asked me to do this—like late August, early September—she had me create a shopping list, a dream list of the best of everything. When I arrived, it was all here: booze, wine, glasses, accessories, everything. That's what money can do. It makes things happen easily and quickly."

"Think you will stay in New York?" Sue asked, trying to keep the conversation going.

"I don't know yet. Part of me still wants to be a ski bum before I get too much older—you know, while my knees are still solid—and get by tending bar or doing other pickup jobs." He scanned the room before turning his attention back to Sue. "I've been rambling on about myself. How did you end up being a cop, a pretty woman like you? You look more like a model."

"Great line, Matt. Do you use that one often?"

"Never. What I mean is that the work you do has got to be

tough. Like tonight, having to be the bearer of such bad news. Have you considered doing anything else?"

"I've been thinking about going back to graduate school. Maybe doing something in the arts. I took some pottery courses as an undergraduate. I loved working in clay, but I don't imagine you can make a living throwing pots. I've also played with the idea of going to law school. Would you recommend it?"

"I don't know. The competition—it's tough. The classes are just a grind. But maybe the biggest downside is when you graduate and pass the bar, you probably have to be a lawyer. I mean, by then you've invested so much time and money. I'm not sure that's what I want to do for the next forty years."

"How about being a bartender?" Sue quipped.

"That would probably be more fun. But my mother wouldn't be impressed. Looks like I've got some business," he said, glancing toward the bar. "Nice talking to you. Hope we can chat again before we're liberated from this blizzard."

Ray was approaching the table as Matt departed. He noted Sue's melancholy expression as she watched Matt walk away.

12

Ray was relieved to call it a day. He found the lakeside exterior door at the south end of the main building blocked by a snowdrift. Together, he and Sue were able to push it open and make their escape through the deep snow to the cottage.

Ray tried to unlock the door with the key card. After several unsuccessful attempts, Sue pulled off a glove and took the card from Ray's hand. The green light flashed on her first attempt. "It's all in the wrist, Ray," she teased.

Sue settled on a bench in the entrance hall and unlaced her boots. After removing them, she set them on a boot tray at the bottom of the opposite wall. "The bartender is an interesting guy."

"'Interesting,' that's all you're going to say?" pressed Ray. "He seemed to be really chatting you up."

"I was asking most of the questions. He's smart, has great eyes, and a wonderful smile. So what's the story on Sarah James? I've never seen you desert a plate of gourmet food before."

Ray busied himself with taking off his parka. "Yes, Sarah James," he said.

Sue waited a moment but got nothing. "So did you find out what she's doing here? Alumni work? Fundraising?"

"That would have been my guess, but no. Seems she is a Leiston School alum and a member of the winter camping group from twenty-five years ago." Ray stared off into the distance. "I'm a bit baffled. We spent a lot of time together for a few months. She never mentioned that she had been a student at Leiston. The history she shared with me was all about her son not doing well in public school and moving here so he could attend Leiston."

"Did you ask her about it?"

"Yes. She passed it off as something that never came up. I guess that's possible, but it's not totally plausible. When she told me about her son coming here, there was no suggestion that she had had any previous experience with the school. I would have remembered that. It's like I never really knew the woman," he mused.

Sue stood and brushed the remaining bits snow off her parka before hanging it on a large peg above her boots. "Join the club, only insert 'man' for 'woman.'"

"I understand," he responded.

"You must be exhausted. We should figure out the sleeping arrangements."

As Sue led the way through the short hallway into the living room of the cottage, her attention was immediately drawn to the bedroom door behind which the body of Bitsy Morgan lay. The door was ajar. She pushed the door open, flipped on the lights, and peered down at the carefully wrapped body. "That's strange," she said, looking at Ray. "We didn't leave the door open." Returning the room to darkness, she pulled the door shut, then pushed against it, making sure the latch caught.

She crossed to the other bedroom door, pushing it open without touching the knob. "Ray, this door has also been forced. The strike plate has been torn out of the frame."

She turned on the lights by pushing her elbow against the rocker switch. The contents of Bitsy Morgan's luggage had been emptied onto the carpet. "Let me shoot some photos, just for the record."

Ray peered into the room from the doorway as Sue circled the area snapping photos. "And they didn't even pull a search warrant," he observed.

"Why didn't they just take the bags?" she asked. Then she answered her own question. "They were probably looking for something that could be easily hidden under a jacket. Dragging the bags would have been too conspicuous."

Ray crossed the bedroom to the sliding patio door and opened the curtain. The security bar was up and the door was open wide enough for someone to slip out. He stepped outside and swept the area with the beam of his flashlight.

"Anything?" asked Sue as he stepped back into the room.

"Footprints disappearing into the snow. If they were still here, they would have heard us come in. And while we were chatting they would have had lots of time to make their escape." He paused for a moment. "We left the patio door open in Bitsy's bedroom, so that's how they got in. Not finding what they were looking for there, they searched the living room and kitchen, then broke into this room. As soon as they heard our voices, they did a quick exit." Ray inspected the door. "Home level construction. You could easily tear this lock out with a hard shoulder against the door."

"The duffel was dumped and perhaps picked through," said Sue. "The roller was opened, but the contents don't seem to have been disturbed—yet. We interrupted the process."

"How about her purse and computer bag?" Ray asked.

Sue pointed to the top of the dresser. "Up there with our packs. They're kind of beat up. Her things look like our stuff."

"The plot suddenly thickens. What were they looking for?"

Sue passed Ray a pair of latex gloves. "Let's see if we can find anything unusual, out of the ordinary, whatever."

They organized the contents of the duffel bag on the floor. After a careful inspection, with photographs and detailed notes, they repacked it. Then they worked their way through the contents of Bitsy Morgan's carry-on bag.

Sue looked across at Ray. "Nothing, at least as far as I can see."

"Let's check her purse and computer bag."

"There's nothing unusual here," commented Sue, looking at the contents of the purse carefully laid out on the surface of a small desk. "She travels light. Wish I could winnow my junk down to this level."

After Sue returned the items to the worn leather bag, Ray passed her the computer bag. She unzipped the main compartment and removed a MacBook, a manila folder, and a glossy booklet.

She briefly looked through the publication. "Impressive," she said as she passed it to Ray. "Someone spent a lot of time and money putting this together."

"Yes," he agreed as he flipped through the pages. "Looks like Gordon was keeping his minions busy pulling this event together. It's all here: then and now photos, CVs, brief histories. You could catch up on your classmates on your way in on the plane. And these photos, they must be from that camping trip. Lots of snow and petulant-looking kids in period parkas and huge backpacks. This will help us sort out the cast of characters."

"And look at this," said Sue, holding up a thick binder. "*Bitsy Morgan's Wilderness Journal.*"

Sue spent a few moments flipping through the pages, stopping occasionally to read a paragraph or two aloud to Ray. "It looks like Bitsy kept a day-by-day diary of the trip. I think we've found something to read this evening."

Sue looked over at Ray. "It's cold in here. Would you turn up the heat and get a fire going? I'll check with dispatch and see what's happening with the storm and road conditions. I gave them the info from Morgan's driver's license before we went to dinner. Maybe they've found some next of kin."

Ray started building a fire. "Just think, you could be in Chicago right now, lingering over a romantic meal or having a nightcap in some cozy neighborhood bar."

"Yup. Instead I'm snowbound with a bunch of spoiled adults, trying to figure out their crazy games."

From her tone, Ray couldn't tell which one Sue actually preferred.

"Before you crash, Ray, Jennings, as promised, has sent me a list of everyone here—guests and staff. You might want to look it over." She passed Ray her iPad.

13

Ray was awakened by a muffled thumping. He wished it away, but the pounding continued. Finally, willing himself awake, he searched for a light switch in the strange surroundings. He flipped the switch several times, and when the lights failed to go on, he searched for his phone. He used the gentle glow to find his trousers and then guide him toward the door of the cottage.

He pulled the door open and Gary Zatanski entered, carrying a flashlight.

"Ray, I need your help," he said, shivering as he spoke.

"What's happening?"

"There's been a fight or something. People hurt, bleeding, people out in the storm."

"And the power?"

"It's been out for more than an hour."

"Ray?" Sue said.

Zatanski followed him into the living room. Ray could see her wrapped up in a blanket on the couch near the fireplace.

"What's going on?" she asked sleepily.

"Better get dressed. There's been some kind of an incident."

"I am dressed. I just need to find my boots."

Within minutes they were clothed and jacketed. Just before they ventured out into the storm, Zatanski passed each of them a flashlight. "The switch is on the bottom," he instructed.

With Zatanski leading the way, they plodded through the even deeper snow, the bitter wind biting into any bit of exposed skin. Once inside the main building, he guided them to the north wing of the structure. They entered a large room. In the dim light of randomly placed candles, Ray could see furniture had been toppled and that the room was in disarray.

"Where are the injured?"

Zatanski used his light to survey the room. "Over there on the couch."

Ray found Sarah James on one end of the couch, holding a bloody towel. Matt, the bartender, was at her side. Richard Gordon was at the other end. Jennings Bidder was attending to his needs.

"Anyone else?" asked Ray.

"Yes, the tall woman, the doctor," answered Zatanski.

"Alex," mumbled Sarah.

"She was following Tony, trying to calm him down," offered Matt. "They went outside."

"Gary, we need some first aid supplies," said Ray.

"There must be a kit in the kitchen. I'll see what I can find."

Ray crouched near Sarah. "What happened?" He directed the question to Matt. Sue hovered close by.

"I was cleaning up the bar area by candlelight. I heard what sounded like an argument. Then there was screaming and crashing, sounded like stuff being thrown around. By the time I found my way in here things seem to be over."

"It was nothing, really," interjected Jennings Bidder. "A little misunderstanding. People have just had too much to drink. It's not a police matter. This is a private party."

Ray moved close to Sarah. "I need to look at her injury," he said to Matt. "Take the towel off the wound."

Matt slowly lifted the makeshift dressing away from her face.

Ray inspected the wound as Sue illuminated the area. Sarah squinted and used her hand to shield her face from the light.

"How bad is it?" Sarah asked, keeping the eye on the injured side closed. Her speech was slurred.

"You've got a nasty cut just above the eyebrow. There's a large bruise, too. You're going to have a shiner by morning."

"A what?" she asked, struggling to understand what he had just said.

"A black eye."

"OK," he directed Matt. "Keep some pressure there above the eye until we get that bandaged.

"What happened?" he asked Sarah.

She looked dazed. "There was an argument. It was something about what happened. Tony, he just lost it. Alex and Richard, they were trying to hold on to him. I just got hit somehow. I think Tony was trying to punch Richard. He got me instead." She closed her good eye.

"I can't follow. You've got to tell me more. Did you fall?"

"Back off, Sheriff," Matt said. "This woman is hurt. And she's—"

"Open your eye, Sarah. You have to stay awake till we get you bandaged."

She partially opened her good eye. Ray lifted his light just enough to see if the pupil was dilated. It wasn't. But her eye was bloodshot, and the lid was drooping, signs of hours of hard drinking.

"Are you hurt anywhere else?" he asked. She closed her eye and shook her head back and forth slowly a few times.

"Keep her awake until we get her bandaged," said Ray to Matt.

He and Sue moved to the other end of the couch. Jennings Bidder was holding a plastic bag filled with ice against Richard Gordon's head.

Bidder removed the bag and Ray inspected Gordon's scalp. The lower portion was carefully trimmed. The longer hair on the top was carefully combed over. He could see a large bump on the top left side of Gordon's head. There was a small laceration at the center of the bump.

"How did this happen, sir?"

"I don't know. It was crazy."

"He's part of our security staff, ex-military." Jennings explained. "Mr. Gordon knew Tony was having problems. He reached out to him. Gave him a job."

"Where is Tony?" asked Sue.

"I don't know," Jennings said. "Sarah and Richard, they were trying to keep him from hurting himself."

"Was he drinking, too?" asked Sue.

"We were trying to limit that," Jennings said.

"So where is Tony now?" demanded Ray.

"He's out in the storm," exclaimed Alex, coming into the room from outside, brushing snow from her hair and clothes. "I tried to stop him. I couldn't. He's too strong, too out of control. I followed him out. He knocked me down and then dashed off. He was heading down the bluff toward the lake. There wasn't anything I could do."

14

~~

S lowly Ray and Sue trudged away from the dark monolith of the house as they followed the trail of Tony Messina. From the beginning it was an exhausting slog, at each step their snowshoes sinking into a thick, heavy blanket of snow.

Even in the blizzard conditions, they could make out his jagged trail. His path ran down the steep slope toward the lake. Initially, Ray broke trail, then let Sue take the lead, and they continued to switch positions periodically. Their thighs burned as they struggled to move forward through the deep drifts. In places where the wind had blown the snow cover away, they encountered steep walls of sheer ice. The hardened steel rims of their shoes cut into the surface, providing some traction, but not preventing an occasional fall. After crossing the ice, it would take a minute or two to locate Messina's trail again, the beams of their headlamps limited by and dulled in the blowing snow.

Ray struggled to keep up with Sue, the icy air burning his nostrils with every inhalation. He was breathing fast and hard. Sue slowed and Ray took over the lead, setting a pace he could maintain. They reached the bluff over the Big Lake. The sound of the wind was overtaken by the percussive baseline of the pounding surf. Messina's tracks led toward the beach. They couldn't see the water in the darkness, but they knew what they were about to confront.

Ray moved forward, stopping briefly at the top of a steep, ice-covered slope. He paused, looking for other routes. He jammed the teeth of one shoe into the ice, tested the grip, then slid the second snowshoe ahead. Suddenly he felt his footing give way. He tumbled forward and slid down the steep slope, his fall finally arrested as he dropped head first into a deep drift at the foot of the dune. Headlamp gone, entombed, Ray struggled to orient himself in the total darkness. He freed his arms, first one, then the other, and pushed the snow away from his face. He rested for a moment, taking several deep breaths, then started moving his body from side to side, bit by bit liberating his limbs. His legs were caught somewhere above him, the snowshoes hindering his efforts to free himself. For a moment he felt trapped. Then he started pushing back the icy walls with his arms and legs. Slowly he clawed his way to the surface and pulled the rest of his body into a position where he could regain his footing. He recovered his headlamp and hat near the top of the deep pit he had made as he plunged into the drift. He stood for a long moment to catch his breath, then slid down the last small ridge to the water's edge, guided by Sue's light.

"You OK?" Sue yelled, cupping her hands close to his ear, trying to be heard over the roar of the pounding surf.

"Yes."

"Which way?" she asked.

Ray pointed north. A few hundred yards up the beach they found Messina huddled against an embankment, his body pulled into a fetal position. He was without a jacket, one shoe missing.

Messina stirred as they stood over him. His eyes widened as he scrambled to his feet, his face contorted with fear. He was motionless for a few seconds, then he turned and dashed into the water. He splashed forward into the surf, a breaking wave suddenly tumbling him backward. Ray dashed into the receding water and grabbed a leg, pulling Messina toward the shore. Ray and Sue pulled him to his feet.

Messina twisted violently free from their grasp, throwing elbows and fists. He caught Sue on the side of the head with a powerful blow, knocking her off her feet. Then he swung at Ray, the blow hitting just below his left shoulder, much of its power absorbed by the thick parka.

Ray crouched, then swung back, putting his body behind the punch. He felt his gloved hand make a solid connection. Messina crumbled. They dragged him away from the water.

Ray pulled off his jacket, and he and Sue struggled to get the stuporous man covered.

"What about you?" she asked.

Ray patted the thick vest he was wearing. "Fast," Ray said, motioning toward the hill.

Side by side, with Messina between them, they began their climb toward the ridge line. Their progress was controlled by the steepness of the terrain. On the most abrupt slopes they crawled forward, one step at a time. It was a team effort, both of them using their legs and upper bodies in unison to lift and pull Messina's limp form forward. They settled into a routine: one foot forward, drag Messina between them, then the other foot forward, slowly repeating the process over and over again.

At times their progress was limited to only a few inches at a pull. A few times they lost their grip on his body, and they would have to slide backward and start again. When they encountered ice, they would circle the area until they found footing again. On the gentler slopes they were able make slow, steady progress, sometimes as much as ten or twelve steps, before they would have to pause to catch their breath.

Throughout the exhausting climb, Ray tried to stay focused on the slope in front of him, the tiny piece of real estate illuminated by his fading headlamp.

As they neared the top of the ridge line, Ray noticed a sudden glow. Moving closer they could see a series of floodlights illuminating the area behind the mansion. The power had been restored. Almost at the point of total exhaustion, they trudged forward to the lakeside entrance of the mansion.

They were suddenly surrounded by a crowd, people sliding in to carry Messina away, then someone helping Ray, releasing him from his snowshoes. Ray crawled through the door on his hands and knees, then stretched out on the carpeting of the brightly lit interior, closed his eyes, and started to drift away. He could feel someone tucking a warm blanket around him.

When he opened his eyes again, the swirl of activity continued.

He was being pulled into a sitting position, Sarah on one side and Matt on the other.

"Drink this. It will help you warm up," she urged, bringing a steaming mug close to his face.

Ray took a tentative sip of the hot, sweet, lemony brew. He could taste rum or brandy in the mix. He was too weak to object as he continued to take sips of the warming liquid.

"How are you doing, Sheriff?" Alex's face was close to his.

"How is Sue?"

"She's good. She's up and moving around."

"And Messina?"

"We're working on warming him. He's in a hot tub of water. Don't worry. I have four people looking after him. He should be in an emergency room. We're doing what we can with what's available. Do you understand what I'm saying?"

Ray nodded.

"I've checked your hands and feet. You've got good circulation. We're going to get you in a warm bed. Try to get some sleep. Everything is under control."

15

Ray opened his eyes to the dimly lit surroundings. He pulled himself up a bit and looked toward his legs and feet. He could feel the weight of several thick wool blankets.

He rolled his head back and rotated it from one side to the other, trying to work out the pain and stiffness in his neck. Then he freed his arms from the blankets and stretched them slowly above his head, pushing one out, then the other, filling his lungs, pushing back at the stiff, sore muscles. He felt sleep pull at him again and struggled to wake up.

"Any interest in some coffee?" Sue asked.

Ray swung his feet off the bed and sat up. "What time is it?" he asked as he accepted the Thermos mug from Sue.

"It's getting close to noon," she said. "I've been checking in on you for several hours. You were out cold. Dr. Bishop was here about an hour ago. She said you seemed slightly feverish. She wants to check you over when you're awake."

Ray sat and sipped his coffee. "That was a bad dream, wasn't it?"

"Yeah."

"You OK?"

"Yeah. Sore and tired."

"What about Messina? Is he all right? Who's taking care of him?"

"A constantly expanding cast of characters. Gordon's air crew—a pilot, first officer, and steward. Seems they all double as members of the security team. The steward, Conrad, is also an EMT. They're all ex-military."

"Where the hell were they?"

"Probably sleeping soundly in the staff quarters. I imagine

Jennings Bidder would have used her own people if she had been in control of the situation, but Gary Zatanski decided to rouse us.

"Anyway, those were the people who took charge when we got back. They were just on their way out to search for us. Conrad got on the phone, maybe it was a sat phone, getting expert advice on how to care for Messina. They ended up warming him in the bathtub with people supporting his body. When they got his core temperature high enough, they put him to bed in the staff cottage."

"I have no memory after getting back other than just sort of collapsing."

"Yeah, it looked like you passed out. You got a lot of attention initially from Conrad, the EMT. You don't remember any of that?"

"Was there a hot toddy involved?"

"Yes, hot and strong. I'm not sure that's what Conrad meant when he asked someone to get you a hot drink. But you stopped shivering and went to sleep. It took four of us to drag you back here."

"What did you do then?"

"I went back to the main building. I was wired. Matt made me a toddy, or maybe two. Then I came back here, wrapped myself in some blankets and slept on the couch. I woke up a couple of hours ago and wandered back over looking for coffee and something to eat. Other than Jennings and members of the kitchen staff, no one was stirring. I got some coffee and a croissant and lingered a bit as people had started to traipse in. What a sorry looking lot.

"I came back here and checked on you, then I went to work. I finished Bitsy's memoir, took a long hot shower, and then I talked to dispatch. We've got another twelve, fourteen, sixteen hours before the storm blows out of here. Everything in the region is shut down. They won't even begin plowing until early on Monday. But dispatch says things have been very quiet. Everyone is hunkered down."

"How about power outages?"

"They're scattered across the region, but nothing is going to happen until the plows can get back on the roads. We'll just have to hope people without power can use their woodstoves or fireplaces to keep warm."

"So how did the power here get restored?"

"My question exactly. I asked dispatch to check on outages. The utilities aren't showing any in this area."

Ray sipped some coffee. "No reports, interesting. Lots of stuff going on here. Let's talk about what happened last night. What's your take on it?"

"I started an incident report. As people were arriving for coffee this morning, I pulled them aside and got statements. I'm talking about Jennings, Sarah James, Matt Reed, Richard Gordon, and Gary Zatanski—all tell the same story to an amazing degree. Tony Messina had some sort of episode. No one is very specific as to the nature of that episode. When they tried to bring him under control, they were injured. They're all sure he didn't intend to hurt anyone. No one wants to press charges. They just want to get Tony some help."

"Didn't someone say he was part of Gordon's security detail?"

"Yes," Sue answered. "I asked Jennings about that. Tony Messina and Richard Gordon were roommates at Leiston and have remained friends over the years. Messina had made a career of the military, special forces or something. He did multiple tours in Iraq and Afghanistan before retiring. Once he was out of the service, his life fell apart — divorce, problems with alcohol and drugs, etc. Jennings said her boss couldn't allow that to happen to a friend. He threw Messina a lifeline, a job with a lot of extra support to get the guy through a difficult time."

"And how's that working out?"

"Jennings couldn't explain what happened, said maybe he was off his meds and that he wasn't supposed to have any alcohol. She assured me that they would take care of the problem. She said, 'Messina is family.' They will make sure he gets the best of care."

"It's a pretty screwed up family."

"You need to read Bitsy's journal. It's required reading if you want to understand this drama. And while you're doing that, I will see what else I can find out about this cast of characters."

16

"How are you?" asked Jennings Bidder as she wrapped her arms around Richard Gordon. Seconds later she pushed him away. "Can't I show my concern without you grabbing my ass?"

"It's in your job description, isn't it?"

"You've reassembled your high school harem. Let them take care of you."

Jennings was always taken aback by his ability to deflect any sort of criticism. It was as if he could shut down his hearing to anything that might cause even a few nanoseconds of self-reflection. She remembered being charmed by him early in her employment. He was rich, powerful, and in control. It took her some time to admit to herself that she had fallen into intellectual and physical subservience to him. *Stockholm Syndrome*, she thought, *time to walk away from the money and prestige.*

Richard sighed loudly. "To answer your question, my head hurts from where that bastard hit me. I got a big, ugly bump that's going to be hard to hide and harder to explain to business associates. This whole event is turning into shit, and now I can't even end it because we're fucking trapped here by the snow. When's the airport going to reopen?"

"Best estimates are sometime late tomorrow, at the earliest. It all depends on the weather. And no one is going to the airport until the roads are plowed."

"Hire a helicopter, at least for us. Get one from Chicago or Milwaukee, it's just across the lake."

"Richard, helicopters don't fly in heavy snow, and who's going to plow a landing zone?" She wondered if she should keep her mouth shut. "I was worried about this venue right from the beginning. You insisted. You said it was important to be here, but you never explained why it was so import to be in this specific locale."

"Look, I tell you what you need to know," he snarled. "I pay you to facilitate things, to make things happen, and to anticipate problems. But you're not my shrink, you're not my confessor, and you don't know the whole story."

"You pay me to cover your ass. I need some control over your public events if I'm going to manage your image." She struggled to control her anger. After several deep breaths, she continued. "I've done a lot to rehabilitate your image over the last couple of years. I haven't made you squeaky clean—no one could do that—but my spin has made you look a hell of a lot better." Jennings wondered how far she should push him.

"Why are we here?" she asked. "You've kept me in the dark right from the beginning. I've never known enough of your background with these people to be able to anticipate problems like what happened with Tony. And now things are totally out of control."

"How was I to know fucking Bitsy was going to croak?"

"Richard, that one is no big deal. People die. Dr. Bishop says she had a heart condition."

"But she shouldn't have died here. Now we've got the sheriff poking around."

"One percent of the population dies every year. She needed to pass somewhere. And the sheriff and the sergeant are just doing their jobs, Richard. They see Bitsy's death for what it is. And it's probably good that they are here. Without them, we might have lost Tony. We might have ended the weekend with two bodies. That would have brought a lot of attention from both the police and the press."

"My people could have found Tony."

"Sure, after someone got 'your people' out of bed, briefed them on the situation, and sent them off inadequately dressed for the conditions to find a path that had already disappeared in the snow. Richard, we are lucky that Sheriff Elkins and Sergeant Lawrence were here. And now that we're going to be here for at least one more day, we've got to make sure nothing more happens. No repeats of last night."

"It was all Tony."

"That's a bunch of crap, and you know it. It was about drugs and sex and a whole lot of shit that happened on that infamous camping trip and in the intervening years right up to the present. It was about a dark history that you and these people share. I don't want to know the details. I have no interest in wading through the blood and gore of your old school ties. My job is to keep you smelling clean, and like I keep saying ad nauseam, that's hard to do."

Richard exhaled sharply, "OK, shit, well keep things cool. Are we OK on food?"

"No problem. We are well provisioned for several days, that was part of a contingency plan."

"OK, then, just keep everyone fed and the alcohol flowing. We'll make it through another day."

"We need to cut back on the booze. Matt has been instructed to let people get happy, but only so happy. No more sloppy drunks."

"How about Tony?"

"The aircrew has worked out a shift system. And Dr. Bishop is trying to figure out his meds. I told you not to hire him. He's a liability."

Jennings watched him redden and knew she had pushed him too far.

"God damn it, Jennings, it's about loyalty. That's something you image people will never understand. It's about blood. It's deep, primordial."

"So Tony is some sort of a relative?"

"No, but he might as well be. It's a male thing."

"Yeah, great. And Richard, no drugs tonight. Who brought the coke, by the way, was that part of Matt's job?"

"Sarah, I think. She liked coke back in the day."

"You think? Do you ever tell the truth? And you're worried about the Sheriff. No drugs and you have no worries. But if they see people using, they will tear this place apart."

"Let's do the fencing matches tonight. Can you get everything set up in the gym?"

"Everything was ready last night, but you told me to stop."

"It would have been all wrong, Bitsy's death and all."

"Suddenly, you're Mr. Sensitivity."

"OK, the fencing match, that's our plan. Keep people busy this afternoon. If you can, get people into the gym beforehand to do some practicing. And show off the trophies. Make it a big deal. Then we will have a long leisurely dinner followed by the tournament. That will take a big part of the evening, you know, with the video replays and all. Then we'll do the awards and finish off with some drinks. Your job will be to get people off to bed. Get the staff to help you make that happen. OK?"

17

Ray set the manuscript on the coffee table and looked across at Sue on a couch opposite his.

"You've finished?" asked Sue.

"Yes, every word."

"What do you think?"

"Morgan, she wrote a lot better at fifteen than I ever did."

"Yeah, same here."

Ray pondered his answer. "Gordon, he seemed to be a real rotter back then," he said. "But I grew up with lots of guys who were like that. Most got beyond the throbbing hormones and the adolescent alienation and anger and became reasonably good human beings. I don't know what to say about Richard Gordon, the adult version. He's a successful entrepreneur, apparently, able to organize and bankroll this event. Looks like most of the people on that camping trip cleared their calendars and made it here for the weekend. It's unclear to me that the animus that might have existed back then has completely evaporated over the years." He looked over at Sue.

"I can't read the situation here," said Sue. "I've had limited conversations and mostly with staff members. Gordon's people are very professional. And that Bidder woman, she's constantly circling, keeping us walled off from the Leiston alums."

"Maybe that's just part of her job, keeping the cops away from the invited guests. At this point she's probably trying to make sure nothing else untoward happens this weekend."

"We need a whiteboard," said Sue. "I want to start graphing this, seeing if I can connect the dots."

"And what would you put at the top?"

She pointed to Bitsy Morgan's journal.

"Drugs, sex, rock 'n' roll," Ray said. "Where isn't that part of the unwritten curriculum—the things kids believe are lost on the adults around them."

"Come on Ray, it's more than that. Bitsy is describing possible criminal acts, things like Tony's injury and Etienne's disappearance. Bitsy clearly states that the group agrees to stick to a story that won't get them kicked out of school for violating the zero tolerance policy."

"Yes," agreed Ray.

"The unanswered questions have to do with the two Yoopers and the missing teacher, Etienne Falconet. I Googled his name. Lots of Etienne Falconets, but no one the right age or with the personal history to be this Etienne Falconet. Then I called the Marquette County Sheriff's Department. Their Central Dispatch is covering the phones."

"What did you learn?"

"I talked with one very weary woman. Their weather is as bad or worse than ours. Everything across the U.P. is shut down. I explained to her why I was calling. That got a bit of a chuckle out of her, especially the 'twenty-five years ago' part. She suggested I call again during the normal work week, which she quickly modified to late sometime next week, saying it was going to take days to dig out and return to normal."

Ray, still a bit groggy, thought about what Sue had just told him. "He taught French and took the kids to France, according to Morgan's diary, but was he a citizen of France? He could have been . . ."

"Canadian or Belgian or bilingual. With a French-sounding name—real or assumed—and competence in the language, it would probably be easy to pass yourself off as something you are not, especially in the great American Midwest."

Ray chuckled, "I sense some cynicism about our relative provincialism."

"Can you tell the difference between Québécois and Metropolitan French or Belgian French or Swiss French?"

"No, can you?"

"Well, a little," she replied cautiously. "Four years of high school French, four more in college, one semester in Paris during my junior year. Truth be told, at that time I was more interested in art than language, but my French was good enough to navigate around the country. I could order meals, buy railroad tickets, ask directions, and chat up French guys. And back then I could hear the difference between Québécois and the Paris variant. I'm not sure I could do that anymore. But my point here is that the kids couldn't hear the difference and the people who hired Falconet probably couldn't either. And who knows about his credentials. Were they real, enhanced, or totally false? I wonder what, if anything, exists in the Leiston School files."

"So what are you thinking?"

"Put yourself in his shoes. What if he's a complete impostor? He probably would think that this disastrous trip would make him the center of attention. And if that happened, he would be exposed."

"And would that be so awful? He would probably be fired, but . . ."

"What if this was a pattern? Morgan's diary implies that he was sleeping with some of the girls. What if this was his MO? Etienne gets jobs at small prep schools, accepts meager pay to get access to young girls. A suave, good-looking man would probably quickly have a gaggle of adoring admirers. And when things start to get too hot, so to speak, he gets fired or quits. Then he reinvents himself and finds a new gig, some other school in need of a French teacher."

"But wouldn't they check his credentials?"

"Twenty-five years ago, I wonder. The Internet has changed everything. Your former love interest, Sarah, didn't she run the business side of the Leiston School administration for a few years? Do you think she might have looked through old personnel files just out of curiosity, I mean, given her history with the group? If it had been me, I would have been going through the old personnel files the first time I had the opportunity."

"That's probably why you ended up a cop."

"Come on Ray, that's just human nature. Sarah would be curious about what happened to Etienne. She might have had a crush on him or perhaps . . ." Sue let the thought hang. "She'd want to know if there was anything interesting in the files. And if she stayed close to any of the girls in the group, they'd want to know, too."

"And if we weren't here?" asked Ray. "What if the EMTs had handled the call and nothing looked suspicious or unnatural?"

"Yeah, this wouldn't be of interest to us. We'd have more immediate fish to fry. But we are here, and my brain needs something to chew on. If this doesn't interest you, read a book."

"I didn't bring one, and I have yet to find a library or even a bookcase around here."

"Why don't you download one?"

"And read it on my phone? I couldn't do that."

"Luddite," she teased.

"What's happening in the outside world?"

"Dispatch says things are quiet. The snow emergency and travel ban is currently in effect until 10:00 a.m. Monday. You need to be available for a conference call tomorrow with the other county emergency managers. The current forecast calls for the storm to start losing its intensity sometime in the early morning."

"I'm always amazed by how heavy snow brings things to a standstill. Other than an occasional house fire or impending birth, the phones stop ringing," Ray said.

"Yup, the wife beaters and husband bashers have hopefully established a detente, the drunks and druggies can't use their cars to resupply their habits, teenage boys can't get out of their driveways, and the embezzlers can't get to the office, although some them probably work their magic from home. I guess we'd have to turn off the Internet to bring total peace to the valley."

"And what are you going to do?" asked Ray.

"First I'm going to find a Diet Coke, and then I'm going to see if I can get some real food. I wonder if Chef Michel has the makings for a cheeseburger? And once those two cravings are satisfied, I'm going to try to get access to Tony. You know, official business."

She gave Ray a mischievous smile. "Need to dot the i's and cross the t's on an incident report. That's the way we do things in this jurisdiction. Do you want me to come and get you before I try to talk to Tony?"

"I wonder how much Jennings will try to interfere."

"Yeah, she'll probably be wearing her lawyer cap rather than her media engagement hat. What are you going to do?"

"After a long, very hot shower, I'm going to nap." Ray yawned as if on cue. "You should probably try to get some rest, too. Tonight I want our presence to be obvious, almost intrusive. Let's try to make sure nothing more happens, and we can get these people out of here sometime tomorrow.

"If the autopsy turns up anything suspicious, we'll figure it out later. And while you're getting that Diet Coke, see if you can get anything out of Matt about the possible use of the other kind of coke."

18

S ue had Matt add a couple of lemon and lime pieces to her
Diet Coke.

"It helps to kill the flavor," she said. She glanced across at
the mirror behind the bar and pushed her freshly shampooed hair
around.

"Why do you drink the stuff?" Matt asked. He motioned to the
shelf of bottles behind him. "Look at all this high end booze. I could
make you something really exotic. I seldom have access to stuff at
this price point."

"I'm not much of a drinker, and when I do, it's mostly white
wine. But those toddies last night, they were just right, warmed me
right up, and I had no difficulty falling asleep, even though I was on
an adrenaline high."

Matt reached back and pulled a pear-shaped bottle from the
bar, setting it in front of Sue. "I've never served this stuff before.
It has a satiny quality, lovely and smooth. While I was making you
the toddy I was sampling it. Ended up having a couple of toddies
myself. Between the two of us, we had five or six hundred dollars
worth of brandy."

"But you only used . . ." Sue pointed to the liquor level in the
bottle.

"Yup," he answered. "If you have to ask the price, you can't
afford to drink this stuff."

"What else was in the toddy?" Sue asked. She liked his warm,
engaging smile. The color of his hair fascinated her.

"Trade secret. If I give all my magic away I'm no longer the
wizard." He gave her a soft punch on the shoulder. "I'll see if your
burger is ready."

Sue watched him disappear, then turned and toyed with the swizzle stick before taking a sip of the cola. She pulled her phone from an inner pocket and scanned her emails and messages. There was nothing of importance and no word from Harry. *He had to know about the storm. At the least, wouldn't he check to see that I got home safely?* she thought. *Even if we had a major falling out and he was the one doing the traveling, I would be calling or messaging. How did I become an absolute nonperson in his life? Does he really despise me? What did I miss? I thought I knew him.*

Sue was jolted back to the moment as Matt slid a carefully plated meal in front of her.

"One Kobe beef patty topped with aged Vermont cheddar and a thick slice of grilled pancetta on a sourdough roll with hand-cut french fries on the side—no pickle or onion. Chef Michel apologizes for the lack of foie gras and truffles. He's struggling with the exigencies of frontier living. He has dubbed this creation his *Northwoods Blizzard Survival Burger.*"

"I notice you're having the same," she said as Matt settled on a stool across from her.

"What can I say, I'm a Midwesterner at heart." He smiled. "That said, this is a bit over the top."

Sue took the first bite and savored the mixture of intense flavors. "Wow, this is like . . . I've never had a burger like this."

"Chef Michel's mantra is that you need the best ingredients to make the best food."

The conversation slowed as their attention turned to the food.

"Where exactly are you from?" she asked.

"Suburban Chicago."

"Where, specifically?" she asked.

"We moved around a lot. My father was in real estate. Do you know Chicago, like the western suburbs?"

"The city a bit, but not the suburbs. Which place did you like best?" She waited for him to finish chewing.

"Probably Glen Ellyn. That's where I went to high school, Central High. How about you?"

"Michigander through and through—born, reared, educated, and still here."

"I know you're not drinking alcohol, but this beef demands just a little bit of red wine to really enhance the flavor. I have an exceptional Cabernet Sauvignon open. How about just a bit, a half glass or so? I won't put it in a wine glass. The secret will be ours."

She hesitated a long moment, then gave him a nod.

"Good decision," he said, smiling warmly.

He poured the wine into two whiskey tumblers, setting one next to Sue's cola glass. "The bouquet will be a bit lost, but I think you'll find the Cab will do something wonderful for your palate."

Sue sipped the wine, slowly swishing it around her mouth, and then she swallowed. "Amazing."

"Yeah, it is, isn't it? I used to think all this food and wine stuff was a lot of pretentious junk. Now I have to confess that there really is something to it."

"Is it safe for a bartender to drink on the job?"

"In my experience, there are two types of bartenders: the ones who don't drink, and the ones who are constantly sipping on something but don't seem to ever get inarticulate. I'm usually in the first group. My drink of choice is black coffee." He motioned toward the tumbler, "This is not my MO."

"How about drugs in New York bars?"

"There's probably the total spectrum, from opium dens to places where they're not tolerated. I don't really see them in my tiny slice of the world."

"How about the private parties you work at?"

"Again, I know it happens, but I don't see it. My clients like fine wine and rare whiskeys. Most of them seem perfectly satisfied getting totally shit-faced on high-end booze."

"So last night's festivities . . . they were just alcohol enhanced?"

Matt chuckled softly, "Are you morphing over to your detective persona?"

"I'm always trying to figure out what really happened. When we get called, it's usually after the fact. So I'm always curious about what happened before; what's the backstory. At times I'm trying to unravel long complicated histories."

"Well, I can't tell you much about last night. Everything was pretty much over when I came on the scene. But there's a lot of history between these people, you know: old romances, sex, things that happened decades ago. That said, I didn't see any drugs."

"How about Tony?"

"I don't know. I met him when we first got here. You don't have to spend much time with him to know something is really wrong. The man has trouble making eye contact. When I've tried to engage him in conversation, I don't think we're on the same wavelength."

"Was he drinking?"

"I was told not to serve him, and I didn't. That said, all my extra supplies are stored in a room right off the kitchen. Tony is both a guest and a staff member. He's got full access to the place. It would have been very easy for him grab a bottle or two."

"Jennings seems to be a very interesting woman," observed Sue. "She organized this whole event, right?"

"Yes, but I've never gotten good vibes from her about this trip. This is something her boss wanted to do. Jennings' focus has been changing the public's perception of Gordon. She's been trying to recast his image. The former tabloid playboy and unscrupulous tycoon is now being depicted as a responsible, public-spirited businessman."

"For what purpose?"

"That's an interesting story."

19

"**A** bit early for a beer," commented Ray as he settled across the table from Sarah James in a small dining room near the kitchen. He was still struggling with the realization that he didn't really know this woman.

"Early? Even in central time it's after noon, Ray," she responded, squinting her right eye a bit, her left eye totally swollen shut. "You were always somewhat of a prude. Bit of the hair of the dog, this. Champagne headaches—the bloody worst. And this on top of it." She made a flaccid gesture toward her face with her right hand. "How bad is it?" she asked.

Ray had seen many battered women over the years—black eyes, broken noses, torn and bloodied lips, sometimes a broken jaw or missing teeth. There were times when he could hardly control his anger at the abuser. Fortunately, the immediate care of the victim helped him maintain a professional focus. As he looked across at Sarah, he wondered if she was the victim of an assault, or, as she claimed, just the recipient of an errant punch.

"Did you look in a mirror?" he asked.

"Just a peek. It's looks awful," she said. She drained the glass and set it on the table in front of her. "I needed to use my fingers to pry my eyelids open. I can see OK, it's just the swelling."

"I wish we could get you to an ER."

"Do you think it's that serious?"

"I always try to err on the side of caution. I would feel better knowing that your injuries were just bruising, a contusion, and nothing more. As soon as we can get out of here, you're going to the hospital."

"So if it's just bruising . . . ?"

"Things look really awful the first few days and then they start to resolve. The bruised area changes color a few times before the normal skin tone returns."

"What do I tell people when I get back to the office, that I ran into a door?"

"You might try the truth. These things happen."

"The truth is boring, and this doesn't reflect who I am."

"So what really happened last night?" Ray asked.

"I drank a lot of champagne, way too much. I don't remember a whole lot. I'm not much of drinker, you know that."

"Yes," said Ray, looking over at her empty beer glass. "Anything else or just champagne?"

Sarah was slow to answer. "Late in the evening, people were passing a joint or two. We were remembering the trip, trying to sort of evoke the whole experience, you know. Are you going to arrest me?"

"Tell me about the trip. That's why you're here after all. I've been hearing bits and pieces."

"It was a long time ago, Ray, a long time ago. I don't remember too much, not like some people. Alex, she seems to remember everything. I mostly recall being cold, incredibly cold. And there was more snow than I'd ever seen. We were freezing and hungry, and outdoor toilets, you know, like pits in the snow. Some of the kids thought we were all going to fucking die."

"You didn't hike into a blizzard, did you? There must have been some good times before the storm hit."

"It was all right at first. Of course, we took supplies along—cigarettes and a little grass, some pint bottles of booze. Just normal teenage shit. Come on, Elkins, you were a kid once. You probably did the same, although you're probably too pious to admit it."

"And somewhere along the line your teacher went missing?"

"Yeah, that was just at the end, shortly before Mike, the school bus driver, rescued us."

"Tell me about the teacher."

"Yeah, Etienne, it was strange. Some of the kids thought that he was just pissed at us and left us. You know, let these little rich kids figure it out. And I think that's possible. My memory is that he was sort of a socialist. It's a French thing, you know. Those people are always going on strike."

"But his disappearing, that had to be a big thing. Leiston is a small school. There were only a handful of you on the trip. Did you guys like him, hate him?"

"He was OK. Some people liked him a lot. More than they should have."

"What does that mean?"

Sarah poured the remaining beer from the bottle into her glass and downed it. "Why are you asking me these things? It doesn't matter anymore. That all happened so long ago. It's ancient history. And you're making my head hurt more."

"Come on, Sarah, the 'more than they should have' part, what does that mean?"

"Teenage girls, Elkins. Hormones, competition, romance. We didn't know much about the world, but we thought we knew everything. High school girls and faculty men. Things happen. You know that. It's in the papers every day."

"Didn't you and the others wonder about what happened to him?"

"Sure we did, lots. But the adults at the school, the other teachers and the administrators—especially the administrators—were totally tightlipped. And even Mike, the bus guy, who talked all the time about everything, his lips were sealed. When we came back from Christmas break there was a replacement French teacher, some dumpy woman they found in town. And fencing came to an end, at least for that year. Elkins, I'm getting bored by this conversation."

"But you must have speculated amongst yourselves . . . ?"

"Yeah, for a while. But we moved on. We were thinking about college, graduation, stuff like that. We figured the adults knew what they needed to know. They could figure it out."

"And when you came to work at Leiston, didn't you tell me that you took care of human resources?"

"I looked after all the business functions with the exception of accounting."

"You must have still been curious about Etienne. Did you look to see if there was any information on him in the old files?"

"Why don't you just leave this alone? No one cares."

"The files, Sarah?"

"OK. There was a file, just like the others from that time, but it was empty. Someone had cleaned it out. I don't know why they left the empty folder. They should have tossed that, too."

"How did that strike you?"

Sarah looked down at the table and slowly pushed the glass and the bottle away from her. "I think the administration back then just wanted the whole thing to go away. There were a lot of rumors floating around about Etienne. Who knows, they probably hired Etienne without checking his credentials.

"The reality was that we were all put at risk on this camping trip. The administration had not done enough to ensure our safety. So this is what I think, if you want to know. The administrators, they were in total 'cover your ass' mode. They just wanted to blot Etienne out of existence, pretend like he never happened."

"And last night, did Etienne Falconet play a role in that argument?"

"No, nothing like that. It was just people drinking too much. I don't even remember what the argument was about. Something involving Tony and Richard. When the fists started flying, I was just trying to get out of the way. Unfortunately, I didn't duck or weave at the right time."

"Were you and Richard classmates the whole four years at Leiston?"

"No, the last two. He had been kicked out of at least two other schools out east, you know, prestigious places like Exeter, Choate, and Deerfield. At least that's what he said. With Richard you can never tell. He makes things up as he goes along. Anyway, he made a big deal of getting expelled from 'the best prep schools in America.'"

"How did he end up at Leiston?"

"His story at the time was that his father had endowed something to get him in. 'Money makes things happen' was his pet phrase back in the day. He let us all know he was a trust fund kid. He didn't have to play by the rules."

"Doesn't sound as if you liked him much."

"I didn't, at least in the beginning. But Richard sort of grows on you. He liked to break the rules, and I was into that, too. Lots of sneaking off into the woods for a quick smoke. Sometimes he had a pint, too. In the months before graduation we were a couple, a brief hot and heavy teenage romance. "

"Which ended with graduation?"

"He went off to Yale, legacy admission, and I ended up in East Lansing. We saw each other occasionally for a few years. He would send me an airline ticket. Then the relationship ran out of steam, totally."

"And Tony, was he part of your group?"

"Yeah, he roomed with Richard. And even back then Richard always seemed to have lots of money—cash, credit cards, too. He treated Tony like an employee, his errand boy. Tony didn't seem to mind. What you've got to understand, Ray, is Richard was really cool. He was fun, too. He was always making things happen. Now he just seems so serious."

Sarah leaned forward and pushed herself up from the table, using her hands to steady herself. "Ray, there was a lot I liked about you, but sometimes I thought you were a real bore, insufferably so. I am going to take a very long bath followed by a nap."

At the door, she turned back toward Ray. "If you're that interested in what happened to Etienne, you might want to talk to Mike Kniivila. He would be better at speculating what happened to Etienne than anyone else. I saw him having brunch with Gary Zatanski a little while ago. Maybe he's still there."

20

Mike Kniivila pushed back his breakfast plate and turned toward Gary Zatanski. "I told you I didn't have a good feeling about this," he said. "I should have kept my sorry ass in Florida. I don't need any of this."

"Stop your bitching. You got a free trip and a couple of thou extra in your pocket," said Gary.

"And now we got a sheriff sniffing around. What was in the past should have stayed there. This whole thing was just asking for trouble."

"What was I supposed to do?" asked Gary. "Richard Gordon knows how to pull the strings. He makes things happen. Whenever it looks like we're about to go belly-up, Gordon comes through with a check. So when he calls the headmaster with an idea—I should say when his people call the headmaster with an idea—we all are ordered to make it happen."

"I never liked that sniveling little bastard," said Mike. "Cocky as hell, you know, a real smart-ass breaking all the rules. He was always into some bad shit. And he'd get the other kids in trouble, too. But they'd often end up taking the rap. Gordon and all his money, even as a kid he was able to buy his way out of things."

"But you took some of that money, Mike. You're sure as hell not clean."

"And sorry I did, too. It seemed innocent enough at the time. You never know how things are going to play out. And if any of this starts floating to the surface, Gary, you'll be in the net, too."

Ray grabbed a fresh cup of coffee before approaching the two men huddled close in conversation. "May I join you?" he asked, knowing that by all appearances he was interrupting a private conversation.

"Please," answered Gary Zatanski, motioning toward the chair directly across from him. "Sheriff, this is Mike, Mike Kniivila. He's a long-term employee of Leiston School. Perhaps you two have crossed paths before."

"Never had the pleasure," said Kniivila, standing and extending a hand. "Before moving south I saw the sheriff on the news a few times. I've never had the honor of spending time in the local hoosegow, but I heard the food was pretty good." He held Ray's hand for a long moment before slowly settling back into his chair.

"How are you feeling today?" asked Zatanski, looking over at Ray.

"A bit tired," he said, trying to control a yawn.

"That's a hell of a hike you guys took, even under the best of conditions. I don't think I could have made it. And the storm, that's as bad as I've ever seen it. What you and that sergeant of yours did is just amazing. You saved that poor bastard's life."

"You look like you could use a nap too, Gary," Ray said. "Bet it's a lot easier looking after teenagers than these forty-somethings."

"Yup, I now feel guilty about bitching about the kids. I prefer them to this lot."

"How's Tony Messina?" Ray asked. "I haven't been able to see him today."

"Contained and being looked after by Gordon's staff," Zatanski said. "I think as soon as the roads are clear enough for travel, they will whisk him out of here. He'll probably end up in a private hospital, at least for a while. I heard Jennings Bidder talking about damage control."

Zatanski gestured toward the man next to him. "Mike here was the headmaster's right-hand man back in the days when these guys were in school. In fact, Mike chauffeured them to the U.P. in the school bus and is responsible for rescuing them. In today's world of social media, he would have become instantly famous, the hero of snowmegeddon. Back then he was just a working stiff doing his job."

"That's all it was, Gary, I was just doing my job," Mike responded.

"The people at this gathering, Mike, they all know that you saved their bacon. That's why it was important for you to be here. Some things Gordon gets right."

"I think I've got some of the dots about this trip, but no way of connecting them. Perhaps you would help me with that?" said Ray.

"Mike is just the man to do that, Sheriff. And if you two will excuse me, I got things to do."

As Ray watched Gary stand and move away from the table, he wondered if the sudden departure was precipitated by his interest in the backstory of the reunion.

"I hear the weather was much like this when you rescued the kids," said Ray.

"It was just like this, Sheriff, only worse." Mike pointed to the dense, swirling snow just beyond the wall of glass at the front of the room. Tall drifts were now cutting off the first four or five feet of the view. "We now got that fancy name, polar vortex. Then, it was just another badass storm. It pounded us for days and dumped snow across the region. The whole U.P. was closed—Route 2, 41, the whole nine yards. Nothing was moving. Power was out most everywhere. Some of the drifts were six, eight feet high. Those storms, they're always worse in November when Superior is still warm. I don't understand the science behind it, but I've lived through lots of them, especially when I was a kid on the Keweenaw. Back then we sometimes didn't go to school for weeks."

Kniivila paused, his voice dropped. "I would be happy to tell you more, Sheriff, but I got a question for you first."

"Go ahead."

"Bitsy Morgan, she was such a special kid. Can you tell me what happened to her?"

"We won't really know anything for sure until after the autopsy, but it appears that she died of natural causes."

"I just saw her for a few minutes that first night. She gave me a big hug and said we'd have to get together, she had a lot tell me. She'd called me in late September, asking if I was coming up. I hadn't decided yet. She's one of the reasons I came. She said she had found her journal from the trip. She was going to make a copy and bring it to me.

"And then suddenly she's gone. And it's the strangest thing, you know. When your sergeant made the announcement, people seemed stunned for a bit, said a few nice things about her. Then it seemed to me the party just went on."

"You knew Ms. Morgan well before the camping trip?"

"In those days I was head of maintenance and grounds, but I also would run kids to town, and my shop was open to them to do all kinds of stuff, you know, like to sharpen skis or skates or work on school projects. I got to know the kids pretty good, better than their teachers sometimes.

"Bitsy came to Leiston as a ninth grader and she was a young one at that. Kind of small for her age. Something bad had happened in her life, like her father died or skipped out on her mother. Bitsy, she needed to be driven to town every week to see a psychiatrist. I spent a lot of time with her, especially during her first two years at school. She was sensitive like, kind of fragile. But sweet and real nice, appreciative of everything that you did for her." He took a shaky breath. "I've been grieving, Sheriff, grieving on my own. Maybe I take these things differently being old." He pulled off a pair of gold-rimmed bifocals and wiped at one eye with the back of his deeply tanned hand. "Doesn't seem like anyone else much cares. I'm so sorry I got talked into coming back here for this event. I've had enough sadness in my life in recent years."

"How is it that you are here?"

"Richard Gordon's woman, whatever her title is, the one with the last name first . . ."

"Jennings Bidder."

"Yah, that's the one. She called me in September. Said the group wanted me to be here, kind of like they were all beholden to me, not in quite those words, but I think that's what she meant. I live in

Florida—started in the coldest peninsula in the country, doing my final lap in the warmest. She arranged everything, I mean everything. Hasn't cost me a dime. People have been nice and all, but I'm not needed here. I'm not part of their world. I'm just an old guy with gray hair, what's left of it."

"I heard about the students getting trapped by the storm and how you managed to get a school bus through almost impassable roads to get close enough to snowshoe in and check on them. And then you hiked out and arranged for their rescue. That story says a lot about you, Mike, and it says a lot about your character."

"Thanks."

"There's one part of the story that I don't understand."

"What's that?"

"The teacher who was acting as their guide, the French teacher."

"Yah, Etienne."

"What can you tell me about him? Did his family contact the school looking for him after he disappeared?"

"Not that I know of. The poor man. He was in over his head with those kids, the storm, everything. From what the kids told me after, he did hold things together pretty good till close to the end. But he didn't have experience with anything like that.

"The original plan was that he was supposed to go along as an assistant on that trip. Julie Jensen, a science teacher, was supposed to be trip leader till she hurt her back. That woman was tough as nails, stronger than most men. I think she had been a drill sergeant or something, Green Berets, too. When I heard Jensen was out, I went and told the headmaster to cancel the trip, but he wouldn't listen.

"He said they were closing school for Thanksgiving break, the staff was all on vacation. I guess he didn't know what to do with the kids, figured things would work out OK. I warned him about the weather. Told him that Yoopers know how to deal with these conditions. They heat with wood, they hunker down and make do till the storm passes. But to put kids up there near Superior in tents, that was just frigging crazy. He looked me straight in the face and said that he had every confidence in Etienne. He was more than a little irritated at me for questioning his judgment. So I drove the kids up to the McCormick Wilderness and dropped them off. Then I went on to the Keweenaw to see family and do some deer hunting. As soon as the storm hit I started to worry about them. I was stranded myself for a few days. When the roads became passable, I come back to check on them."

"And Etienne?"

"He had left the day before, that's what they told me. I didn't see hide nor hair of him when I snowshoed in. When I came out I called the sheriff's department to get help. I asked if he had called, told them he was missing. They hadn't heard anything from Etienne."

"Did you file a missing person report?"

"No. I reported it to the headmaster, but I didn't do nothing formal. I thought Etienne was just holed up somewhere and would show up. I mean, where was he going to go? And I was busy, Sheriff. I was babysitting those kids at a hotel. I was on duty like twenty-four hours a day till the roads got good enough to take them back to school.

"I asked the headmaster what was he going to do about Etienne. He just told me to leave it alone; he was going to take care of it. And I confronted him a number of times over the next six months. The answer was always the same, he was making inquiries. The last time we talked, he told me that Etienne had been seen working as a ski instructor somewhere north of Montreal."

"Did you believe him?"

"I knew he was a good skier. I used to drive the ski bus to the slopes every Friday afternoon. I skied with him sometimes and watched him do some teaching on the slopes. In fact, Etienne was a hell of a skier. So it did make some kind of sense. But I did worry about it. I didn't see Etienne just leaving the kids and walking away. Then the headmaster told me in no uncertain terms that it would be better for the reputation of the school if we just closed the chapter of that book. I felt like it meant my job if I brought it up again."

They sat in silence for several moments. Ray wondered what, if anything, Mike was leaving out of the story.

"And the Leiston School campers, how do you find them twenty-five years later?"

"They were kids then, not much different from any other kids. You know, people would say to me, 'What's it like working with those rich kids?' They never quite believed me when I told them that the Leiston students weren't much different from anyone else. Yah, they come from more money than most, but they had the same teenage bullshit to figure out."

"Which of the kids from that group do you remember best?"

"Bitsy, of course, and also Alexandra. She always had a commanding presence. That hasn't changed. And Richard Gordon, he always seemed a bit shifty. I guess he's made that work for him. That guy has the big bucks. I never really liked him much, still don't. He could be super nice to you or a complete shit. The rest of the kids I don't remember so clearly. They all seem to blend as the years pass. You know, people grow and change, usually for the better I think. That's probably true of this group. They seem to be leading respectable adult lives.

"Can't wait to get out of here, Sheriff. I got a real bad case of cabin fever. And I want to forget about this once and for all. It's best not to go back, Sheriff. That's what I've learned from this trip. I don't want to think about this no more."

21

S ue found Ray sitting at the small table in the kitchenette of their cottage. "Looks like you found something to read," she said, noting the pile of books on the table in front of him.

"Some of the Leiston School yearbooks from about the last three decades, the only reading material in the whole place. I've selected the few that include our current cast of characters. There is not much print, mostly pictures. It's interesting to see what these people looked like 25 years ago."

"Like?"

"The boys, they all had hair, lots of it. The world isn't fair. And I did find something that I know you will find intriguing. It's the book on the top of the pile, where the pencil is sticking out."

Ray watched as she picked up the book and settled into the chair across from him.

"Eric Matthew Reed," she said, a few seconds after opening the book. "I don't frigging believe this."

"And notice his home town?"

"Royal Oak, Michigan. He gave me all this stuff about being from suburban Chicago. I wonder what else he didn't bother to mention."

"Not really a lot of family resemblance," observed Ray. "Matt doesn't look much like Sarah."

"No, not much at all. Different hair, eyes, body type. I wonder what Matt's father looks like."

Sue studied the picture for a long moment, then asked, "How did your conversation go with . . . should I say Sarah James or Mom? She didn't happen to mention anyone by the name of Eric Matthew Reed?"

"No, he didn't come up. Wish I had stumbled on this earlier. That said, she did tell me a number of interesting things." Ray recounted his conversation with Sarah.

"Elkins, you're a Nick Carraway kind of character," said Sue. "People just seem to tell you things, even when they don't want to."

"It wasn't quite like that," Ray responded. "She was really hung over and kind of hostile, especially by the end of our conversation. Besides, she wasn't really giving anything away."

Ray looked away, then refocused on Sue. "Do you find me boring?"

"Where did that come from?"

"Sarah said I was an insufferable bore."

Sue chuckled. "I think I have to invoke the protection of the Fifth Amendment."

"Come on, you can do better than that."

Sue sighed resignedly. "Ray, you're very intense. You're passionate about everything you do, and you're working or busy with something all the time. You're not the kind of guy who lingers over meals making small talk or takes leisurely Sunday drives. Personally, I like that about you. That's the way I am, too. But I can see that would drive a lot of women nuts. Sarah is probably one of them."

"She never said anything while we were seeing one another."

"My memory of the relationship is that she ended it suddenly, and then she got out of Dodge. So that's your answer. She figured it out and probably saved both of you a lot of pain. Any other great discoveries while you were wandering around?"

"As a matter of fact, yes. The issue of the power suddenly going off. I found the electrical panels for the main building are in an equipment room just off the kitchen. It would have been easy to slip in there and pull the main disconnect."

"And who would have access and know what to do?" asked Sue.

"You don't have to be a genius to get the power turned off. The people with easy access to the area include the kitchen staff, Matt, and Gary. That doesn't preclude someone else sliding in there and flipping a switch. And while I was looking at the panels I noticed an automatic transfer switch for a backup generator. There's a door in the equipment room that opens to the outside and sure enough, there was a backup generator sitting right next to the wall. I got enough snow off the top to lift the cover. The unit was turned off; it wasn't in the standby mode."

"So Gary would have had to know about the backup generator?" said Sue.

"I would think," he responded.

"You got a possible scenario?"

"Wild speculation at best. Someone turns off the power to create havoc. Is this some sort of a prank or something more sinister?"

"What if Gary shut off the power with the hope that people would retire early, letting him get some sleep?"

"Possibility, and he would probably know how to keep the generator offline, too. And speaking of Gary, he introduced me to Mike Kniivila, the bus driver and rescue guy on the U.P. trip."

"Did you learn anything more than what was in Bitsy's diary?"

"One interesting piece. According to Kniivila, no one, not Leiston's headmaster or anyone else connected with the school, ever filed a missing person report. The headmaster told Kniivila to 'leave it alone.'"

"Did he speculate on what might have happened to Etienne?"

"Not that he shared. He said he confronted the headmaster about Etienne's disappearance and was told there was a possibility he was working as a ski instructor in Canada. At one point he felt the headmaster might fire him if he kept bringing it up, so he dropped it and got on with his life."

"That's bizarre."

Ray nodded. "Did you get to talk to Tony?"

"They let me see him, but I think it was sort of a setup. He was out cold. Dr. Bishop was there. She told me they had him out of bed earlier, and that he had eaten some breakfast. She assured me Tony was back on his meds and appeared to be 'responding in an appropriate manner to his environment,' whatever that means.

When I questioned her about last night's violent incident, she told me everything happened so quickly that it was over before she was fully aware of what had occurred. When I probed her on the events that preceded the violence, she said she had had too much to drink and didn't know what triggered Tony's anger. Then she gave me some verbiage that his explosive behavior was consistent with the symptoms of post-traumatic stress disorder.

"At that point Jennings Bidder, who was monitoring our conversation closely, interjected that Richard Gordon was very concerned about his friend and would be 'allocating the necessary resources' to take care of the problem. Jennings told me that Mr. Gordon was 'enormously grateful' to the two of us for saving his friend's life," Sue noted.

"Yeah, the posse arrived on time. It strikes me as funny, though, that Mr. Gordon couldn't thank us himself."

"True, but given his demeanor, not surprising. Jennings also introduced me to the people looking after Tony—the flight crew— who double as a security detail. These were the people who were coming to our aid last night. I have to admit, they were barely on my radar. It was interesting seeing them in the light of day."

"Do they look up to the job of keeping Tony under control?"

"Yes. They are all young and ex-military types. Megan, the pilot, is very petite and strikingly beautiful. She looks like someone from central casting, long blond hair and a very worn leather jacket, à la WWII fighter pilots. The first officer is African American, handsome man, Nick Speyer. And then there is the flight steward, Conrad Voight."

"And?"

"Well, everyone was sort of bundled up. Not Conrad—nylon sleeveless red t-shirt, totally ripped, lot of tats, shaved head. Maybe a gold earring, I'm not sure. If he didn't have one, he should've. Conrad had *Special Ops* written all over him. And there seemed to be some chemistry between him and Megan. Looks like Gordon likes to surround himself with beautiful people.

"Anyway, before I made my exit, Jennings puts her hand on Nick's shoulder and assures me Tony will cause no further problems. It was such an interesting gesture. There were a lot of hormones in the air and the suggestion of some very complex relationships. I wish you could have seen it, Ray. Pure theatre."

"How about your conversation with Matt?" Ray asked.

"In light of what you have just discovered, I need to rethink everything he told me. That said, he's a very pleasant guy. I can see why he's a successful bartender. And he did share something that's quite interesting. Remember Jennings Bidder told us her job is to positively engage Mr. Gordon with the world? Matt says that Gordon is fishing for some high government appointment, like an ambassadorship. It's Bidder's job to make sure the public forgets about his fairly outrageous personal life and a whole raft problems in his corporate career—ethics violations, lawsuits, bankruptcies."

"Sounds like he has the perfect credentials to help move the country forward," said Ray.

"There's one more thing—I love this gossipy stuff—Gordon's personal staff, he likes to surround himself with bright, competent, attractive women. And while it may not be in the job description, it seems that . . . well you know where I'm going with this. According to Matt, Jennings arrived on the scene just as Gordon was parting with wife number four. It was a bit of a public relations train wreck because the poor woman had just been diagnosed with an aggressive form of breast cancer, and their prenuptial agreement left her with nothing. Gordon had been getting his share of ink in the *New York Daily News* and across the Internet.

"Jennings," Sue continued, "is apparently a crisis management whiz. She was brought on board to help minimize the damage to Gordon's already less than pristine reputation, which apparently she did with great success. She was soon promoted to the chief of his personal staff. Before long she was rumored to be keeping a toothbrush and comb at his penthouse. But alas, Mr. Gordon has a short attention span and soon moved on to a new piece of eye candy, and Jennings went back to being just another employee. Matt says Jennings knows she's on her way out. She's already talking to headhunters."

"How does he know all this?" asked Ray.

"The friendly neighborhood bartender—a lot cheaper than a therapist."

"Remind me not to hang out in bars," said Ray.

"And then, as if her ears were burning, Jennings came and found me at the bar and wanted to know how quickly the roads will be cleared so that Richard Gordon can get to the airport. I explained the priority system we use, but she didn't really like my answer. She was wondering what could be done to expedite their travel. She wondered what you might be able to do. I told her I'd pass on the question."

"It's rather tempting to get all the county's plows organized to rescue the two of us from this crowd," said Ray, "but that's not the way things work. I think we're all going to be stuck here for much of the day tomorrow. But our first job is to make it through the night."

"You're right, Ray. Our first job is to make it through the night without anything else happening. And I think you should ask the road commission to make a deviation from their priority plowing. We need to get these people out of here before someone dies."

Alex was curled up on a couch near a carefully banked fire in the media room, a large comfortable space just off the great room connected by French doors, one of which was slightly ajar. The sounds of tables being set for the evening meal filtered in.

Alex looked away from her novel toward the glowing coals. She had read the opening page of the book several times without much comprehension. Her mind was on other things. Her attention shifted to a knock on the door a brief moment before it was opened. A tall thin man entered the room, and then completely closed the door.

"I hope I'm not interrupting you. I'd like to have a word."

"Please join me," Alex said, gesturing toward the couch facing hers. "I've seen you lurking about, Scott Shelby. And that's my memory of you. You were always there at the edge of the action, observing what was going on."

Scott smiled and looked slightly abashed. "Yeah, that's me, or at least that was me back in the day. I was very shy. And I was only a freshman. Junior and senior girls were very intimidating, especially you, Alex."

"According to the background information Richard sent out, you're an Episcopalian priest."

"Yes," he responded, "and you're a psychiatrist."

"Wife, children?" she asked.

"My wife died several years ago, breast cancer. Both of my children are now in college. And you?"

"I've been married twice, but no children. I've probably been overly focused on my professional life, and my personal life has suffered." She paused for a moment. "There's something you want to talk about?"

"Yes. I was hoping that I could have a conversation with you, but it's sort of a private matter, and you've always been surrounded by other people. It goes back to the trip."

"Yes. And I can see you there. The tall, skinny, redheaded freshman who was mature beyond his years. You were there helping Etienne. And when he left to get help, Etienne sort of put the two of us in charge."

"Yes."

"And for the rest of the year, you were always around. Fencing, student council, and lots of informal gatherings."

"Yes," Scott admitted, blushing. "I had a crush on you, but I did my best not to show it."

"And this is what you wanted to talk with me about?"

"No, not at all. I wanted to talk about Etienne, his disappearance. It bothered me at the time, but I was so young I didn't know what to do. In fact, that's the only reason I came. I wanted to see you again and ask you if you ever learned anything more about his disappearance. It seemed to me that, well I don't know exactly how to phrase this, but you two had a special energy between you. I mean . . ."

"Tell me what do you know about Etienne's disappearance," probed Alex.

"Next to nothing. He left our group to get help, and then we never saw him again. After that no one ever talked about it. And when you guys graduated, even any memories of Etienne were scattered to the wind. At the time, I knew something was desperately wrong, but I didn't know what to do. And this has continued to plague me over the years."

Alex looked away for a long moment, then refocused on Scott. "Well, I don't really have much to tell you. You probably know everything that I know."

"Why didn't you do more? Even way back then, you had a presence, Alex. Adults took notice of you. If any one of us could have taken the Etienne thing further, it was you."

Alex played with her braid as she chewed on her lower lip with her upper teeth. "Oh Scott, it was so complicated. Like you're suggesting, I was involved with him. And then I caught him cheating on me. I was angry and hurt. And then he disappeared and we . . ."

"We took the oath, didn't we."

"Scott, you were one of the few innocents in the group. I was a self-absorbed teen. I had been admitted to Columbia, and I was afraid that if I got kicked out of school my admission would be withdrawn. It wasn't right. I knew it then. Over the years I've searched for Etienne. Some of my tech-savvy friends have helped me search for him. I've never found anything. In truth, I'm here because I was told if I showed up I'd learn more about Etienne. That hasn't happened yet."

"And that was the carrot that was offered you? I bet that enticement came from Richard or that Jennings woman."

Alex nodded affirmatively. "What enticed you here?"

"Jennings, she obviously did her research. I've been a United States Fencing Association referee for years, mostly on the collegiate level. Of course she wanted me to be part of the alumni group, but she especially wanted me to come and be the referee at Richard's survivors tournament. She offered me a generous honorarium and said that she'd arrange to have me picked up in a private jet."

"And that carrot worked?"

"No, not really. I told her to keep her cash. I drove my beater Subaru. That's more my style.

Scott looked at Alex. "I sense you don't want to be here anymore than I do. Are we the outliers?"

"That's an interesting question," said Alex. "I have a feeling we are just the props in one of Richard's newest schemes. And it scares the hell out of me also."

22

Jennings met Ray and Sue as they entered the great room for the evening meal. The long banquet table had been separated into three tables. Jennings, referring to a seating chart on a legal pad, guided them to their places.

Moments after Sue and Ray were seated for dinner, Matt brought Sue a Diet Coke with wedges of lemon and lime. He lingered near her, asking if there was anything else she needed, at one point gently resting a hand on her shoulder. His smile was warm and welcoming. Sue beamed back, thanking him before he departed for his post behind the bar.

"Why the smirk?" she asked Ray.

He just nodded his head, feigning innocence.

"It was that obvious?" Sue finally said.

"Obvious to me," Ray responded. "Probably not to Matt. You gave him that special smile of yours. What was it you once told me, the rush smile, the social chairman smile, something connected with your sorority girl years?"

"That was probably my rush smile, lots of teeth and sparkly eyes when I'm really thinking about something else." Sue paused for a moment and dropped her voice before continuing. "This is a person I'll probably never see again. Why did he need to tell me stories? I don't understand guys. They're either spouting exaggerations or fabrications."

Ray was still mulling over what to say about his gender when Jennings appeared at the table.

"Welcome, Sheriff and Sergeant Lawrence. Once again, Chef Michel Daudet has delivered a series of small miracles under the most challenging of conditions. Please help yourselves to the buffet."

When they returned with their entrées, Tony, surrounded by his minders, had been installed at the other end of the table. Ray quickly identified the members of the flight crew from Sue's descriptions as Jennings provided formal introductions. Then Jennings escorted Tony and his protectors to the buffet. Ray watched them move as a group, keeping Tony contained between them. Conrad, the tall burly one, had his hand on Tony's shoulder.

"Good descriptions, Sue," said Ray. "I can identify the characters without a program."

Jennings rejoined them, occupying a seat in the middle of the table, a buffer between Ray and Sue and the aircrew and Tony.

"We will be plowed out tomorrow, won't we, Sheriff?" Jennings pressed.

"Yes," answered Ray.

"Can you estimate about what time the roads will be open?"

Ray explained again that the road commission follows a priority system and that it was still impossible to estimate when they might be plowed out.

"Can't you expedite the process?"

"Sorry, no," he answered.

Jennings excused herself and left the table.

"You're not giving her the answers she wants to hear," commented Sue. "And you seemed grumpy, too."

Ray gave her a weak smile. "These people seem to think they can fix every problem, including the weather, by throwing money at it."

When Jennings returned to the table a few minutes later, she turned her attention to Megan. In the small snippets of conversation that Ray could hear, Jennings was clearly on task, trying to work out tentative flight schedules with the pilot. Then the conversation moved back and forth between Jennings and all the members of the flight crew.

Looking down the table, Ray's observations reinforced the things that Sue had shared with him earlier. There seemed to be some chemistry between Megan and Conrad, the steward. Conrad seemed to be doing all the talking, and Megan appeared to be hanging on to every word. Ray also observed Jennings was chatting up Nick, the first officer. He couldn't help but notice a level of informality between them, Jennings dropping her usual officiousness—even smiling—almost appearing relaxed and happy. And then there was Tony, without affect, not making eye contact or conversation, eating silently, looking like a wounded dog.

After dinner everyone was invited to an adjoining room for coffee and desserts. Ray and Sue sipped their coffee from a vantage point near the door as the dining tables were moved off to the side of the great room. Members of Gordon's staff—Jennings, Nick Speyer, and a couple of members of the kitchen crew—scurried about, installing a fencing piste in the center of the long dimension of the room and arranging chairs along each side. The bright LEDs of the scoring machines flashed as Speyer checked the equipment.

Slowly the group moved back into the great room, and Richard—dressed in a white fencing uniform, the mask lifted away from his face, and holding an epee in his right hand—came to the center of the piste.

"Well, you guys will remember that one of our planned events for this gathering was a tournament to determine the best fencer of the class of 1990. And, of course, we didn't get to that. Something about alcohol. In some important ways, we were shaped by experiences on the piste during those years. We learned about courage and how to face adversity. I think we all became braver, more confident due to the many hours we spent in controlled confrontation." He paused and eyed the crowd, his gaze slowly sweeping back and forth.

"I keep an epee in my office, close at hand, the one I used here at Leiston, to remind me of all those life-changing lessons. It's about steel, isn't it? Steel and blood, and never being afraid to confront what's in your way. We survived the worst Mother Nature could throw at us because we are warriors. And a quarter of a century later we are successfully making our way in the world because of the lessons of steel and blood."

Gordon brought the blade to his lips, then away in a long, sweeping papal gesture. "My friends, the survivors, I salute you."

Ray carefully eyed the crowd. There was some clapping, stomping of feet, and cheering. But Ray thought most of it was coming from Gordon's employees, rather than his classmates.

After the applause subsided he continued, "You've got to know that I hauled all this stuff out here at great expense. When we've finished and the championship trophy has been awarded, Matt will be ready to serve some exquisite bubbly as we close our celebration of surviving the great storm. Little did we know we would have to survive a second great storm. Again, my thanks for being here and being the part of the group that kicked the gales of November in the ass, not once, but twice."

Gordon bowed to the crowd and waited for the applause, which was brief and polite. Sue looked over at Ray and rolled her eyes.

"We're just going to be using epees tonight. I know most of you don't remember the rules for foils, and I was afraid of putting a saber in the hands of Alex the slasher," Gordon leered in her direction. "There's piles of extra gear over there, if you need anything. It's all new, not like the junk we used to use. So let's get dressed and warmed up. Let the games begin."

23

The crowd briefly dispersed, then started to assemble again, most of the returning alums clothed in fencing uniforms. Ray noted that in addition to Leiston alumni, some of the members of Gordon's staff were suiting up.

"Looks like a few ringers," he observed.

"Do you think members of the entourage would dare defeat His Majesty?" Sue asked.

"Probably not a good move if you want to stay employed," he answered. Like Mike Kniivila, Ray had a bad case of cabin fever. "I need to get out of here, just for a few minutes."

"Lead on," said Sue. She followed him across the Brobdingnagian entrance hall and out through the mansion's massive front doors. The snow was cleared away from the walk for a few yards, and they stood in the lee of the building in silence for a few minutes, the wind still howling and snow swirling around them. Any way he cut it, Ray didn't see how this evening could end any way but badly.

"What's going on?" asked Sue.

"I'm the proverbial stranger in a strange land. I can't grok much of what's happening."

"Ditto. You probably want to be in your kayak trying to stay upright in rough water."

"Not today. Today I'd take a glassy surface, the water mirroring the shoreline. I'd like to be watching the bow wake angling away from my boat, my breathing and paddle stroke falling into a steady rhythm."

Sue looked at him for a long moment, then shivered. "Best we go back in."

"I feel safer out here," he responded. Then he followed her back inside.

Sue found Matt standing behind the bar.

"Rosy cheeks, you must have been outside. What can I get you, another Diet Coke? Or how about an Irish coffee to warm you up?"

She pondered the choices for a long moment, finally saying, "I shouldn't, but I'd like the Irish coffee. Just a bit of whiskey, enough to add the taste, nothing more."

"I can pass the bottle across the top, just a splash," he said, beaming at her, showing dimples she didn't quite remember seeing before. "Perhaps you'd like one of these while you're waiting." He reached under the bar and produced a small silver plate. Chocolates were arranged on a paper doily. "They're solid chocolate, 88 percent, with a lovely, creamy consistency. There must be some extra cocoa butter in them to give such a satiny finish."

"Is this part of your usual service?" asked Sue, feeling some of her anger drift away. Still, she wondered what his reasons were for misrepresenting himself.

"Just taking care of the regulars. In fact, one of the hallmarks of the bar I work at is these chocolates. The owner discovered a long time ago it was a way to keep our female clientele coming back. Marketing, you know—complimentary chocolates and overpriced drinks. As we were planning this event, Jennings specified these chocolates, instructing me to bring an ample supply."

"She likes Irish coffee, too."

"Yes, it's her winter drink. She probably likes it too well." He caught himself. "I'll get your drink started."

Matt filled a glass with hot water and waited a few minutes for the glass to warm. Then he poured off the water and set the glass on the bar in front of Sue. He poured an amber stream of steaming coffee into the glass, filling it more than half way. She watched as he added more than a touch of whiskey.

"And here's the coup de grace," he said. "Double cream. You can get this in New York and probably nowhere in the Midwest.

It's flown in from the UK." He held out the container and carefully eyed the label. "In fact, this stuff is the real deal, the mother lode, processed in the Republic of Ireland."

Matt inverted a spoon and held it at the surface of the coffee. He slowly poured the viscous liquid onto the spoon, allowing it to slowly spread across the surface of the coffee. He placed the glass on a cocktail napkin and slid it in front of Sue, setting a long handled drink spoon on the right side.

"Enjoy."

"No cherry? No Reddi-wip?"

"Chicago," he shot back.

"Detroit?"

The repartee suddenly slowed. "Yes, Detroit, too. And Des Moines, Milwaukee, and West Moline. Mountains of Maraschino cherries, rivers of Reddi-wip, and piles of ground cinnamon or nutmeg."

"Matt, you've never told me your last name."

"The first rule of bartending, Inspector. Never give out your last name or your phone number, unless, of course . . ."

"Of course," Sue repeated, blushing. "Jennings has your phone number," she teased.

"Strictly business, strictly business. The work she's thrown my way has helped me survive New York's outrageous prices."

Sue didn't believe the 'strictly business' part of Matt's answer. She suspected Jennings could arrange for pleasure when she needed it, with Matt or a number of other people.

"I see that Jennings is suited up to do some fencing. Is that part of her background?"

"Jennings, yeah. She was a big time fencer at Penn, part of a championship team. She never made it to the Olympics, but I heard she was really good."

"Fencing, is that a job requirement to be part of Gordon's personal staff?"

"Can't hurt, as long as you remember whom not to beat."

"So Jennings gets your last name, and I don't," Sue teased. "I'm not the stalker type, Matt."

"Sorry, it's all about maintaining the code of my profession. No offense. I find you very attractive, too. That said, sometimes we just have to answer to a higher calling."

"Well, how about this, is Matt your first name or your middle name?"

"Middle."

"Why don't you use your first name?"

"I don't like it, never did. If I look at myself in a mirror and say the name, it's just not me. Do you know what I mean? As soon as I was in school, I dumped my first name. I told all the kids and teachers to call me Matt. It took me a while to get my family to stop using it."

"You know it's funny, when I look at you I don't think just of Matt. I can think of other names that would work."

"Like what?"

"Mmmm, how about Eric?"

Sue watched the smile disappear from his face.

"What's going on? Why are you toying with me?" He looked tense and angry.

Sue pondered his question. Why was she bothering? It wasn't the first time a man had lied to her, and she knew it wouldn't be the last. This was really about her trip to Chicago, she thought. It was about the extra toothbrush, it was about the anger she had been pushing back into her subconscious for the last several days.

"My boss is a reader," she said. "There's nothing much to read around here. He ended up with a stack of old Leiston yearbooks. And guess what, he found your picture and then connected the dots to your mother. And after he pointed this out to me, I did a quick Google search. You never lived in Chicago, there's no Glenbard Central High School in the 'burbs."

"Did you run my name in NCIC?"

"Damn straight. Checked you out in several databases."

"And?"

"You know the answer. Other than a couple of speeding tickets when you were in your late teens, you have had no encounters with law enforcement. And the rest of the things you told me about yourself all seem to be true. So why this fabricated story about Chicago?"

"I'm sure you figured this out already, but here's the story. Sometime in the early fall, my mother told me about the reunion during one of our Sunday morning phone conversations. When we first talked about it, she said Richard Gordon, one of her classmates, was really pressuring her to attend. I could tell by her tone that she was conflicted. It had been a bad experience, something she had spent years trying to forget. In later conversations, she seemed to soften, and said she would probably make the trip. She had been planning to come to New York to spend Thanksgiving with me. She had to get time off from work, figure out flights, that kind of thing. I was trying to get theatre tickets and work out a schedule. And then suddenly, by some strange coincidence, I got a chance to fly out and be the bartender at the very same event."

"It's an almost unbelievable coincidence," said Sue.

"I guess it would sound that way, but it's true. Jennings has been getting me bartending gigs for several years. I couldn't believe it when this opportunity came up. I thought it would be great fun. My mother and I would be able to spend some time together. I'd get to meet some of her classmates at Leiston. And we'd have this secret that no one else would know about."

"Oh, come on, Matt, there must be some people here who would make the connection."

"No, not really. I've never met any of her classmates. And no one from the school is here other than Gary Zatanski. She hired Zatanski years ago when she worked at Leiston—he's sort of a friend. She called him and explained the situation. He was happy to go along with the charade."

"Have you misled me about anything else? Did you give me the full story about what happened last night?"

"I told you everything I know about it."

"And your mother has told you nothing more?"

"No. If there is anything more, she's disinclined to share it with me. I mean, we all have our little secrets, don't we? I think she deserves her privacy without her kid prying into her life."

Matt gazed at Sue for a long moment, and his smile returned. "Are you going to finish the chocolates? They don't constitute an attempt to bribe, Sergeant."

"Are your plans still on for Thanksgiving?"

"I don't know. She's really upset by the shiner. I think she's planning on going into hiding until all the bruising disappears. I just wish I could get her out of here. She seems to have been shattered by this whole experience."

24

Sue found Gary Zatanski leaning against an archway at the side of the great room watching the pre-tournament warm-ups.

"How's it going?" she asked.

"I'm counting the hours till they're gone and I can get my life back. How about you?"

"The same. I want the body out of here, and I want out of here. I'd like confirmation that there is nothing untoward about Morgan's death. And if there is, unfortunately, these people will be scattered to the wind, and we will be left with a very difficult investigation."

Zatanski nodded but didn't say anything.

"I was just talking to Matt Reed, the bartender. I guess you know him?"

Another nod.

"Come on, Gary, you can do better than that. He told me the whole story."

Zatanski exhaled sharply. "It's no big deal. There's nothing illegal going on here."

"I'm not suggesting that. I was just wondering if there are any other relationships I should know about, maybe something relating to the camping trip."

Zatanski yawned, bringing his hand to his mouth. "Sorry, it's been a long several days. To answer your question, there are no other secret relationships that I know about. Sarah called me weeks ago, explained the situation. Her kid needed the work. Why not? Perfectly innocent, wouldn't you say? Sarah was always good to me, and Matt, a real nice kid when he was here, not like some of the other Leiston brats.

"Is there some weird stuff going on here? Absolutely. But I don't know what it is. I don't know if it's based on things that happened when they were at school or things that happened later. But this isn't a happy group. I could sense that Friday afternoon when they started arriving. I've seen a lot of alumni groups come and go at the school. I've never felt vibes like this. I think these people mostly hate each other. I hope no one gets hurt during this frigging tournament. I just want them to go away."

Sue slid into a chair next to Ray. He was sitting at the back, away from the action, looking at his phone.

"We're getting lucky," he said, pointing to the radar image on his phone. "The monster is finally blowing out of here. What happened with Matt?"

"Everything was cool. His explanation made good sense."

"So he's forgiven."

"For the moment. What's happening here?"

Ray held out a diagram showing the pairings. "This is where we are. Started with eight, now we're in the last bout of the final four. I don't quite understand what's going on. Everything happens so fast, but when there's a hit—"

"A touch," Sue corrected.

"Yes, a touch. When there is a touch, the lights flash. It looks very high-tech." He pointed toward the piste. "That's Jennings and Alex. My money is on Alex. She seems more aggressive."

After the winning touch, the combatants pulled off their masks, came to the center of the piste, and briefly grasped one another's hands.

"You were right, Ray. Alex is in the final round."

"Who is the umpire?" asked Ray. "I've seen him around. One of the alum?"

"Referee," corrected Sue. "That is Scott Shelby, the other freshman on the trip."

"You've met him?"

"Yes, I had a brief conversation with him. He seems very quiet and introspective."

Ray nodded, signaling that he had heard her. "This will be interesting. The final bout. Richard Gordon and Alex Bishop. Any bets?"

"I'm trying to stay neutral," chided Sue.

Gordon was on the piste. Nick Speyer, one of the flight crew, was connecting him to the wire and checking his epee. Alex was at the back of the piste, her mask still off, wiping sweat from her face. Then she moved onto the piste and waited to be wired into the system.

The combatants came to the center of the piste, saluted the referee, raised their weapons horizontally, and then saluted each other. They moved to the opposite end of the piste and pulled on their masks, the heavy metal screening obscuring their faces.

The referee stood near the center. "*En garde,*" he instructed. He waited for a few seconds. Each combatant signaled that they were ready. "*Allez,*" he commanded.

The fencers started moving to the center of the piste, weapons extended, left hands trailing. Ray suddenly felt electricity in the room. There was no immediate contact, just weaves and bobs, parries and ripostes. They were about the same height, thin and athletic. Alex's movements were ballet-like, delicate and graceful. She seemed to anticipate Gordon's every move, responding instantly to each aggression. Gordon was more physical, stamping on the piste, beating against her blade, charging forward at the slightest retreat.

Gordon got the first touch, and the second, each time scoring as he charged past her. On his third attack, Alex dropped low and lunged forward, striking his knee. She quickly got two more touches before the referee halted the action for the end of the first three-minute period.

In the opening seconds of the second period Gordon charged again. Alex held her position, stretching out and reaching deep, catching him under the arm, the scoring box flashing her touch. Gordon continued forward, his body crashing into hers, knocking her from the piste.

"Halt!" The referee's command was sharp. He moved to Alex's side and helped her regain her footing. Ray watched the brief conversation between the referee and Alex. He assumed the referee was checking to see that she was uninjured.

Then the referee turned his attention to Richard Gordon. Ray couldn't hear that conversation either, just the tone. It appeared that Richard had been given a warning. The chatter that had filled the room early in the bout faded away. All eyes were on the rivals. A number of smart phones were being held aloft, capturing the action. He looked over at Sue. Her phone was in the air, too.

Once the combatants were in position, the bout began again. Alex became the aggressor, quick ripostes to each of Richard parries, skillfully repelling each of his offensive moves. She picked up three more touches to his one before the end of the period.

In the first minute of the final period, Richard tried his aggressive move again. He charged forward, attempting to get a hit as he ran past her. Ray thought Alex had clearly anticipated the move. She dodged to her left and struck the elbow of Richard's outstretched arm. He tripped over her right leg and tumbled forward, landing in a prone position.

"Halt!" The referee dropped below Ray's sightline. Then he stood, Alex at his side. Richard was soon back on his feet, bending to retrieve his weapon. Again, Ray could hear the tone of the official's dispassionate caution.

"En garde . . . Allez," commanded the referee once he had returned to his position. Ray thought Richard, moving slowly, looked like a heavyweight in the closing rounds. Alex, still appearing fresh, became the aggressor, scoring several more touches before the clock ran out.

Ray watched as Gordon pulled off his mask and met Alex at the center of the piste, his face flushed, dripping with sweat. Alex extended her hand. Richard suddenly swung a closed fist toward her face. Alex ducked the intended blow and sprang forward, wrapping her arms around Richard, driving him backward, and knocking him off his feet. By the time Ray got through the crowd, they had been separated. Conrad was holding onto his boss, the referee blocking any further advance by Alex.

Jennings was standing at the center of the piste, scanning the crowd, assessing the situation.

Ray knelt next to Conrad. "Stay with your boss. I don't want any trouble tonight."

Conrad nodded. "Yes, sir."

Sue caught Ray's arm as he moved back. "What did you see?"

"Misdemeanor assault on the part of Richard Gordon. I'm not sure what to say about Alex. It looks like she might have gotten a couple of slaps or punches in. You've got video. This can wait till morning. See if you can persuade Matt to close the bar. Let's be very visible until everyone drifts away. I want this to be an early evening."

25

Ray was pulled from a troubled sleep by frantic pounding and then the panic-stricken voice of Gary Zatanski. As he quickly dressed, Ray listened to Zatanski's report that Tony Messina had overpowered his keepers, shot and wounded Conrad, and then fled in the same direction as he had the previous night, down the dune toward the lake.

Two nights in a row, the same sort of violence with the same purported perpetrator, Ray thought as he left Sue to attend to the injured while he pursued the reportedly crazed Tony Messina into the night again. He carried a stun gun and handcuffs in exterior pockets, and a Glock tucked away in an interior pocket.

Ray moved out of the shadows of the main building and past the cottage occupied by the flight crew. A gibbous moon hanging in the steel gray sky reflected off the undulating mantle of snow. He stopped and surveyed the landscape, his eyes slowly adapting to the tenebrous terrain. He moved forward again, lifting his right snowshoe and pushing it forward, then following with the left, planting and moving arms and poles and feet in a slow, labored, rhythmic dance.

He stopped a second time, breathing hard, the polar air biting into his exposed skin, burning his nose and throat with each inhalation. The vast hillside opened below him, glistening in the moonlight, running down to the dark water. Ray found a trail in the enveloping gray shroud that draped the hillside.

He carefully worked his way down the slope in a zigzag pattern, controlling the angle of his descent. Finally he paused at the water's edge, the place where the path disappeared. The wind had abated, but the residual energy of the storm was still in the water.

Broad lines of rollers marched toward the beach in the moonlight, finally dissipating where the water had cut into the snow.

Ray surveyed the scene, then turned south, moving on the level plain a few yards above the water. He stopped from time to time to check the dark objects he encountered, some snow covered, others bare in the icy wash. Most were weathered logs and other bits of flotsam. One, from a distance, had a humanoid form. As he moved closer he could see the outline of a deer, a buck, one set of antlers and the left leg above the sand, both rear legs, uncovered, reaching toward the water, moving slightly with the final wash of each wave. He pushed on his flashlight and inspected the carcass, looking for wounds or signs of trauma. He saw none, at least not on the exposed side. The sleek muscular body had yet to be ravaged by scavengers. Ray stood for a long moment, taking in the grace and beauty of the animal, wondering how it had ended up on the shore, probably at a distant point from where it had gone into the water.

He switched off the light and waited for his eyes to adjust again to the darkness, then he continued on, stopping at a dark shadow in the water: a heavy wood picnic table, legs skyward, pushed up against the shore, each wave washing over part of the inverted top. Ray walked on for another ten minutes, then retraced his steps, past the table and the deer, back to the trail he had made descending the slope. As he headed northward along the beach for a few hundred yards, his attention was pulled to a dark shape in the water. As he drew nearer, he saw that it was nothing more than a huge boulder. Beyond it was another form, low and partially submerged. Another boulder, part of a field of stones that formed a shoal close to shore. He had paddled his kayak past these obstructions many times and wondered about their origin. Were they dropped by a glacier as it retreated northward?

Stopping, he surveyed the beach beyond. He could see the waves breaking over the large rocks near the shore and several more dark shapes ahead. First he encountered the remains of a tree trunk. Then he carefully crossed a section of dock, much of the decking broken or missing. He was thinking about turning around when he saw the dark shadow in the water. Ray switched on his light and moved the beam along the form. The head and arms were awash, rising and falling with each wave. One foot, shoeless, appeared entangled with the ancient roots of a driftwood tree. The other foot, also bare, was partially buried in the sand.

Ray unclipped his snowshoes so he could move around in the water. He photographed the body from different angles, carefully plotting his course, avoiding waves that might wash over the top of his boots. Then he freed the corpse from the sand and roots and pulled it onshore and up over an embankment, safe from the encroaching water. He knelt at the side and rolled the torso, bringing his light to the face. Empty eyes stared skyward. Ray's thoughts flashed back to the man he had seen at dinner: a frail droid-like character held on a short leash by his minder, Conrad. Why was this man dead on the beach? How could he have overpowered his keepers?

Ray took a few more photos, then tried to phone Sue. The call failed. Strapping on his snowshoes, he stamped out the surrounding area for a few minutes to make the body easier to find. Then he began to climb back up the steep hill in a slow, measured pace, his thoughts focused on events and images of the last many hours.

"Anything?" Sue asked, standing at the crest of the hill near the mansion. Above them, the night sky was starting to fade behind the creeping fingers of dawn.

Ray stood still for a long moment, catching his breath. "Yes. I found him in the water, facedown. I pulled the body high enough on the bank so it wouldn't drift away. What about the injured?" he asked as he stooped to release his snowshoes.

"Conrad took a bullet in the left shoulder and has a nasty scalp wound. Alex says his collarbone is fractured. She got the bleeding stopped and bandaged both wounds and immobilized his arm. She's more concerned about Megan, the pilot. She's suffered a concussion. Alex said they both need to be in a trauma center as quickly as possible, especially Megan. I've started the process. We'll evacuate them by snowmobile to the township fire department. They're in the process of clearing a landing site for the EMS chopper."

"How did Messina get free? It doesn't make any sense."

"Just a few sketchy pieces. Somehow Messina got loose. He had a club of some sort and was able to disarm Conrad. I guess there was a struggle for the gun, and Conrad ended up taking a bullet."

"And Megan, how was she injured?"

"That's unclear at this point. The place is busted up pretty good. Hopefully, they can tell me a lot more after they've been treated for their injuries."

"How about the other pilot?"

"Nick? I don't know. He doesn't seem to have been there. How about the body?"

"See if dispatch can organize another snowmobile crew to collect it as quickly as possible. I'd like to get it to town for a preliminary autopsy. I'd like to know about time of death and cause of death. Given the size of the drifts and the steep terrain, it's not going to be easy to get sleds down there. Some of the locals will know the best way to get to the beach."

Ray followed Sue the rest of the way up the hill, listening to her side of the phone conversation.

26

Ray could see Gary Zatanski on the other side of the glass as they approached the central doors at the back of the mansion. He pushed one of the two doors open and held it as they entered.

"You found him?" Gary asked.

"His body," answered Ray.

"There's another body," said Zatanski.

Ray looked at him, he could see the horror in his face. "What?"

"It's Gordon," he responded. "He's got one of those swords right through his heart. Must've been Messina. Body's cold. Been dead awhile."

Ray thought the man appeared to be in shock. His words came slowly. His face had a grayish tone.

"Where is he?" asked Ray.

"In the owner's suite."

"Who discovered the body?"

"The Jennings woman."

"Anyone else been in there?"

"Other than the killer, I don't think so. But who can tell with this group? I got it locked now."

"When did you hear?"

"Ten minutes ago? I was just coming to find your sergeant when I saw the two of you." Zatanski exhaled noisily, "I didn't sign on for this shit."

"Are you OK?"

"I don't know. I'm having some chest pains, and I don't have my meds with me."

"Let's get you lying down. What do you need, nitroglycerin?

"Exactly," he answered.

They guided him into the great room and onto one of the leather couches. Sue placed a pillow under his head, another under his knees. Ray sat at his side on a couch while Sue put in a call to dispatch requesting emergency medical response for an apparent heart attack.

Ray could see that Zatanski was still agitated. "You've secured the area," he said. "Try to relax. Help is on the way."

Jennings, dressed in heavy fleece warm-ups, stood at the door of Richard Gordon's suite. Her face was contorted by anguish. She reached out to Ray. He held her as she collapsed into tears. Eventually she pulled away from him. Sue passed her some tissue.

"Something was wrong, I just felt it. When I got here, the door was open. Richard was on the floor. There was a sword sticking out of him. I got close enough to see that he wasn't breathing." Jennings collapsed into tears again, this time reaching for Sue.

"And you stayed here after summoning Gary Zatanski?" asked Sue.

"Yes, he went in. I didn't follow him. And when he came out he told me to guard the door until he came back."

"You did your job. Thank you. Would you like Sergeant Lawrence to accompany you back to your room?"

"I'm OK. I'll go back and get some clothes on."

They watched her depart. Sue passed him a pair of latex gloves.

"Do you want to dust the door handle?" asked Ray, pointing to the long, elegant lever.

"Yes, later. We need to protect it. Probably lots of prints there, maybe even the perp's."

Before he inserted the key card, Ray gently pushed the door with a gloved hand. The door easily yielded to pressure. He pointed to the damaged frame. "Someone was in a hurry to get in."

All the lights were on. They carefully took in the scene. Richard Gordon's body lay on the floor in the wide expanse between the two king-sized beds. A pair of silk pajama pants covered his lower body.

They moved closer. Gordon was stretched out on his back. His head leaned limply to the right. His arms were at his sides, his hands open, palms facing up. His mouth hung ajar, eyes open. An epee protruded from his chest.

"My God," said Sue.

"Yes," agreed Ray. "But almost no blood. He was already dead when he was stabbed."

"Yes, that's weird, isn't it? I'll need some time to work this scene, both of the scenes, actually. As soon as the injured are transported, I'll see if I can send the bodies the same way. And I'll see if dispatch can get Dr. Dyskin on his cell. I'd like his recommendation on where we should send the bodies. I'll get everyone here assembled, make sure we have a complete list, and then start trying to figure out who knows what. Fortunately the weather is on our side. We have a captive audience, at least for a while."

Ray stood in front of the group that had been assembled in the great room. He glanced over his notes, then asked, "Is everyone here?"

"Everyone is here or accounted for," answered Jennings Bidder, who was standing at his side.

Ray looked out at the people, clustered in two groups—the Leiston alums and the employees of Richard Gordon.

"Good morning. It's been a long, difficult night. Let me brief you on what we know at this point. Then Ms. Bidder will update you on possible travel arrangements and address any concerns you may have.

"Sometime after 4:00 this morning I was awakened by Gary Zatanski, the Director of Security for Leiston School. He reported that there had been a shooting in the North Cottage, the building occupied by the flight crew. Sergeant Lawrence and I followed him to the site of the shooting. There were two injured people. Conrad Voight, the flight steward, had a bullet wound in the left shoulder. Megan Bartoli, the pilot, had sustained a head injury. The alleged assailant, Tony Messina, was seen fleeing the building.

"Sergeant Lawrence stayed with the injured to provide first aid and begin working on their evacuation to a trauma center while I pursued Mr. Messina. I'm sorry to report that I eventually found Messina's body in Lake Michigan. Soon after I returned to the mansion, Mr. Zatanski informed us that Richard Gordon had been discovered injured and unresponsive in his quarters. We have since determined that Mr. Gordon was a victim of homicide."

Ray paused and looked at the haphazardly dressed group. Some were weeping, most appeared fearful.

"We are in the process of moving Mr. Voight, Ms. Bartoli, and Mr. Zatanski, who has a heart condition, to a freshly plowed landing area at the township fire department. From there they will be transported to our regional trauma center for treatment.

"At this point I have to ask for your help. I will be interviewing each one of you. Please think carefully about what you saw and heard last night after the fencing matches. Did you witness or hear any arguments or conversations that might be related to these incidents? Also, did anyone hear a gunshot? Did you see or hear anything else that was suspicious or that might be related to this case?

"But before I begin, Ms. Bidder has some announcements."

Jennings stood at Ray's side. "I don't know quite where to begin. One is never equipped to handle events of this magnitude. I do want to assure you that we will be taking care of you. Obviously, the tentative travel plans that I laid out for some of you yesterday are no longer operative. I've only been able to make a few phone calls since this all happened. Some of our people in New York are starting to work on the transportation problem. We hope to be able to get you out sometime tomorrow."

The members of her audience groaned. "I know, I know . . . ," she said. "The sheriff tells me that the plows are on the roads now that the snow has stopped, but it will take time to dig out. And then there will be the issue of finding flights."

"How about our pay?" The question came from one of the food staff.

"Whether you are a regular employee of the company or

someone with a special contract for this event, you will be taken care of. I assure you."

"So we're trapped here till tomorrow?"

"That's my best guess." She turned to Ray. "Sheriff?"

Ray stood. "Yes. It will probably be tomorrow morning before the roads out here are open. In the meantime, two areas of the mansion are active crime scenes: the first floor of the owner's wing and North Cottage. The bodies of the deceased will be transported as soon as possible—in the case of Tony Messina, as soon as a crew can get to him on the beach, and in the case of Richard Gordon, as soon as the crime scene has been processed.

"Please make yourselves available to me and to Sergeant Lawrence for questioning by remaining in the common areas or in your assigned rooms. I will be conducting interviews in the private office off the kitchen."

Ray looked over the group. No one moved for a long moment. Then they began to move away, alone or in small groups. He could feel the undertone of grief, sorrow, and fear.

27

Jennings Bidder was the first to be interviewed. Ray studied her face closely as they sat across from one another at the table in the small office adjoining the mansion's commercial kitchen. The room was stark and sterile: white walls, light-gray industrial furniture. The terracotta-red tile floor provided the only hint of color.

Ray started a recorder app on his iPhone, identified himself and Bidder, and gave the date, time, and place of the interview. He placed the phone on the tabletop between them.

"Where should I start?" asked Jennings, her hands gripping a heavy cream-colored coffee mug.

"Let's start with the last match, the fencing match and events that followed. And take me through this morning when you found Gordon's body."

"The match, you saw what happened. It was a disaster. All the people with their iPhones. Within seconds it was all over the Internet. I've been working so hard to shape Richard's image. How do you put a spin on gross stupidity?"

"What was that all about?" asked Ray. "There must be more to the story than just losing a fencing match."

Jennings took several slow sips of her coffee. "It's complicated. There's a lot of history, and I was only privy to a bit of it—the part that Richard wanted me to know. It doesn't matter now. First, Alexandra Bishop didn't want to come to this event. It took a lot of persuading. Again, I don't know the backstory, other than Richard and Alex had been friends or at least classmates at Leiston.

"The tournament was supposed to be a focal point of this gathering. Richard was really involved in making sure I got everything right. He had scripted it all, picked out the equipment, everything. Usually he just told me what he wanted and expected me to figure out the details. Not this time. And he started taking fencing lessons months ago. The part of his script that he didn't share was that he was going to win, be the best fencer in the place. He didn't tell me that directly, but it was obvious as hell. And somehow it involved Alex. With Richard it was often about a woman and usually about power and control.

"So the tournament, it didn't happen Saturday night as planned. Morgan's death threw a damper on things, and everyone got way too drunk to fence, especially Richard. But by Sunday morning, when it was clear we weren't going anywhere, the fencing match was back at the top of the list. I told Matt to limit the alcohol until the event was over. Then he was supposed to break out some very good champagne. As you know, it didn't happen the way it was planned. It was hardly the time for a celebration."

"So after the event, you left with Mr. Gordon?"

"Yes, with Conrad's help. It's sort of dangerous to strong-arm your boss, but Conrad has a way of doing it. It's happened before, usually when Richard was drunk and needed to be brought under control. Conrad hustled Richard back to his suite and stayed with him, first in the suite and later just outside the door. I stayed with him to talk him down. When he really screws up like that, he doesn't want to talk about it. He just wants to pretend it didn't happen. That said, he wanted me to call his lawyer immediately. He wanted things in place in case he was going to be charged with assault. Then he wanted me to collect everyone's cell phone. I told him that wouldn't happen."

"Did he or anyone else bring an epee back to his suite?"

"No. But there was one in the room. In fact he picked it up sometime before I left the room and smacked at one of the pillows a few times before tossing it on the bed."

"Then what happened?" asked Ray.

"Alex arrived and started talking to him. Whatever had caused the flare-up on the piste was history. They were having a friendly conversation. I stayed around for a while to make sure the cordiality was continuing. Finally, the conversation seemed to be getting very personal, and I thought it was best to make my exit. So I told him I was going and asked if there was anything else that needed to be done. He told me he wanted to see Megan before he went to sleep. He wanted an update on the weather and when he might be able to get out of here. He seemed desperate to get back to New York and forget this whole experience. That was one of the remarkable things about Richard, his amazing capacity to move on from a disaster."

"Disaster? I don't understand."

"Well, it's about prestige and position. Let me give you some background. A couple of political operatives had been hitting him for big donations, suggesting that he might land an important job in the new administration, maybe even an ambassadorship. I think he was mesmerized by the prestige attached to a high government position.

"That said, he had accumulated lots of negative publicity over two decades—questionable business deals, messy divorces, yada, yada, yada. I totally reimaged him—entrepreneurial genius, civic leader, and philanthropist. It's amazing how many impressive sounding boards you can be named to by spreading around a little cash. I'd done a good job of molding a positive public image. Until last night when it all unraveled."

"So how did this happen?"

"Well, because he kept me out of the loop. He was never honest about why he wanted this event. Now I think I get it. There was some dark secret that he was concerned about, something that might be uncovered if he was rigorously vetted for an important position. Don't ask me what that something was. My speculation is that Richard saw a path to removing the problem. Somehow that was supposed to happen this weekend."

"So that's the last time you saw him alive, when you left him in the room with Alex Bishop, with Mr. Voight still standing guard?"

"Yes."

"And did you tell the pilot, Megan, that he wanted to speak with her?"

"I relayed the request through Conrad."

"And during the night, did you hear anything? You are in the next suite, right?"

Jennings looked down at the table and toyed with her coffee cup. "No, another room became vacant, and I moved there."

"Why?"

"It has nothing to with this."

"Ms. Bidder, this is a murder investigation. I'll decide what's relevant and what is not. Please proceed."

She cleared her throat and then looked directly at Ray. "Matt, the bartender, was concerned about one of the guests, Sarah. Seems she's . . . his mother."

"And you had no previous knowledge of that relationship?"

"None at all. I was quite surprised to learn they're related. Anyway, he wanted to share her room. She was frightened and asked Matt to stay close. He wanted me to know he had made the move, and when I learned that his room would be empty, I asked if I could use it, and he was nice enough to give me the key card. Quite frankly, Sheriff, I was worried about what Richard might do. He was not particularly stable on the best of days. I wanted some distance from him."

"You were afraid of what Richard might do to you specifically?"

Jennings nodded reluctantly. "Yes."

"What are we talking about? Some kind of violence?"

"We had been in a relationship. I was reestablishing boundaries. I was afraid he would become violent if I refused him. I've seen flashes of that before."

"So that's where you spent the night, in the room that had been assigned to Matt?"

"Yes."

"Is there anyone who can verify that?"

Ray held Jennings in his gaze. After a long silence, she looked up at him.

"I was with someone."

"Who?"

"Nick Speyer, one of the pilots. I've been seeing him occasionally. Not in New York, just when we're traveling."

Ray gave her a questioning look.

"He's married. His wife works for the company. If she found out, it would undoubtedly be unpleasant for everyone involved."

"And you spent the whole night with him?"

"He slipped out during the night so he wouldn't be seen by other members of the staff. I assume he went back to his room."

"So tell me what happened this morning. When did you go to Richard Gordon's room?"

"Richard wanted me to wake him up by 7:00. He was probably hoping that I would have all the travel arrangements taken care of. So I got up early, showered, and arrived at his suite at seven. I brought him a mug of black coffee. The door was slightly ajar, which seemed odd. My hands were occupied, so I pushed it open with my foot. All the lights were on. I walked in and set the coffee on a table near the window. I saw his feet first. Then I moved around the bed and saw the body."

"And then?"

"I knew he was dead. He was just lying there with his eyes open. I ran out of the room in a panic. I don't even know where I was going, but in the hallway I ran into the Leiston security guard, Mr. Zatanski. I have to say that it was strange to find him there—it seemed like he was just lurking around in the hallway. So he came back into the room with me. He checked Richard for a pulse, which is something I never even thought to do. Then he told me we needed to secure the scene. He asked me to stand outside to make sure no one went in while he went to find you. It was all I could do to stand there until you arrived. I just wanted to run away. I couldn't believe Richard was in that room, dead."

"Do you know anyone who wanted Richard Gordon dead?"

Jennings laughed abruptly. "Lots of people passionately dislike him and will probably be happy to hear that he's dead. That said, considering the possible consequences, I don't know anyone who would off him."

"How about you, Ms. Bidder. Did you kill Richard Gordon?"

"No, Sheriff. I had a better plan. I was leaving the company. I had reached the tipping point months ago."

"What was it like working for him?"

"In the beginning it was a dream job. I was doing exactly what I was trained to do: turn a pig's ear into a silk purse, with all the requisite spinning and media manipulation. But I realized a few months ago that I was trying to achieve the impossible. When I finally figured that out, I was held captive by his golden handcuffs. He could be charming, almost magnetic, but the monster was always just below the surface. But the money was good, especially in a tight job market. That's the only reason people put up with his crap. Anyway, I've got a new job starting in January, less money, but I'll be able to look at myself in the mirror again."

"It was that bad?"

"Worse than you can imagine. I was starting to lose my sense of self, my ethical center. I can't say I'm sorry I've been given an early parole. Are we done?"

"For now," said Ray. "I'll probably need to talk to you again."

Ray watched her depart. He reflected on his own limited contact with Richard Gordon. He hadn't seen either the charm or the monster. His impressions were limited to someone who was distant and arrogant.

28

Ray looked across the table at Dr. Alexandra Bishop.

"How are you?" he asked.

Alex inhaled slowly and bit at her upper lip. "Physically, I am very sore. That was a hard bout. I'm reminded that I'm not seventeen anymore. But that's nothing. The soreness, the bruising will resolve in a few days. Emotionally . . . I'm exhausted . . . confused . . . and conflicted. It will take me a long time to make sense of what's happened over the last few days."

"Can you tell me about last night?"

"So much happened. Where do you want me to start?"

"How about your fencing match?"

"Sure. If you watched any of the preliminaries, I'm sure you noticed the farcical nature of the whole event. You saw a group of middle-aged, out-of-shape people playing with epees. Most of those folks hadn't touched a weapon since they left school."

"Yes," said Ray. "That was quite obvious. But it wasn't true of you or Richard."

"That's right. We both continued fencing in college and beyond."

"Up to the present?"

"Yes, for me. I don't have the right temperament for yoga. Richard's assistant made a big deal about Richard wanting a rematch. Let me explain. We had a tournament during graduation week. It was just open to seniors. I won. The first time a woman had ever captured the school championship. That's what the rematch was all about. Jennings stressed Richard thought it would be the highpoint of the reunion. She said he was back into fencing and had been taking lessons from an Olympic coach."

"So that was enough of an inducement?"

"No, not at all. I had no desire to see Richard again. But Jennings kept waving another carrot in my face, although I'm sure she had no idea about our history."

"The other carrot?"

"Ms. Bidder said if I came to this reunion, Richard would give me a clue to what happened to Etienne Falconet."

"The fencing master, the teacher who went missing," Ray filled in.

"Hmm. How do you know about Etienne?"

"I've been hearing bits and pieces of that story since we've been here. What happened to him? People don't just disappear."

"I don't know. At the time, they—the school people, the adults in our world—made it sound like Etienne had just taken off. Like he had screwed up and put us in danger and then ran away from his responsibilities. That just wasn't true. It was just the opposite. I tried to tell people that, but I was just dismissed. And I guess after a time I wanted to believe their story, too. It would have meant that Etienne was safe. That would have taken away at least part of the pain."

"You and Etienne . . . ?"

"Yes. The first real love of my life. Nothing like it before or perhaps after." She looked away.

"How would Richard have known what happened to Etienne Falconet?"

Alex's eyes met Ray's. "He never admitted to knowing anything—back then, anyway. But I never trusted him. You see, Richard and I started dating when we were juniors. It was hot and heavy. We were quite the number. It was all glandular—mostly about sex and drugs and alcohol. In truth, neither one of us knew anything about relationships. And then Etienne came into my life. It started during the study trip to Paris the previous spring. Richard wasn't on that trip. The other kids thought Etienne was spending his time with a French girlfriend. Etienne joked about my seeing Paris on my back. When we got back to school, I broke it off with Richard. He went completely crazy, even staged an attempted suicide. Fortunately, the school year ended, and we went our separate ways for the summer. He did try to contact me, but when I didn't respond, I thought he'd get the message and be over it by the time fall rolled around. He wasn't, but by fall Etienne and I were together. Under the adult radar, but of course some of kids had figured it out.

"Richard did all kinds of silly adolescent things to win me back, mostly involving gifts of alcohol and other forbidden items. When that didn't work he threatened to expose our relationship to the administration. Richard always had a camera in his hand, and I imagined that he had a portfolio of incriminating photos.

And then during the trip Etienne just disappeared. It made sense that Richard had been involved in getting him to go away for good. In fact I still believe that Richard was behind Etienne's disappearance. So like I said, when Jennings told me that if I showed up Richard would solve the Etienne mystery, well, I just had to come. But it was against my best judgment. I knew that Richard might not tell me anything at all, that he might not even know anything to tell. But I had to try."

"So did you and Richard get back together after Etienne disappeared?"

"Oh, hell no. We became mortal enemies for the rest of the school year. We were the best fencers in the school; no one could compete. Our battles on and off the piste were legendary. There were a couple of times we threw down our epees and resorted to slugging it out until the adults could separate us. The scary thing is that Richard and I were a lot alike then. We were both from really screwed-up families. And we were both bundles of insecurities and anger. I really didn't like the person I was back then. It took me years to even begin to figure it all out—lots of failed relationships, way too much alcohol. During medical school I started to get a sense of who I wanted to be. That led me to psychiatry."

She looked steadily at Ray. He peered into her hazel-green eyes. He felt drawn to her, yet remained circumspect.

"Aren't you going to ask me if I killed him?"

"Did you?"

"No."

"At this point it appears that you were one of the last people to see him alive. You went to his room?"

"That's true. Part of the deal as Jennings spelled it out was that if I showed up and participated in the fencing tournament, Richard would tell me what had happened to Etienne. Ask her, she'll tell you. I kept my part of the bargain. And then you saw how it ended, that prick slapping me and all and his goons dragging him off. I thought he'd find a way to sneak back to his jet and get away without telling me what I came here to find out. There was no way that I was going to let that happen. So I went to his room."

"And?"

"It was the same old bull, the Richard I knew at seventeen, with the same testosterone-charged adolescent male brain behind a middle-aged face. It was his locker room patter—something to the effect that after we had screwed our brains out he would tell me what he knew.

"I reminded him that wasn't part of the deal. And his comeback was that I had agreed to a fix. He was supposed to win. That's what Jennings had negotiated. I was the one who didn't keep my end of the bargain."

"Was this true? Had you agreed to lose?"

"Oh, hell no. You don't know me. I would have never done that." Alex paused a moment. "Richard, he had been sipping from a bottle of champagne the whole time, and by now he was sloppy drunk—he could never hold his liquor, even back in the day. He was mumbling how he needed this video, the importance of looking young and vital. He's into some new ego trip.

"Then he tossed me an epee. It looked familiar. It was my old practice epee, part of my kit from high school. It had disappeared from my locker just before graduation. I asked him how he'd gotten it, and he said he'd stolen it. Then he told me I was his first real love. Talk about melodrama. Eventually, I tossed the sword back to him. It was too tempting holding on to it. I was afraid I might do something stupid. Anyway, he made a clumsy attempt to catch it and missed. I took that as my cue to get out of there, and I headed for the door.

"He pleaded with me to stay. When it was clear I wouldn't listen, he said that if I wanted to know what happened to Etienne, I should go ask Mike. That was it. I left feeling angry and used."

"Did you see anyone when you left Mr. Gordon's room?"

"No one. Everything was quiet, at least between Richard's room and mine."

"How did you know it was your sword? Don't they all look alike?"

"Yes. All of our swords came from one supplier. But there were two special things about my epee. First, the wrapping on the handle was different. Mike helped me with it when the original wrapping on the grip fell apart. He had some soft doeskin that he cut into narrow strips. It had a nice feel; I really liked it. And there was a second thing. When we disassembled the sword to do the wrapping, I marked the hand guard with my initials. Those guards are soft aluminum. Mike had a set of tools with hard steel letters, the whole alphabet. You'd strike them with a hammer to make an impression in the aluminum. So as I held that epee in Richard's room, there were my initials, pretty beat up but still very visible."

"So have you talked to Mike?"

"No. I'll probably ask him about it if I happen to run into him, but I don't think it's worth pursuing. It's just Richard's usual BS. How would Mike know anything? I mean, I wish there was something. I would like a resolution—it's the only reason I came back to this godforsaken place. I'd like to put all of this in the past. I'd like to know that I wasn't a player in some dark tragedy."

The interview drew to a close. Alex departed. Ray thought about Bitsy's journal and the Latin phrase attributed to Alex, *Mendacium Donec Moriamini:* Lie Till You Die. He wondered about the veracity of Alex's story. If her tale was mostly fiction, she was a very convincing liar.

29

Ray found Matt Reed working in the bar area, an alcove at the side of the great room. "Looks like you're packing up," said Ray. He noted that Matt's usually preppy attire had been replaced by a sweatshirt and jeans.

"Yes," responded Matt. "The party is over, finally."

"I was wondering if I could have a word?"

"Yeah, I guess," Matt responded unenthusiastically. He followed Ray to the kitchen area and the small office where the interviews were being conducted. Ray turned on the recording app, set the phone between them, and read the pre-interview boilerplate aloud.

"Good cop, bad cop?" Matt asked. His usual geniality was gone. There was an edginess to his tone.

"How do you mean?"

"Usually your sergeant is the one questioning me. I assume she's the good cop, so you must be the bad cop."

Ray smiled wryly at the idea. "Nothing of the sort," he said. "But Sergeant Lawrence is tied up at the crime scenes. Matt, I wonder if you could give me a timeline of your whereabouts last night after the fencing tournament."

"I had been instructed to have lots of champagne available for a final celebration, which was part of the plan from the get-go, from my first planning meeting with Jennings back in New York. So I had set aside a couple of cases of really good stuff. It was all iced and ready. But the way things ended, it was not a celebratory moment. People kind of lost it after that. I had opened several champagne bottles, but before I could fill many glasses, a few people were just grabbing the bottles. Some of the staff were leading the rebellion— the kitchen crew and the pilots. They were snatching liquor bottles, too. A bit of a palace revolt, it was. I didn't promote it, but I didn't try to stop it. I just backed up and let it happen. Truth be told, I grabbed a bottle of champagne and the last really good bottle of scotch and walked away. I had more than fulfilled my contract."

"What did you do then?"

"I went to my mother's room. I drank scotch neat; she sipped champagne from the bottle, sloppily. We had a long, increasingly inarticulate conversation. Nothing was held back, no secrets. Sort of a sad commentary on our relationship.

"We eventually fell asleep—or passed out, if we're being technical here—and woke up with bad heads. When we emerged from her room this morning, the place was in complete chaos."

Ray looked at Matt until the younger man met his eyes. "So you're telling me that you and your mother went to her room and didn't leave again until sometime this morning?"

Matt pressed his lips together, his body moving in a gentle rocking motion. "Yes, well, that was sort of it."

"But you left the room?"

"Do you have a witness saying I did?"

Ray nodded.

Matt's rocking became more pronounced.

"Well?" Ray pressed.

"Yeah, I left the room. Just for a few minutes. I wanted to confront Richard Gordon."

"And did you confront him?"

"No, I was too late. When I got near his suite, I could hear voices in there, two or three of them. Then some heavy banging. I retreated and hid in an alcove around the corner from his suite. Then things went quiet. I heard one door open, presumably the door to Richard's room. Then I heard another door farther away open and close, and I felt a cold gust of air, so I assumed it was the exterior door down the hall from Richard's room. I waited a bit before approaching the room, in case someone was coming back. When I came around the corner, I saw that Richard's door was ajar. I went in and saw him on the floor."

"Where?"

"Between the beds. He was lying on his back, and his eyes were open, looking at the ceiling. I was really drunk, the world was whirling, but I could still tell something was wrong with him. I kicked his foot, but he didn't respond. I knelt beside him. He wasn't breathing. And that's when I started to freak out."

"Did you see any wounds?"

"No, nothing like that. He was just lying there on the floor."

"So what did you do?"

"I just got the hell out of there. I didn't want to get blamed for whatever might have happened to him. I was freaking out."

"You didn't call for help?"

"No. I was trying to distance myself from the man and the crime, if one had been committed."

"Richard Gordon was your employer. Your mother was his guest. Wouldn't you feel an obligation to—?"

"Not at all, not to that man. And under common law, I was under no obligation to report a possible assault or his death."

"Let's not quibble about the law. Obviously there's hostility on your part toward Richard Gordon. You said you went to confront him after having a long talk with your mother. Was it about something concerning her?"

"It's a long story."

"I've got the time."

Ray watched Matt consider his options. Finally, Matt blurted out, "My mother has been involved with Richard since they were at school here. He's always had some kind of sick hold on her. And I was part of the collateral damage."

"Are you telling me that there was an ongoing relationship between them that lasted more than twenty-five years?"

"Essentially, yes. She's never been totally honest about it, at least not with me. I guess there are things you don't tell your kids."

"And how were you part of the collateral damage?"

"I think my mother's continued relationship with Richard was one of the causes of my parents' divorce, not that my father was a complete innocent. The divorce took place about the time that Richard was named to the Leiston School Board, and I'm sure he paved the way for my mother getting an administrative job here. From that point forward they had a monthly rendezvous until he left the board."

"So what exactly were you going to confront Richard about?"

"You know, I don't even remember now. My thinking was so muddled at the time. I just had a kind of primordial urge to protect her from him."

"Nothing more specific?" Ray pressed. "Nothing about getting back at him for something he did here, at the reunion?"

"OK, fine. Last night she told me it was Richard who slugged her on Saturday night, not Tony. By the time I arrived on the scene, Jennings was already spinning the story that Tony was the culprit, but last night my mother told me it started with Richard getting angry with her and slugging her in the face. Tony apparently stepped in and clubbed him in response."

"Do you know what sparked Richard's outburst?"

"That she wouldn't tell me other than it was something that happened long ago, something best forgotten by everyone."

"You're being here, it's almost an unbelievable bit of serendipity."

"Agreed, but that's all it is. Six degrees of separation and all that. I met Jennings a couple of years ago by chance, when she came into the bar where I was working. I couldn't have planned that meeting if I'd tried. I didn't know that Jennings worked for Richard until months after we first met. I had been somewhat aware of my mother's relationship with Richard for a few years."

"You still haven't told me why you decided to sign on for this weekend gig."

"Two things. First, I was going to get paid a lot of money. Second, I was going to see this Gordon character up close for several days. I wanted to get a sense of the man who has been such a major player in my mother's pattern of self-destructive behavior."

"Did you hold him responsible?"

Matt shook his head. "We all have to learn to swim with

sharks—the users, the sociopaths, narcissists, and other nut jobs of the world. She wasn't an unwilling participant in their relationship. Richard's pull on her was some sort of strange addiction, one that I didn't understand. One that I still don't understand. To me, he was obnoxious and overbearing."

"So last night, by your own admission, drunk and with new knowledge of how Richard had physically assaulted and battered your mother—"

"True, and I know where you're going with this, Sheriff. My confrontation with him was going to be verbal. Nothing more. And a shouting match never happened because he was dead when I found him."

30

Matt lead Ray to his mother's room. Ray waited outside while Matt went in to see if his mother was dressed to receive company. A few minutes later he reappeared and guided Ray in. Sarah was seated at a small table holding onto a coffee mug, her head tilted forward, her shoulders collapsed. Ray settled into the chair directly across from her. She slowly lifted her gaze and looked at Ray.

"Are you OK?" Ray asked. "We could probably do this later."

"I'm hungover, confused, and grieving." Sarah paused for a long moment, wiping away tears. "Matt wanted me to get this conversation over with. My kid has decided to take control of my life. What do you need from me?"

"I'm pulling together loose ends. I need you to confirm a few things. I will be recording this." He set his phone on the table between them, started the app, and ran through the boilerplate.

"Tell me about last night."

"Like what?"

"Everything you can remember, from the end of the fencing match until you woke up this morning."

"Richard was never a gracious loser. Alex is fast. She avoided his slap."

"Is that how Richard hit you?" asked Ray.

Sarah eyed him suspiciously. "That was Tony."

"No, Sarah. It's time for truth telling. Richard hit you."

"Well, it was very confusing. I was smashed. We all were. It might have been Richard. It doesn't matter."

"It does matter, Sarah. It does matter. Why did Richard hit you? Have you looked at yourself in the mirror this morning?

That wasn't a playful slap or an accident. There was a lot of anger and rage directed at you. What was going on?"

"I don't quite remember. Maybe it was Richard who started talking about Huck and Judd, like he was trying to find out what we remembered."

"Huck and Judd? I'm not sure who you're talking about," Ray said, keeping his cards close to his chest.

"They were guys that showed up one of our last days at the campsite. One night Richard passed out pot brownies and some kind of liquor laced with something, LSD I think. The results were almost catastrophic. He was in big trouble, so he just disappeared, ran into the woods with his sleeping bag. Late the next afternoon he wanders back with two rough-looking characters, you know, beards, foul smelling. All three of them looked drunk. In the end these two Yoopers started a fight with Etienne. He kicked their asses royally and made them leave. I was happy to see them go. All the girls were, if you know what I mean.

"So the other night, someone brought up Huck and Judd, and Alex picked up on it right away. I don't think she was as drunk as the rest of us. She got rather aggressive, asking Richard if he had some involvement with them. And then Tony asked him if he had hired Huck and Judd to come to the campsite and make trouble. You know they broke Tony's leg, really badly, a compound fracture.

"Then I asked Richard point blank if he had hired Huck and Judd." Sarah paused for a long moment. "It was even stronger than that. I accused him of hiring Huck and Judd. And I think I went on to accuse him of setting up the whole thing to get at Etienne. He just frigging lost it. He smashed me. Not a slap, a closed fist.

"I remember Tony pushing him away from me. Then he smacked Richard hard several times. That surprised me—Tony had always been such a sycophant, always doing Richard's bidding. I guess he finally had enough."

Sarah slowly sipped her coffee before continuing. "Tony probably had the inside story on Huck and Judd. He and Richard, they were really tight. Is any of this making sense? I know I'm giving you bits and pieces and everything is out of order." She looked at Ray and waited for his response.

"The possibility of Richard being involved with hiring Huck and Judd . . ."

"Yes. In retrospect, it's so damn obvious, isn't it?" said Sarah. But it never crossed my mind. I was really into Richard. I was happy when Alex dumped him. The two of us, Richard and I, didn't really hook up until the camping trip. From that point forward he became my addiction—sex, drugs, and some weird hold on my psychological needs."

"Do you have any evidence that Richard might have arranged for these men to come to your campsite?"

"None. But I can tell you this, and my apologies for the cliché, but Richard could always think outside the box. And he always had lots of money and knew how to use it. In many ways, he was much more mature than the rest of us. He knew how to use money to manipulate people. If he wanted to hire a couple of goons to humiliate Etienne in front of Alex, he'd find a way to do it. I mean, him running off looking drug crazed and then wandering back to the campsite a day later in the company of those two guys, that's all fairly improbable. And then Etienne just disappearing. I wonder if Richard paid Etienne to go away. That seems highly plausible, but I guess we will never know."

"Your relationship with Richard, it continued from the time you were in school?"

"Matt told you that?"

Ray nodded.

"Did I want Richard dead? Did I have a motive?"

"Did you? The man seemed to have quite a hold on you."

"No," she said. "I didn't want him dead." A fresh flow of tears started from her eyes, and she wiped them away almost impatiently. "He was an addiction, but my cure wouldn't come from killing him. I have a new therapist in Chicago. She's been helping me work through my twisted relationship with him. I now understand that it hasn't been about Richard, it's been about me. It has always been about me. Richard just fed into my . . . I don't know what to say, my need for dysfunction, for drama. Saturday night just confirmed why I needed to get him out of my life. I was finally able to admit the kind of person he really was. Getting hit in the head was a good thing. It finally knocked some sense into me. No, I didn't kill him. I had no motive."

"Do you know of anyone who wanted him dead?"

"No, not dead. Lots of people here have reasons to dislike him. But killing Richard, no, not in our group. I don't know about his staff. I'm really hungover, Ray. Is there anything else?"

"Let's go back to last night just for a minute. I'm trying to map where everyone was. What did you do after the fencing match?"

"I went back to my room. Matt joined me a few minutes later, and we had a few drinks. Well, more than a few. We had a heart to heart. Then I crashed."

"Did either of you leave your room during the night?"

"Well, I didn't. And Matt had had at least as many drinks as I had—and he was drinking scotch. I can't imagine he went anywhere after I crashed."

"That's about it, Sarah. I might have more questions for you later."

"Whatever. I'm surprised by one thing."

"What's that?"

"You didn't ask if I was seeing Richard when you and I were dating."

"It's not germane to the investigation," he responded.

"Elkins, you're a real pain in the ass. You need to get in touch with your feelings."

31

"Sheriff, I was wondering if you had any news on Gary Zatanski," asked Mike Kniivila. They were standing in the great room near a breakfast buffet.

Ray looked up from the screen of his smart phone. "Morning, Mike. I just got a message. Gary and the others have been transported to the medical center. Gary is in the cardiac care unit and is reported to be in stable condition."

"Good to hear. Glad you were able to get him out of here so fast."

"Mike, I need a word."

"Anything, Sheriff."

They went through the kitchen and into Ray's makeshift interview room.

Ray started his recording app. "Your name keeps coming up, Mike," he said, "as someone who knows so much about the history of Leiston School. You're a legendary character. When I talk to people, I keep hearing, 'Mike would know that.' And you're part of a very positive memory for this group, the way you came back to check on them, hiking through the fierce storm and organizing the rescue."

"It was nothing special, Sheriff. I was just doing my job." Mike rubbed his knuckles against the three-day stubble on his cheek.

"I saw you sitting off to the side at the fencing match last night," commented Ray. "What did you think?"

"Until the end, it seemed like old times. I mean, Alex, I think she was probably the best fencer the school ever had."

"So you got to know her a bit when she was at Leiston?"

"Yeah, better than most."

"How so?"

"Well, she was always in my shop. She did all the repairs on her fencing equipment, even the electrical stuff. She wanted my help, but she wanted to do things herself, get what I'm saying? And the same was true with her skis. She was probably the best skier that ever came through the place, too. She won the regionals starting when she was a sophomore. Never won a state title, but finished pretty high up. She probably needed better coaching and equipment to really be competitive, especially the coaching part. But let me tell you, the other kids, they'd bring their skis by and expect me to tune them. Not Alex.

"I carted the fencing team all over Hell's half acre in the school van—a twelve-passenger Ford. We went to Detroit, Grand Rapids, even Chicago, as far as Cincinnati once. On those long drives you learn so much by just taking in their conversations. And I drove the bus for the weekend ski trips. Even though other staff members were supposed to help chaperone, they sometimes sent me alone, so I was the only one with the kids. I skied with Alex and the other kids lots of times. There was always lots of chatting and kidding around, and you gradually learn about their classes, their teachers, their families, what they think about things."

"Sounds like you really liked Alex."

"Well, I did. Liked them all. Well, most of them. But Alex was special, smart as a whip, and she had that physical confidence that you see in really good athletes. You should have seen her ski. She really had balls, you know what I mean? For Alex, the slopes were never too steep or too bumpy. None of the boys could stay with her. And foul mouthed, too. She was a head turner, still is."

"Some people have told me that there were inappropriate relationships between some students and some of the Leiston faculty."

Mike shook his head. "You know," he said, "in high school our government teacher told us about John Locke, what he wrote about the social contract, and that always stuck with me; I always followed it. He said that we all have a responsibility to maintain social order.

And in a school, like Leiston, adults have to put responsibility above their basic urges. I can say I did that, but I'm not so sure about some of the other adults at Leiston."

"Are you thinking about anyone in particular?"

Mike played with the stubble on his chin. Ray could feel his discomfort.

"Well, the French instructor, the fencing coach, Etienne, he crossed the line."

"What does that mean?"

"He was messing with some of the girls."

"Alex included?"

"Yes, she was one of them."

"That's a serious accusation."

"Yeah, I know. But Etienne really didn't try that hard to hide what he was doing. He had built a love nest in one of the storage rooms in the fencing building. I was over there one day doing some maintenance work, and I found this mattress and pillows. And then I was there another time—I wasn't trying to catch them or anything; I'd rather not have known about it at all—and I hear giggling and such, and then Alex comes running out of the storage room in her underwear. She was so embarrassed, and I was, too. I just got out of there fast. Then Etienne came to see me the next day, brings me a bottle of wine, wants to have a man-to-man about the ways of the world. He asked me not to say anything, you know, to the headmaster. This little secret should be between us."

"Did you go along with Etienne?"

"Oh, hell no. I went right to the headmaster, Colonel Wallengate. Did you ever know him?"

"No."

"The board brought him in to try to shape things up, you know, the teachers, the kids, all of the rest of us, too. The school was getting a reputation for being way too loosey goosey. So they found this ex-military guy to reintroduce discipline, as if there had ever been much. Well, Wallengate, he looked the part. You know, steel-gray hair and mustache, and that erect military bearing like he had a broom handle up his ass. As a headmaster he was a complete failure. By the time he got here he was already starting to lose it. His first major decree to restore order was the creation of a cocktail hour for the faculty, I guess like something they do before the officers' mess."

"So you took this problem, your concern about Etienne, to the headmaster?"

"Yes, late one afternoon. He was already in his cups. He offered me a glass of whiskey. During my more than three decades at the school, he was the only headmaster who ever had alcohol in his office. He didn't last."

"So how did he respond to your concerns about Etienne?"

"First he started telling me about his time in Brussels at NATO headquarters and how he traveled extensively in France. And then he rambled on about how Europeans in general, and the French in particular, have a more mature, relaxed view of sex. And if Etienne was having a dalliance with one of the girls, it was more a reflection of his nationality. Wallengate said that Etienne just didn't understand American culture. He promised me that he would have a word with Etienne and straighten him out. Can you imagine, he would have a word with Etienne? But what could I do, the maintenance guy trying to straighten out a retired brigadier general?"

Ray nodded. "Yes, that must have been tough."

"We're tuned to the same channel, Sheriff. We know right from wrong."

"Absolutely, Mike. You can probably help me with something else. I'm sure the campers told you all about the two guys that wandered into the campsite a day or two before you organized the rescue. I think their names were Huck and Judd."

Mike nodded to the affirmative. Ray was watching him closely.

"Yeah, the kids mentioned them. A couple of real Yoopers, I guess, going on what they told me. Rough-looking guys with big beards."

"Well, here's the deal, Mike. There's been a suggestion that Huck and Judd showing up and their fight with Etienne, that was all staged. That somehow Richard had managed to hire these two guys and that it was all part of a plan to embarrass Etienne. It has been alleged that Richard had put this little charade in place to try to win Alex back."

"Well, Sheriff, I wouldn't know about that. I do know that Richard was a scammer, even back then. I heard from some of the other staff about him trying to buy grades he didn't earn. I never seen a kid with that much money. The sad thing is that money talks. You know what I mean? He usually got what he wanted."

"Considering how you felt about Etienne," Ray said, "you probably wouldn't have minded it much if you heard that he had gotten his ass kicked. I mean, Etienne was breaking the rules, messing around with underage girls, including Alex. Creating his own little harem while the headmaster was looking the other way."

"Yeah, you got that right."

"Well, Mike, I'm with you on that. What's interesting to me is how Richard, if he was indeed behind hiring these Yoopers, Huck and Judd, was able to pull it off. I mean, he must have been very clever to find those two. And then there were some fairly complicated logistical problems, getting Huck and Judd to the right place, a remote campsite in the U.P. And there's the whole issue of timing. Again, let's say Richard was involved. Today he'd just use his cell phone, he'd call them or text them. But back then it had to be much more complicated."

"Yeah, I see what you're saying. Let me think. I remember the kids mentioning about Richard wandering away for a day or more. And when he came back, he was with those guys, so yeah, he must've known that they were out there somewhere. There must've been a plan so he could find them. Otherwise it would be easy to get lost up there permanently. People disappear into the woods and are never seen again. Happens most every year during deer season."

"Yes, that's my thinking, Mike. Richard was following a very good plan. And you know what? I think it was your plan."

"No, no way. Where did you get that?"

"Not long before Richard was killed, he told someone if they really wanted to know what happened to Etienne, they needed to talk to you, Mike."

"Richard was always a liar, always. Anyone will tell you that."

"But in this case it's true, isn't it, Mike? Richard had you hire a couple of goons to mess with Etienne, didn't he? And to your way of thinking at the time, it was probably the right thing to do."

Mike looked down at his coffee mug, then away from the table at the tile floor. Finally, he looked up at Ray. "It was a good plan. I just didn't get it right. How was I to know he was so good at Kung Fu or whatever. The plan was not to hurt him. We only wanted to make him look cowardly in the eyes of the girls. It all seemed so easy, and it all went so wrong. It's been eating at me for years, Sheriff. But I couldn't walk it back."

"Who were the guys, Mike? Huck and Judd? I assume those weren't their real names."

"Well, Ted, he's the one I knew. My nephew, my sister's boy. It was him and a friend, his roommate. I think his name was Merle, something like that. They were students at Northern. They were a bit older. They'd been navy buddies."

"Yoopers?"

"No, downstaters, at least my nephew. He grew up in Wyandotte. I don't know about the other kid."

"The logistics, Mike, how did you make this work?"

"Not so hard. After I dropped the kids off, I spent the night in Marquette with Ted and his buddy. Then I dropped them off the next day when I was heading to the Keweenaw. They were going to make the job part of a deer hunting trip. They skirted the Leiston kids and set up camp a couple of miles on. It was all worked out when Richard was supposed to find them. Course things didn't go right . . . first the weather, then Etienne beating the hell out of them. Plan was that I'd pick them up at the trailhead. That didn't happen because of the storm. I ended up hiking in to check on the kids. Ted and his friend, they had to find their own way back."

"Did they tell you what happened?"

"Well, after the rescue, and after I got the kids settled in the hotel, I went over to Ted and Merle's apartment. They said Etienne got the best of them. And it looked like it. They was beat up good. They wanted their money. I paid them and that was that."

"Etienne going missing, were they connected with that in any way?"

"Sheriff, at the time we didn't know he was missing. Later on I did talk to Merle about it. I stopped off to see Ted. He wasn't there, so I talked to Merle. He said they caught up with Etienne the next day, messed him up pretty good. I asked if they killed Etienne. He said no, but he wouldn't tell me nothing more."

"Where is he now?"

"According to Ted, he hit an ambulance head-on on his Harley sometime after the bars closed one night. This was years ago. Ted said it was bound to happen sooner or later. Merle was always living on the edge."

"How much money are we talking about?"

"Five hundred each. A lot of money back then, especially for college kids. And you know what? Richard wanted his money back, said I didn't fulfill my end of the bargain. But when Etienne never showed up again, he stopped bugging me."

"And you never pursued this any further with Ted?"

"No. Truth be told, I haven't seen him for years. He didn't even show up for my sister's funeral. He sort of disappeared from the family."

"Tony Messina was badly injured during the confrontation between Etienne and Huck and Judd. Don't you take any responsibility for what happened?"

"That wasn't in the plan. That wasn't supposed to happen. It was—what do they call it?—collateral damage. It was an accident. The kid got in the way."

Ray sat silently for a short time. He was trying to control his anger.

"Mike, I'm mapping out where everyone was last night. What did you do after the fencing match?"

"I went over to the bar. People were just grabbing bottles. I got some bourbon and went back to my room. I had a few drinks, more than I should have, but I wanted to make sure I slept. One of the problems of old age, I just don't sleep. Are you done, Sheriff?"

"Just one more thing, Mike. Your nephew, you say his name is Ted, but could his name actually be Gary?"

32

~~

S ue caught up with Ray near a coffee urn that had been set up in the great room. The usual elegant array of food had been replaced with the scant leftovers of the weekend bacchanal—a bowl of assorted crackers; a cutting board with a few battered chunks of cheese; a basket of apples and oranges; miscellaneous plastic knives, forks, and plates; and a pile of breakfast bars.

Sue grabbed an apple and some cheese and followed Ray through the kitchen to his small work area.

"Where do you want to start?" Sue asked, carefully centering her iPad on the table in front of her.

"Why don't you go first, Zatanski and the pilots . . ."

"Zatanski is in the cardiac care unit. He's reported to be stable and comfortable. Conrad Voight is in surgery. He's in temporary serious condition, but his injuries are not life threatening. Megan Bartoli, the pilot, was sent on to Spectrum in Grand Rapids via North Flight EMS. She hasn't fully regained consciousness. I don't have any updates on her condition."

"How about the bodies?"

"They've all been removed and are at the medical center. Recovering Tony Messina's body was challenging, lots of digging snowmobiles out of deep drifts. Anyway, autopsies are proceeding as we speak. We should be there but—"

"Fill me in on the scene in the crew's cottage when I went out after Tony Messina."

"Conrad had a bullet wound on the left shoulder. He was losing blood. He also had a couple of scalp wounds with lots of bleeding. And he seemed to be dazed. I think he was concussed. That's about the time Zatanski came back with Alex. She took charge.

There was no fooling around. After she did a quick triage, she told me to arrange for transport ASAP. She got Conrad's bleeding under control, and then turned her attention to Megan, who seemed to be slipping in and out of consciousness. She said Megan was a rush-rush. The evacuation went faster than expected. Four snowmobiles, two with evacuation sleds. The chopper was on the ground waiting at the fire hall when they got back. A few minutes later they were airborne."

"How about the other pilot, Nick?"

"Nick Speyer. I thought he was supposed to be helping manage Messina, but obviously he was somewhere else. Anyway, he discovered Conrad and Megan and then went for help. I guess he found Zatanski sleeping on a couch in the great room. Zatanski alerted us and collected Alex. Anyway, Nick tried to help Alex, but some people just can't deal with blood."

"Did you recover the weapon?"

"Yes, a Sig Sauer."

"Do you have a scenario?"

"Not much. I got bits and pieces from Conrad about Tony Messina getting the jump on them. Remember at dinner last night, Messina looked totally out of it. I thought they were keeping him heavily medicated, maybe even tied to a bed or something. Your guess is as good as mine on how he overpowered Conrad. The guy is massive and totally ripped. Maybe they were asleep and Messina got loose. It appears Conrad and Megan both took substantial hits to the head. I found the probable club, a piece of hardwood, probably oak, about two feet long, maybe three inches in diameter."

"Where did that come from?"

"A stack of wood next to the fireplace. There were several more just like it. An easy grab. I don't know if the clubbing preceded the shooting or vice versa. We'll sort that out when we can interview Conrad."

"How about the Gordon crime scene?"

"A couple of things. Again, I wish Dr. Dyskin had been there. First, the epee sticking out of his chest. Like you noted, that wound was inflicted postmortem. I didn't want to mess about too much, but his chest seemed depressed."

"Anything else?"

"When they were bagging him, the EMT commented on a possible skull fracture at the back of the head. The autopsy will help us reconstruct what happened. Other than that, I didn't find much: a couple of empty champagne bottles, some of his clothes tossed about. No evidence of a major struggle. I did find a couple of buttons, one on the bed, another in the carpet." She set a small evidence bag on the table in front of Ray.

"Woman's blouse?" he said.

"Yes, that would be my guess. And when we were attending to Megan earlier, I noticed her bright red bra. I wouldn't have probably seen it, but her shirt was open. Buttons were missing."

"So what do you think?" asked Ray.

"I don't know. We'll have to get her shirt to do a match. Maybe Gordon was getting aggressive with his pilot, or perhaps it was a preamble to a little rough sex—perhaps consensual, perhaps not. And we both thought it looked like there was something going on between Megan and Conrad. So is he somehow involved in Gordon's death?

"What do you have for me?" asked Sue, looking at his pile of notes on sheets from a yellow legal pad. "What about the usual suspects?"

"If we had a smoking gun or the cause of death, that would clarify this fairly quickly, but no such luck," Ray said. "Matt, Sarah, Alex, and Jennings are professing their innocence. That said, none of them has an airtight alibi." Ray told Sue what he had learned during his interviews.

33

Dusk was settling in by the time Ray and Sue finally were able to get to the regional medical center. Dressed in scrubs, Dr. Dyskin met them just beyond the double steel doors leading into the pathology department. "Where were you when we needed you?" asked Sue, giving him a playful hug.

"In Livonia, watching my grandsons play hockey. For once, Delta was ready when we were. My wife was anxious to get back. Our whole family is coming north for Thanksgiving."

"What do you have for us?"

"This is the preliminary report, of course, since final toxicology will take some time. Should we start with Elizabeth Morgan?"

"Sure."

"You guys did a good job keeping her on ice, by the way. I was rather surprised once I got her open."

"Why?" asked Sue.

"Her age. She had coronary artery disease, very advanced. That's statistically very rare for someone of her years. She was a walking time bomb. I'd like to know more about her medical history."

"So she died of natural causes?"

"I checked the body carefully and reviewed your notes and photos, Sue. Ms. Morgan probably just walked into that room and collapsed. Who knows what precipitated it: the stress of travel, the excitement of seeing old friends, or maybe none of the above. It was just bound to happen."

"What if she had just done cocaine?"

"There's a high correlation between cocaine use and sudden cardiac death. Do you have any evidence that she might have been using cocaine?"

"Not exactly," Sue responded.

"What's that supposed to mean?" pressed Dyskin.

"There was some drug paraphernalia in the room, but it looked staged. I haven't had time to test the bag of powder."

"And I can't tell you any more until the toxicology comes back. Now, the man, Tony Messina, the one who was fished out of the lake. Do you want to see the body?"

"Just give us the results, please," answered Ray. "You can show Sue everything later."

Dyskin emitted a low chuckle. "You're absolutely consistent, Elkins. So here's what you want to know. The immediate cause of death was aspiration of water, drowning. Where was the body when you found it?"

"In the lake, face down."

"And your notes stated that he was taking unknown prescription drugs allegedly for PTSD."

"We might be able to chase that one down, get in touch with his doctor," said Sue.

"Good, can't hurt. Problem is we will never know how he might have dosed. Again, we'll know more with the toxicology. There were probably a number of things that led to his final swim. He had multiple contusions on his hands, arms, and upper body. They appear quite recent. Some looked to be defensive, some are perhaps offensive. It's hard to say. What the hell were these people doing, having wrestling matches?" Dyskin didn't wait for an answer. "The last body you need to see." He looked toward Ray. "You too, Elkins. You will be OK. I haven't started cutting yet."

Sue followed Dyskin into the autopsy room. Ray trailed her, a distant third. He joined them at the side of the autopsy table. Dyskin pulled the sheet off the top half of Richard Gordon's body. "First, there was massive blunt force trauma to the chest. Look at the way the chest is collapsed inward. When we get him open we will find underlying tissue and organ damage." Dyskin circled the depressed area with a gloved hand.

"Someone jumped on his chest or was a skilled martial artist who delivered a well-aimed, deadly kick. I'm not sure this guy would have been breathing afterward. But there's more." Dyskin moved to Richard Gordon's head. "The back of the skull is crushed. It looks to me like there was a blow to the forehead. My suspicion is that the force of that blow caused the rear of the skull to fracture when it was pushed against a hard surface, like a floor. Either of these two injuries would probably have been fatal. I don't know the order in which they occurred."

Dyskin wagged an index finger at them. "When I say force, I'm talking about a lot of power. I'm thinking probably a large, powerful man."

Sue looked Ray. He nodded his response.

"The bit with the epee, that was probably for dramatic effect. Like your notes suggested, Sue, the man was long dead. This was a belated coup de grâce. Any questions?"

"You've given us exactly what we need," Sue answered.

34

While Ray stood at the counter of the nursing station in the intensive care unit filling out the required paperwork to visit Conrad Voight, Sue was just beyond earshot, talking on her phone.

"You'll have to wait a few minutes, Sheriff," explained the nurse behind the desk, a woman in lavender scrubs. "I have to get a doctor to sign off on this." She picked up a clipboard and walked off into an adjoining room where Ray could see men and women seated along a counter, all in scrubs, working at computer screens or conversing.

"Anything?" Ray asked when Sue came to his side.

"Megan Bartoli is conscious and communicating, and it doesn't appear that there is any cranial bleeding. She's being held for observation. The nurse with whom I spoke wouldn't speculate on how long Megan might be hospitalized."

"Sheriff,"—the nurse had returned to her desk—"this is Dr. Kahn, one of our trauma consultants. He'll accompany you to Mr. Voight's room."

Dr. Kahn, young and intense, came around the counter and exchanged handshakes with Ray and Sue. "He's been mostly dozing since we finished attending to his wounds and completed a thorough exam. I will see if he is awake."

Dr. Kahn led them to Conrad Voight's room, where the patient lay on his back with his eyes open, looking at a flat screen television that hung on the wall beyond the foot of the bed. He gave them an uneasy look as they entered.

Dr. Kahn went to the side of the bed. "Mr. Voight," he said, "you have some visitors. Do you feel up to talking with them?"

"I guess I'm good with that," responded Conrad sluggishly.

"It's the sheriff and his sergeant. Under hospital guidelines, you do not have to speak with them at this time. It is your decision, sir."

"It's OK, Doctor. I want to get this over with."

Dr. Kahn moved away from the bed and addressed Ray. "I ask that you keep the conversation brief. If at any time Mr. Voight feels he does not want to continue talking with you, please honor his decision."

Ray nodded his agreement. "Watching a little rugby?" he asked Conrad as he and Sue took up positions on either side of the hospital bed.

"It took me a while to figure out what that was. Those guys are killing each other."

"How are you feeling?" asked Sue, standing on the other side of the bed. She looked at two lines of stitches on his scalp.

"My head aches. The shoulder hurts." He gestured with his hand. "Do you know how Megan's doing? They said they flew her to a neuro trauma center in Grand Rapids . . ." His voice trailed off.

Sue gave him an update.

"Good," Conrad responded. "I couldn't get her to wake up. Then they separated us when we got here. Do you think I could talk to her?"

"Yes," Sue said. "We'll get you the number before we leave, OK?"

Conrad closed his eyes briefly and nodded.

"Mr. Voight, I'm going to record our conversation." Ray held up his phone and hit the record button on the screen. "We'd like you to tell us what happened last night."

"Where do you want me to start?" Conrad asked, his voice going flat.

"Jennings Bidder has told us that you accompanied Mr. Gordon back to his suite after the fencing match."

"Yeah, that's right. Me and Jennings. I was there to provide a little muscle if it was needed. That's not the first time I had to do something like that."

"What happened then?"

"He started to get shit-faced. He had a bottle of champagne

that he was tossing down like Gatorade. Jennings, she has a way with him, she was talking him down. Then Dr. Bishop shows up, the shrink. And after a while Jennings leaves. On her way out, she tells me that Mr. Gordon wants to talk to Megan. He wanted to know when she thought the airport might reopen. I hung around a little bit longer, but the conversation between Mr. Gordon and Dr. Bishop seemed to have settled down, and I knew that as drunk as Mr. Gordon was getting, he would pass out soon enough. I didn't see any reason to hang around there, and Nick had told me earlier that he had somewhere to be, so I went back to the cottage to relieve him.

"Where was Nick going?" Ray asked.

"I don't know. He had places to go, people to see. I'm pretty sure it had something to do with a woman. Megan and I try to keep it professional, you know? We don't date on the job."

"Any idea which woman?" Ray asked.

"Nick didn't say. He keeps his cards close to the chest. When I got back to the cottage, Tony was asleep. I told Megan that Mr. Gordon wanted her to check in with him about possible flight times. I told her that Gordon was pretty drunk, and she should wait to talk to him until the next morning. Megan, she takes her job seriously. She wanted to go check in with him anyway. A few minutes later she headed out."

"And you were left alone with Tony, who was still sleeping?" Ray asked.

"He was out like a frigging log. I didn't think we would hear from him again until the day after tomorrow. He was totally loaded up on all kinds of meds he got from the VA. We made sure he took then." Conrad glanced at the screen, briefly focusing on the players crashing into one another. He looked back at Ray.

"Then what happened, Conrad?" asked Sue.

"I had dropped off to sleep. I don't know how long I'd been asleep when Megan woke me up. She was crying. Her blouse was torn. There was a mark on her cheek where he slapped her, and she was holding her wrist, said she had sprained it. Megan said

Gordon had demanded sex and started pushing her around when she refused. He told her that if she didn't have sex with him, she was fired. I asked if he had raped her. She said no, he was too sloppy drunk to catch her. Like, I just exploded. I started to go out. She tried to hold me back, but I pushed past her.

"When I got to Mr. Gordon's room, I pounded on the door, and when he opened it, I pushed him in the chest and yelled something at him like 'You fucking bastard!' or something like that. I just wanted to smash him in the mouth, that's it, just to make him think twice about ever doing what he'd done to Megan to anyone else. He picked up that sword. He was waving it around my face. And then he said, 'You're fired too, asshole.' He lunged at me, almost nailed me. A switch just flipped in me. I did what I've been trained to do. I kicked him in the chest. He went down. I was on him. I slammed his head into the floor. He stopped moving. And when I saw him just lying there, I knew he was dead."

Ray let Voight's words hang in the air. Quietly, he asked, "Then what did you do?"

"I stayed there, kneeling next to him. I've killed people, Sheriff—I was in the thick of it in Fallujah and deployed twice to Afghanistan. This was a different kind of rage. It was personal. I don't know how long I stayed there with him. Then I finally got up and went back to the cottage. I was worried about Megan."

"Did you think about reporting Mr. Gordon's death to us?" Sue asked.

"I was going to, I swear," Voight said. "But first I wanted to make sure Megan was OK. As soon as I came through the door of the cottage, I could feel something was wrong. Then I saw Megan collapsed on the floor. As I bent over to check on her, Tony hit me. I was stunned at first. Then I reached for him, and he shot me. Then the bastard hit me again. I must have blacked out. The next thing I remember, Nick was there. Then the school security guy, Gary, and you, Sergeant," he gestured toward Sue. "I was pretty confused."

"The gun, Conrad, was it yours?" Sue asked.

"Yeah, I had stashed it under my pillow. He must have found it."

"Tony wasn't restrained?"

"No, like I said, I thought he was totally out of it. Obviously I was wrong."

Ray looked across the bed at Sue.

"What happens now?" asked Voight. "Guess I'll be charged with manslaughter, right?"

"Yes," said Ray.

"You know, Tony was a victim, too. He came back really damaged. I thought I was better than that."

35

"Voight. How do you think that will play out?" asked Sue as they headed toward the elevators.

"You know the variables—the judge, the jury, the prosecutor, the defense lawyers. Given the circumstances that surround this murder and Voight's personal history . . ."

"Well?" prodded Sue.

"I don't know."

As they stood waiting for the elevator, Sue looked at Ray carefully, her gaze sweeping from head to foot then back again.

"Is it that bad?" he asked. "I've been avoiding mirrors."

"A four-day beard, rumpled clothes, and you're in need of a haircut. And you look like you're one notch above sleepwalking. I'm probably no fashion plate either. I'm surprised no one from hospital security has tried to put us in contact with a homeless shelter."

"I'm about to collapse," Ray admitted.

"Ditto. I want my dog and a long hot bath. And food, real food, mac and cheese. Some wine too, or maybe a beer. It doesn't have to be one of those fancy boutique brews. A Budweiser would be OK, just the basics. Then I want to sleep in my own bed for maybe ten or twelve hours. Uninterrupted sleep, no violence, no death, no fighting through blizzards in total darkness. Just sleep. How about you?"

"A shower and then sleep. And maybe Simone should come home with me. It would be nice to have someone sharing my bed."

"I know we have shared custody, but I am the primary caregiver. Besides, I shared a bedroom with you the last two nights, and I didn't get the impression that you needed anyone to cuddle with," she teased. "By the way, when does Hanna come back from California?"

"Sometime next Sunday, late in the day as I remember. I have to check."

"Do you think she'll take the fellowship at Stanford?" Sue asked.

"I don't know."

"It would be hard to turn down. The chance to continue to grow professionally, maybe do something really important, and California."

Ray didn't respond. He was still pondering what Sue had just said when the elevator ding sounded and the doors opened in front of them.

Ray filled out another Law Enforcement Access to Patients and Patient Information form at the desk of the cardiac care unit, and then a young man in blue scrubs led him and Sue to Gary Zatanski's room.

"Gary, you've got some company. Sheriff Elkins and Sergeant Lawrence. Is it OK if they come in and talk with you?"

"Yes, of course."

"Try to be brief," the nurse cautioned. "And remember, per the form you signed, the patient can terminate the interview at any time." The nurse turned toward his patient. "You heard that, Mr. Zatanski, the part about your right to stop talking to these guys?"

"I'm good. No problem," Zatanski assured the nurse. "You can leave us."

"How are you feeling, Gary?" asked Ray, coming to the side of the hospital bed. He glanced at the monitor mounted behind the bed. A series of multicolored lines marched across the display from left to right.

"Much better. As soon as the EMTs gave me some nitro, the pain was manageable. And I feel more relaxed being here, knowing that help is close by if needed. I talked to the doctor a few minutes before you got here. They're going to keep me for a day or two. You know, observation, whatever that is."

"Have you had symptoms before?"

"The angina, yes. And I've been following doctor's orders, you know, avoiding stress, getting regular exercise, and trying to watch my diet. But three days in that madhouse with almost no sleep . . . I'm surprised you two are still standing."

"We're holding on by our nails," said Sue.

"Have you figured out who killed Richard Gordon?"

"Yes, and as soon as the paperwork is completed and I meet with the prosecutor, we will go public with that information," Ray said.

"No hints?"

"Sorry, Gary, we can't do that."

"How about Bitsy Morgan, do you know what killed her yet?"

"She died of natural causes."

"Heart?"

"Yes."

"And Tony Messina?"

"The preliminary findings suggest an accidental drowning—no sign of foul play. There were probably a number of contributing factors. We will know more after we get the results back from the forensic autopsy and the toxicology report."

"I never had much of a sense about Messina, you know. I only encountered him a few times. He must have been deeply troubled."

"Yes," agreed Ray. "Gary, there are a few things I need to get sorted out, and that I'm hoping you might help us with. I'd like to record your answers just to make sure we get things right. Are you OK with that?"

"No problem, Ray. Always glad to help."

"The first thing you can help us with is the white powder and straw we found in Bitsy's room. Sue hasn't had a chance to check the powder yet, but my guess is that it will prove negative for cocaine. And Gary, that whole scene—the Swiss army knife, the baggie with the powder, the piece of plastic straw—it just didn't look right. Sue and I stumble across drug scenes on a regular basis. We know what they look like. And since you were the only one who seemed to have access to her room, we were wondering what you might know about it."

Something flashed across Gary's face—chagrin, maybe, or even embarrassment. "Diatomaceous earth," he finally admitted.

"What?" asked Ray.

"Diatomaceous earth. It's a bug killer, but it's not poisonous. You can eat it. It won't hurt you. I found it in a supply room off the kitchen."

"So you created that little display?" asked Sue.

"Yes, I was hoping . . . I heard a rumor that Richard Gordon liked to ply his friends with coke. So I was thinking that when you saw the body and then something looking like coke, you would disrupt the whole event, maybe even search some other rooms, charge Gordon with possession, maybe send everybody else home. I just wanted it to end."

"Why did you want it to end?" Ray asked.

"I don't know what I was thinking. I was tired of those people from the beginning. I was being hostile."

"And I assume you were the one who slipped into our cottage and looked through Bitsy's luggage?"

"You're way off base on that one, Ray. Why would I do that?"

"You've been a cop, Gary. Think like a cop. Of all the people there, who would know the layout of the cottage? Who would know about the unlocked exterior door leading into Bitsy's room? And when we moved her luggage to our room, who would quickly recognize it among our things? And then when we came in the front door, who would know the best way to slip out without being seen?"

"True, true. But why would I do that?"

"Because, Gary, you were looking for Bitsy's journal, the one that describes everything that happened on the camping trip. Other than Bitsy, there were only two people who knew about the journal. Mike Kniivila knew about it because Bitsy told him about it. And then you knew about it because Mike shared that information with you. I don't know if you acted on your own or if Mike suggested that you should get your hands on it as quickly as possible."

"Why would I care about some twenty-five-year-old journal?"

"Which one were you, Gary? Huck or Judd?"

Gary narrowed his eyes and looked at Ray with something like hatred. Then the nurse came into the room. "You have to excuse me a few minutes, folks. I have to check Mr. Zatanski's vitals. Perhaps you could wait in the hallway until I'm done."

Ray leaned against the wall opposite the doorway to the room. "There are lots of important little details that I don't know."

"Yes, tomorrow I'll get my notes typed up and the recording transcribed, and I know you'll do the same. Then we will be able to sort much of this out."

The nurse emerged from the room and handed Ray his phone, the one he had left lying on Gary Zatanski's bed.

"My patient says he is too tired to continue your conversation, Sheriff. I know you will honor his request."

Ray looked across the table at Sue as she toyed with a plate of hospital cafeteria macaroni and cheese, pushing the pasta through an unnaturally yellow sauce.

"When I said mac and cheese, Ray, I wasn't talking about hospital food. I was talking about the real stuff, or at least Kraft Dinner."

"You could have gone with potato chip–topped tuna casserole," he said, trying to keep a straight face. "You said you were too hungry to take another step."

"And an orange will hold you?"

"It's about the only thing a hospital dietician can't screw up," said Ray.

"Well, I don't think you're going to get Zatanski to talk with you again, not without an attorney present. Where were you going with the questioning?"

"By virtue of his job at the school, Zatanski got dragged into being part of this reunion. It appears that he had reasons for not wanting to be there. I want some kind of closure. I want to know what happened to Etienne. His disappearance is at the center of this whole story."

"What are you going to do now?"

"When things settle down, I'll send a long letter to the Marquette

County Prosecutor's Office on a possible crime committed in their jurisdiction twenty-five years ago. I'll mention Etienne Falconet and note that that's probably not his real name. I'll mention the date he is thought to have disappeared and add that, to my knowledge, no missing person report was ever filed."

"That's sort of the end of it," said Sue.

"Yes, probably a mystery and a crime we will never solve. Eat up."

36

On Wednesday afternoon Ray met Jennings Bidder in the departure area of Cherry Capitol Airport.

"I see some familiar faces," he commented after looking around the area.

"A few people went out on an earlier flight. Most of the rest of us are flying to Detroit, then picking up connecting flights. You said you had a question or two?"

"Yes, I'll be quick. I'm just trying to sort out a few details. Richard Gordon, how did he treat his female employees?"

"Why do you ask? The man is dead."

"Megan Bartoli . . ."

"How's she doing?"

"Better than expected. She should be discharged before the end of the week. Anyway, she has alleged that Gordon attempted to sexually assault her the evening of his murder. I was just wondering if, to your knowledge, anything like this had ever happened before."

Bidder's answer was slow in coming. "Rich, powerful men like Gordon, some of them anyway, seem to feel that all women should submit to their will."

"And this had been a problem with Mr. Gordon?"

"As I worked to rebuild his image, his sexual past had been a problem area, especially with women employees. There were a couple of embarrassing lawsuits that we had been able to settle out of court, fortunately."

"So the possibility of Gordon trying to force himself on Ms. Bartoli, you would not be surprised by that?"

"No, not at all. That would be absolutely consistent with his reckless behavior, especially if he was drinking. You remember,

Sheriff, that I moved rooms that night. I didn't want him to know where I was. And I was glad that I had Nick with me. Why he was dumb enough to try anything with Megan, I'm baffled by that. He had to know she and Conrad were becoming an item. Or maybe he didn't know. Richard was at the center of his own universe, sort of like a spoiled teen. He never seemed to grow beyond that. What's going to happen to Conrad? He's a good guy. This whole thing is a tragedy not of his making."

"He's been charged with manslaughter. I'm reluctant to speculate on what might happen, ultimately."

"Tragic, for him and all of us in lots of ways. My flight is boarding, Sheriff. Is there anything else?"

"Not at the moment. I'll contact you again if I need to follow up. Thank you for your help."

Jennings turned and dragged her carryon toward the gate. Ray located Alex Bishop and approached her where she was standing near the end of the line for boarding. "Excuse me, Dr. Bishop," Ray said. "One quick question before you board. I need closure on a final detail."

"Please make it fast, Sheriff. I don't want to miss this flight."

"After you attended to Conrad Voight and Megan Bartoli, what did you do?"

"I think I went to find some coffee. I was exhausted and stressed to the extreme. I haven't done that kind of medicine for decades. Everything is sort of a blur, you know? I just can't quite remember."

"Any chance you went to Richard Gordon's suite?"

Alex looked at Ray with an impish smile. "Yes, I may have popped in for a word."

"And what did you find?"

"Sheriff, you know exactly what I found."

"Did you check to see if Richard Gordon was alive?" asked Ray.

"No, I checked to see that he was dead. And he was—very dead. From some bits Conrad told me, I had sort of pieced together what had happened. I went to see if Conrad's story, at least that part of the story, was true. It was. Is that all, Sheriff?"

"One more thing. Your epee, was it still on the bed?"

"No. It was on the floor near him. And if you're wondering who stabbed him with it, I wouldn't know. It was probably someone wanting justice for something that happened long ago. An adolescent act. We all have a child still there inside us, don't we, Sheriff?

37

The administrative area of the Cedar County Sheriff's Department was quiet and empty on Thanksgiving morning. Ray Elkins sat at his desk, his door open to a silent hallway, his eyes locked on the screen. His progress was slowed by a clumsily attached bandage on the tip of the fourth finger of his left hand.

As he keyed his thoughts, words became sentences, sentences became paragraphs. In the opening paragraph he provided a summary of the events leading to the disappearance of Etienne Falconet. In later paragraphs he outlined all of the additional information he and Sue had gathered related to Falconet's disappearance, including Gary Zatanski's possible involvement. After completing the draft, he printed a copy and moved over to his conference table to revise and proofread his work.

Sue wandered in to his office with Simone tucked under her arm. She came around the table and handed Ray the terrier. "She needs to bond. The pack has been separated too long."

Glancing down she asked, "What happened to your finger?"

"I was chopping vegetables. Getting a head start on dinner."

"Are you OK? Should I run you into the ER?"

"It will heal. I'm good."

"Read this while Simone and I hike over to dispatch and get a flask of fresh coffee." Ray slid the document in her direction.

"It's all here," said Sue, when Ray and Simone returned. "And as you've already suggested, unless there is an extraordinary development, this will go no further."

"Yes," agreed Ray, his tone one of resignation.

"Dinner, what time?"

"Well, I was thinking we'd gather at 3:00, eat around 4:00. Marc and Lisa are bringing the turkey, dressing, and salad. I'm responsible for the mashed potatoes, roast vegetables, and pies."

"And I bring the wine and champagne. The perfect assignment

for someone with dysculinia. Plus, I remembered which brand of champagne to bring." She gave Ray a teasing smile.

Ray couldn't suppress the grin. He held his injured hand in the air.

"Is that a muffled cry for assistance?" she asked.

"Yes, I would really appreciate the help. Most of the things I need to do require two hands."

"Sure, happy to lend a hand, so to speak. Sounds like we better go to your place and get started on dinner preparations. You're lucky I'm here." Sue stood, then reached down and scooped up Simone. "And she is, too. You'd probably give her way too much organic turkey." Looking slightly abashed, she held him in her gaze. "And I'm really glad I'm here, Ray. And thankful for our special bond."

Author's Note

In the process of writing this book I was aided by many people who shared their knowledge and skills, some of whom wish to remain unacknowledged.

But a special thanks to Henry Davies and Barb Osbon for carefully documenting the trail into the McCormick Wilderness. Their photographs guided my pen in the early part of the book. I also am grateful to Barb for her proofreading prowess.

I am greatly indebted to Heather Shaw for her story editing skills, cover design, and interior layout. I am in awe of her artistic skills and literary sensibilities. Her friendship, sage advice, and diplomatic prodding keep me on task.

None of this would be possible without the support and friendship of the independent booksellers who have been stocking my novels and inviting me for signings and book talks for more than a decade.

Special thanks to Mark Bear for wading out into the surf on cold winter day to get the special shot used on the cover of this book (http://markbearphotography.blogspot.com).

Books in the Ray Elkins Series:

CPSIA information can be obtained
at www.ICGtesting.com
Printed in the USA
LVOW03s1044110417
530396LV00001B/10/P